THE JERICHO COMMANDMENT

THE JERICHO COMMANDMENT

a novel by James Patterson

CROWN PUBLISHERS, INC. New York

The photos on pages 183 and 188 are used by permission of Wide World Photos, Inc.

Inquiries should be addressed to Crown Publishers, Inc., One Park Avenue, New York, N.Y. 10016

Printed in the United States of America

Published simultaneously in Canada by
General Publishing Company Limited

Designed by Ruth Kolbert Smerechniak

Library of Congress Cataloging in Publication Data

Patterson, James, 1947–
   The Jericho commandment.

   I. Title.
PZ4.P31967Je   1979   [PS3566.A822]   812'.5'4
ISBN 0-517-53626-9   78-21241

The Jericho Commandment *couldn't have been written without the help of a former Israeli soldier now living in New York; without the vivid stories of a survivor who had made the pilgrimage to every concentration camp site in Europe—who had also made contact with the radical group known as DIN. Most of all, the book couldn't have reached its present form without the nagging help of the son of a Brooklyn rabbi, who, more often than I would have liked, reminded me to get it down right.*

j.p.

THE PROLOGUE

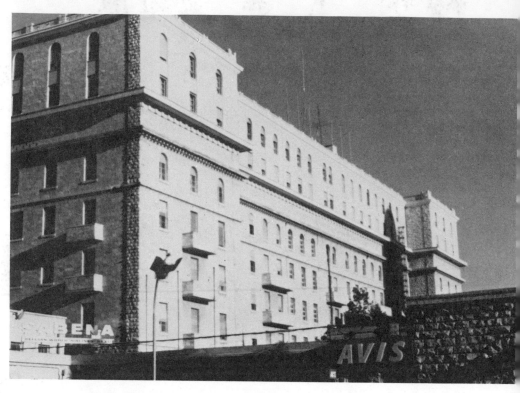

Jerusalem's King David Hotel, where Mrs. Elena Strauss, Benjamin Rabinowitz, and Michael Ben-Iban met for the last time. Also the site where the Stern gang attacked English soldiers and workers in June of 1946.

The King David Hotel, Jerusalem.
October, 1979.
Five months before the beginning.
A benevolent midafternoon sun spattered golden streaks and blown-glass aureoles over the historic domes and needle spires, up and down the gray-yellow stones of the ancient Holy City walls; a bottle of Schweppes Bitter Lemon, a spot of English Breakfast tea, and a sweating-cold Maccabee beer were brought to the three old friends sitting like skittish birds on the pretty hotel terrace; an Arab imam wailed out his afternoon prayers and curses from a distant, crumbling minaret in Old City.

It is a fact recorded in several news correspondents' notebooks—though not as yet in their newspapers—that a sacred, a very secret Jewish brotherhood had existed in Western Europe, in America, in Israel, since the end of World War II. The group was composed of common working men and women—of farmers, entertainers, taxi drivers; of wealthy doctors, solicitors, merchants, rabbis; of important government leaders and elite Army officers.

No matter how these men and women earned their livings, however, the sworn purpose of the cabal thrust another holy and courageous task on them.

They were to remember the terrible Holocaust—every last abhorrent detail of it; they were to protect against another unholy conflagration with their lives if need be; they were to relentlessly hunt down those responsible for the first abomination against the Jewish people and against mankind.

9

The three friends clustered together on the hotel terrace were two of the secret brotherhood's original leaders—plus a woman, a wealthy contributor from America.

Poised as they were in view of the gates of Old City, the three friends made a curious, memorable portrait; a noble picture ready for exhibition in the Jewish Museum.

Benjamin Rabinowitz.

Michael Ben-Iban.

Elena Cohen Strauss.

A combined age of two hundred twenty-six years.

All survivors of the Nazi death camps thirty-five years before.

The previous evening, Elena Straus and Ben-Iban had jetted to Jerusalem after receiving an urgent message from Rabinowitz.

The message had begun:

THE TIME HAS COME TO REMEMBER OUR SACRED PLEDGE . . . I FIRMLY BELIEVE THE FOURTH REICH IS ABOUT TO RISE. IT IS TIME TO CONCLUDE THE DISCUSSION STAGE OF OUR PLAN TO ONCE AND FOREVER STOP THE ENEMY.

Allegro symphony music—some Hector Berlioz—then a BBC news broadcast served as civilized background for twelve or fifteen private conversations progressing in grunts and murmurs on the grandly elegant hotel terrace. The clean smell of almonds and oranges was everywhere in the air.

Out on the streets of Rehavia, Arab cab drivers could be heard mischievously blaring Mercedes taxi horns. Out there too, Hasidim tourists trudged along in their broad hats and stiff beards, pointing at Moses Montefiore's windmill, acting as if the Ba'al Shem Tov himself was standing at every cross street.

In the beginning of their meeting, the three old friends merely chatted.

The most casual talk possible under the circumstances.

They sipped their assorted drinks and they offered opinions on a recent Black September bombing of a children's school bus in Bayit Vegan; they spoke of a best-selling book from England, which had documented that the PLO was receiving huge sums of money from neo-Nazis living in southern France; they gave Freudian interpretations of Teddy Kollek's grand reconstruction dreams for Jerusalem.

Eighty-two-year-old Elena Strauss managed to smile a few times.

Especially when they shared an old story—that was the best.

But when they finally began to talk about the most sinister topic, when the loathsome Reich was brought up, the wizened old woman found that her hands were knotting into tight fists. She found that she could barely breathe. *A single word, a single idea was pounding on her brain.*

Danger.

"No matter what good we are able to accomplish, the Nazis get wealthier and more powerful," Benjamin Rabinowitz began. "In South America. In West Germany and Austria. In Chicago and New York. In the south of France . . . "

"They are indeed ready again, Elena." Michael Ben-Iban elaborated. "I've seen it with my own weary eyes. Their wealth at this time is astounding. Stomach-turning.

"The opulent estates you know about; the gold and diamond reserves. What you don't know about are the legitimate businesses. All over the world. The so-called multinational companies run with the Reich's money. Automobile companies. Oil companies. Communications conglomerates. *Like nothing we've seen before!"*

Benjamin Rabinowitz now began to elaborately review his plan. His proposal to silence the Reich once and for all time. The financing of which was the chief reason for the important Jerusalem meeting.

When Rabinowitz finished, tears were pooling in the soft brown eyes of Elena Strauss. The deadweight sadness and disappointment she was feeling right then were too much for her frail, weakened body. What Elena Strauss had to do next seemed an impossible task. What she had to do almost seemed like a betrayal.

The wealthy American woman stared across the table at hawklike Michael Ben-Iban, perhaps the bravest Nazi-hunter next to Simon Wiesenthal and Dr. Michael Ben-Zohar. She looked at shrewd, feisty Benjamin Rabinowitz. *Such old, old friends, she thought. Such a wonderful, courageous alliance they'd shared . . . even more so, because so very few people knew of their heroics.*

Somehow, all three of them had survived the German death

camps: Dachau, Auschwitz, Treblinka.

They had all been members of She'erit Hapleetch, the *"Surviving Remnant,"* formed when no countries other than the Jewish community in Palestine had been willing to accept large groups of survivors from the death camps.

Instead of planning for the Jewish state, however, they had been among those who planned very necessary revenge and retribution; they had been among those who planned for the future defense of the Jewish people.

Together with forty-four other survivors, they had drawn up the radical brotherhood's priority list for the first Nazi-hunting year of 1946. That first year they had patiently tracked down and killed SS Brigadier General Ernst Grawitz; SS Major Otto Steiner, supervisor of the Belsen gas chambers; SS Colonel Albert Hohlfelder, who had viciously sterilized thousands of Jewish children by mass X-ray exposure.

Through the fifties and sixties, they had diligently *hunted dangerous members of* Die Spinne *and ODESSA.*

They had relentlessly watched for the dreaded Nazi renaissance.

They had remembered the terrible Holocaust—every last abhorrent detail.

"Benjamin, I have listened carefully to your plan, your fears about a new Reich." Elena was finally able to speak again. "I have lived and slept with your arguments, your dark conclusions. I have considered them as carefully as anything in my life. . . . You say you need a great deal of money from me. Seven hundred, eight hundred thousand dollars. I spoke at length with my oldest grandson before I came to Jerusalem. We talked about the Nazis, about the present condition of the Reich."

"They have never been more dangerous than right now," Benjamin Rabinowitz said.

Elena Strauss shook her tiny head. "We think you're terribly wrong," she sighed. "But more important than that, the actions of our group have always been accomplished with great honor, with justice in all our minds. No matter how strong our enemies become, Benjamin, Michael, we must never go down to their Hun, barbarian level. This is the secret strength of the Jewish people, I believe. This is one reason we have survived. *I don't believe we should act against our enemies now. Not in this hateful manner."*

The thin voice of Rabinowitz suddenly rose above the clatter of the King David terrace. It was like the voice of a stern and knowing rabbi rebuking his shortsighted congregation.

"You've lived as a wealthy American for too long, Elena," the old man railed. "You don't understand the terrifying world we live in today. You couldn't possibly, and still talk as you do. The Fourth Reich's money is everywhere, Elena. The Nazi cancer is everywhere. In the Middle East. In America. In Germany, where the Spider's cells are springing up every where. Where little blond-haired children are marching again."

Elena Strauss reached into her purse.

"I have a small check. I want you to continue the search for Bormann, Mengele, Muller. You must! Please! As for the rest, I say *no*. My grandson wants to go to the other contributing families. To the American FBI. If necessary, we would break our vows to stop a dangerous confrontation at this time. . . . You are taking away the last possibility of justice ever being accomplished for the six million! I will not allow this to happen! No! No!" The American woman's face was drawn tight; her eyes were filled with rage.

Neither Benjamin Rabinowitz nor Michael Ben-Iban could believe that Elena Strauss would even speak of breaking their blood oath. For a moment, the effect was numbing. Benjamin Rabinowitz's mouth was filled with bile; he thought he was going to be sick on the hotel terrace.

Elena Strauss was turning them down at the worst possible time.

The elderly woman suddenly stood up at their table. She was visibly trembling, blinking her eyes very rapidly.

"I have been feeling bad this fall. Sick. Old—which I am. I should go back to my room now. This is a hard day for me, too."

Mrs. Elena Strauss bent and gave each of the old men a quick hug. They each hugged her back. The sadness was overwhelming in its intensity. *Thirty-five years* . . . Now, threats! The breaking of oaths! There were tears in all of their eyes at the end of the embrace. It was like the hollow, numb, empty feeling that comes on first hearing of a friend's death.

"Benjamin . . . Michael . . . *Shalom*."

"She is a very, very old woman. A good woman," Michael Ben-Iban whispered, after Elena had disappeared back into the hotel. "Perhaps in a little time she'll come to understand. . . . Benjamin? Are *you* all right, Benjamin?"

Benjamin Rabinowitz folded his thin arms and moaned softly.

"There is no time not to understand. If only I had made her see the terrible danger we know is there, Michael. *The fault is mine.* Oh Moshe, no one but Jews will protect other Jews from our enemies. You know that."

Michael Ben-Iban nodded sadly. He knew. He knew it all too well.

Ben-Iban also knew that the enemy was truly capable of anything now. Even a second Holocaust. Even a terrible bombing right there in Israel. For the first time in thirty-five years, Ben-Iban thought, the Jewish nation could be without an adequate defense. A defense manned by Jews who understood the grave, ever-present danger.

As the two ancient survivors finished their drinks that sad afternoon, the Arab imam was still wailing, still praying from his distant minaret.

The priest's prayer was that God would come and give him back his golden city.

His prayer was that God would come down and kill all of the Jews.

One hundred seventy-four days later, it suddenly began to happen.

On four continents all across the civilized world.

A heart-sinking plot that would be called *Dachau Zwei.*
Dachau Two.

BOOK 1

Dr. David Strauss

PART I

1

Scarsdale, New York.
April 24, 1980.
One day before the beginning.
Along the Chesterfield-gray country roads there were Tudor and Norman mansions with eight-foot-high hedges and pollarded trees. There was a striking chimney-red tennis court with high white referee chairs—where a rich adulteress named Norma Lynch had been shot to death in 1943.

Then there were these rigidly rectangular, crème and lime-green tile swimming pools; and trendy bumper stickers: *Honk if you believe in tennis;* and Post roads, James Fenimore Cooper streets, Leatherstocking lanes. . . .

These things, in fact, were the rule of thumbing one's elegant nose in that part of Westchester County where Dr. David Strauss and Alix Rothman had grown up.

Where the American part of the story has its not so humble beginnings.

Where the nightmares begin.

The April day that made the handsome village infamous had a scratchy, nervous quality about it anyway.

It left an uncomfortable feeling in *Vulkan's* mouth, like sweater fuzzballs under his tongue.

Coughing into a crisp white gentleman's handkerchief, Vulkan watched the others fan away from the wonderfully kept, town children's playground.

The *Hausfrau* (Housewife), a pretty, petite woman—also a frighteningly dedicated warrior—walked away alongside a picturesque fieldstone wall and weeping willow trees on Horse Guard Lane.

The *Soldat* (Soldier) was forcing his great hulking body into a sleek MG Stag parked on Upper North Avenue.

The *Waffen-Fachmann* (Weapons Expert) sat at a bus stop, a copy of a paperback called *The Boat* pressed up to his face. He had on a beige raincoat; snap-brim hat; Weejuns . . . very American-looking.

The beadlelike *Ingenieur* (Engineer) had simply vanished—poof—blended into the residential backdrop like yet another Country Squire station wagon.

Last, the *Führer* was marching off to a chauffeured limousine, which was relatively inconspicuous on the money-lined streets.

The idea of the seven of them taking on World War II code names, meeting on this small-town American street *in 1980*, was preposterous and dangerous, Vulkan was thinking.

Still, the final meeting had to be *someplace*.

The final decisions had to be made before the Final Solution could begin.

Vulkan took out a very beautiful pocket watch, cradling it in the palm of his hand. The man's own face was dimly reflected in the silver lid of the watch. His felt hat, tipped at a raffish angle, was reflected as well.

It was all neatly superimposed over a grand, elegant inscription: *Dachau Konzentrationslager. Sturmbannführer Mann. 1932—*

Agile, piano-player fingers now pried open the watch cover.

Inside was a delicately balanced, silver and ruby-red swastika.

The four crooked arms were pointed and feathered like an Eagle trout-fishing hook.

Overtopping the swastika itself, tiny black hands were ticking off the seconds, days, years.

It was now time to begin.

Again.

One more quick note about Scarsdale, New York, though.

The people who live there, especially the buckskinned, shaggy-haired boys and girls who attend the ivy-covered high school, often complain that nothing meaningful or exciting

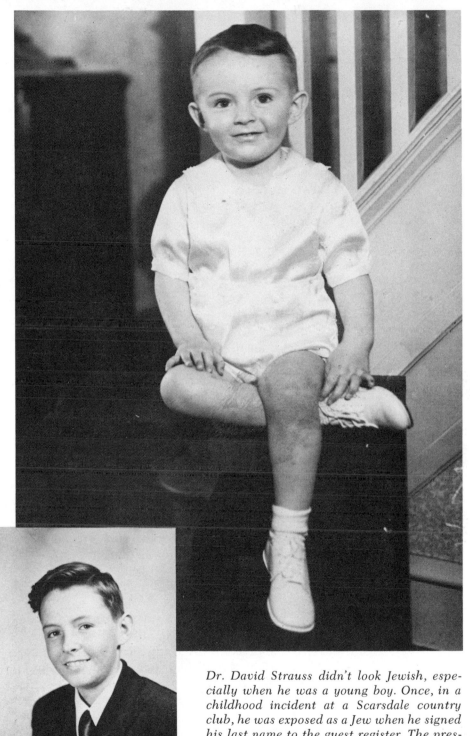

Dr. David Strauss didn't look Jewish, especially when he was a young boy. Once, in a childhood incident at a Scarsdale country club, he was exposed as a Jew when he signed his last name to the guest register. The president of the club came personally to the ten-year-old boy to tell him that he had to leave. It was an unbelievably traumatic moment in supposedly civilized Westchester County.

ever happens in the quiet, wealthy suburban town.

The following night something exciting happened.

Murder was committed in Scarsdale.

The Nazis came to America.

2

Mount Sinai Hospital in New York City, April 25.

The angel-faced teen-ager lying center-stage, sexy Trendelenburg position on the hospital delivery table, was named Katherine Hope O'Neill. Katherine was an anachronistic Irish-Catholic girl from the Yorkville section of Manhattan; she had a brave Kelly-green bow in her shiny black hair to prove it.

The underwhelming color in the Mount Sinai Hospital delivery room was green also. A slightly turquoise, sloshy, seasick green. The hospital setup table was covered with sterile green gowns, green drapes, furzy green sponges. A wrinkled sheet was laid underneath the delivery table like a big green mistake. "The evaporating, dying Cookie Monster," Dr. David Strauss had called it.

At 2:45 A.M., with a cup of lukewarm New York regular and a stale Danish sloughing back and forth in his stomach, the best thirty-seven-year-old Dr. David Strauss could manage for the teen-ager was, "Well, Kath, I guess in about a week or so you're going to have a baby."

"*Booo.*" The head nurse, Mary Cannel, managed a half-smile.

"Hey, what do you guys expect at quarter to three in the morning? Robert Klein? Steve Martin, maybe?"

"How about just Marcus Welby for tonight, doctor."

"All right. O.K. Marcus Welby then." David Strauss grinned. A quick, natural smile that usually seemed to relax people.

Katherine O'Neill's cervix was fully dilated now and she was pushing hard to expel her baby. Draped in still more sterile green cloth, the lower part of the girl's torso was also painted brown with antiseptic wash. "Push! Push! Push!" one of the nurses was chanting like a medieval midwife.

Just a little girl, David Strauss was thinking as he stood over the delivery room scrub basin. Little teen-angel. Soft white Madonna's face framed in lovely rings of black hair. Knocked up on the swinging East Side. Shit.

According to her chart, Katherine O'Neill was seventeen. Unmarried. Uninsured. Probably excommunicated . . . And much too young for having little babies, Dr. David Strauss would have added. Too tiny and narrow at the hips.

Which was probably why the fetal monitor read 101—about nineteen counts slower than it should have been.

David Strauss hurried into a loose-fitting scrub suit. He tugged his sewing-thimble cap over thick black curls of hair. Tied on the mask. Booties. And as he always did right about then, David Strauss suddenly felt a great wave of very adult responsibleness. For the next fifteen minutes or so, he *was* a doctor.

One of the nurses, busy listening to the O'Neill baby with a fetuscope, suddenly called out across the room.

"The heartbeat has stopped, David!"

David Strauss, the anesthetist, and the attending resident ran to the delivery table.

Katherine O'Neill was suddenly undergoing the most severe contractions. The girl was sobbing, calling out a boy's name. The small breasts under her hospital tunic were hard fists with sharp tiny points.

A pair of forceps, specially made in London, appeared in Dr. David Strauss's hand.

Glinting in the overhead kettledrum lights, the forceps descended between Katherine O'Neill's trembling legs.

Then David was hoisting a baby girl up into the limelight, letting its blood rush back for nourishment. The umbilical cord was carefully snipped. David whacked the baby's bottom extra hard.

"Prolapsed cord." The young doctor tried to sound calm and usual. A "prolapsed cord" meant that the umbilical cord had been compressed between the baby's head and the mother's pelvic bone. Oxygen had totally been cut off. The baby girl still wasn't breathing.

Strauss's six-foot one-inch frame was bent in half over the

pale, suffering infant. He blew gently into a tracheal catheter. He was trying to force oxygen into the baby's lungs.

"More heat!" He wanted the Infant Table Warmer.

"Adrenalin," the resident tersely instructed at Strauss's side.

In the terrible machine-quiet of the Mount Sinai delivery room, David Strauss underwent nearly fifteen minutes of the tensest, most draining exercise and strain he could imagine.

Finally, his dark thick head of curls flew back. David Strauss moaned out load. He looked down on the O'Neill baby and she was like a poor sleeping little doll.

"Oh screw me," David said. "Just screw everything."

He walked over to the delivery table and leaned down toward the seventeen-year-old. David Strauss then hugged Katherine O'Neill—something that was so absolutely forbidden by hospital regulations, it wasn't even covered in the regulations.

"Oh doctor, doctor, doctor," the little girl sobbed into his hair. "I just want to die, too."

It was 3:09 A.M. on April 25.

Unfortunately for David Strauss, the death of the O'Neill baby wasn't the worst thing that would happen to him that day.

It wasn't even in the top ten.

Scarsdale, April 25.

Winding along the pretty duck pond and willow tree-infested Bronx River Parkway that night, feeling familiar, pleasant vibrations rising up from their '64 Mercedes 190 (their New York City shitkicker—"the Gray Ghost"), Dr. David Strauss couldn't help thinking that he and his wife, Heather, basically had most of the things they wanted out of life.

Sometimes—after the death of little Katherine O'Neill's

baby for example—David wondered if he and Heather didn't have too much of a good thing.

Less than two months earlier, David was thinking as he maneuvered the too-skinny Parkway lanes, he and Heather had bluffed their way past the stuffed-shirt, bluestocking Co-op board of the Beresford Building on Central Park West. They were now the comparatively young landlords of a high-ceilinged, eight-room park-and-river-view penthouse in one of New York's landmark, snobbier-than-thou apartment buildings.

Right in the lobby of the forty-seven-year-old building, David also owned a neat, oak-paneled office, where he wore a white shirt and Brooks Brothers striped tie every day; where he practiced efficient, sometimes inspired medicine for women ranging from a world-renowned fifty-one-year-old playwright quietly having an illegitimate ("I like to think of her as 'fatherless,' David.") baby on the twenty-second floor, to the more conventional problems of Pap smears, pelvic examinations, yeast infections, menopause, and Premarin dispensation.

Heather, an ear, nose, and throat specialist herself, preferred working out of Mount Sinai on 100th and Madison, but she too loved their apartment in the Beresford.

That night, Heather had worn a formal Yves St. Laurent dress from Saks. She'd also had her long blond hair tipped and sensor-permed at Suga. Heather was looking very spiffy and adult, David was thinking as the two of them sped along.

"Tell me something, David," Heather kept saying as the Gray Ghost got closer and closer to Scarsdale. "Are the rest of the Strausses ever going to like me? At least to put up with me? Seriously, David?"

Which was a funny question in a way, because Heather was one of the most *likable* people David had ever met.

Everyone liked Heather Strauss.

Patients, even the most irascible bastards; New York City cab drivers; the monsignori-venerable doormen and elevator operators at the Beresford.

But. Were the Strausses ever going to like Heather? Well, David thought, even he was puzzled over the answer to that one.

All for three, simple-minded, medieval, and pretty stupid

reasons: (a) On Sunday mornings, maybe twelve times a year, Heather attended services at St. John the Evangelist Church; (b) she ate Oscar Mayer and Nathan's Famous hot dogs; (c) she identified with characters out of *Captains and the Kings* and John Updike, instead of *Seventh Avenue* and Chaim Potok.

In other words, Heather Duff Strauss was a blond-haired, sparkly blue-eyed, wonderfully human and lovable *shiksa*.

David's wife, his best friend, "the top" as the old Cole Porter song had so nicely put it.

4

The Hausfrau, meanwhile, was just finishing her second surveillance walk past the mesmerizing lights of the Strauss mansion in Scarsdale.

She went past the rolling front lawns of the moon-flooded estate, down alongside a long stone wall trailing geranium vines. She approached a thick copse of maple trees loitering at the end of the block, like a shadowy street gang.

In front of her on a taut chain leash, a perky young Irish setter—just bought that night in White Plains—excitedly sniffed its first bed of pachysandra and did its duty on the leafy plants.

With her pretty dog, navy riding jacket, and gypsy kerchief, the Housewife blended quite neatly into the suburban night scene.

The very chic-looking woman estimated that there were now sixty to seventy wealthy American Jews attending the large Strauss affair.

Quiet Upper North Avenue was an impressive parking lot for Lincolns, Cadillac Sevilles, Mercedes 280 Es, Jaguar XJs, and other expensive automobiles.

"We almost have a full house," the Housewife whispered into a transmitter clipped onto her riding jacket.

As she passed a side view of the house, the woman fingered

round, bumpy objects in a special pouch pocket sewn into her sports jacket.

The bumpy objects were white phosphorous grenades, the kind that had been used to raze villages in Vietnam and Cambodia.

At the corner of Post Road, the Housewife bent and patted the young setter's soft smooth head. She whispered into the pup's perked right ear. "Yes, yes, yes. That's a good girl." Then the woman clipped off the chain leash and gave the pup its freedom.

She had killed before, the Housewife was thinking, but never quite like this. The pretty house; cozy North Avenue. It made her shiver to think of the rest.

It was like the first scene in an illustrated children's book.

Up above the Strauss mansion's steep, four-gabled roof a fast moon raced through a high ceiling of poplar and oak leaves.

The estate grounds were like a beautiful, smoky-gray painting that night. Close up, every object was finely etched in black. The skeleton of an old hickory tree. An American horned owl perched on a garage. The strange, strange man in his dark pilot's windcheater; looking like nothing if not a highly skilled housebreaker.

Which was one way to describe the Soldier.

Pressed down close to the loamy, steaming ground, he ran as quickly and silently as his heavy backpack would allow.

He trampled through formal gardens on the East Park side of the Strauss property. Past a red-barn-siding garage with its own private gas pump. Across a mushy bog that rose up to his shoetops; over an unexpected brook; into what looked like an Old World fruit and vegetable garden.

The Soldier stopped and crouched low at a vine-covered gazebo that had seemed to be a small cottage from back around the brook.

"There's a single man out here," he spoke into his transmitter.

Watching the man—who seemed to have come out of the party for a smoke—the Soldier unstrapped his heavy pack. Finally, the man from the party wandered back inside.

The Soldier could begin.

Inside the bag was a curious assortment of supplies. Knotted

27

rags. Different lengths of copper pipe. An American-made Colt Python with four clips. Fuse. A full two-and-a-half-gallon Exxon gasoline can.

Right in the heart of Westchester County, New York, the Soldier couldn't help thinking, as he set to work.

In America.

5

"It couldn't have possibly happened here," a Mount Vernon daily newspaper would postulate the following morning. "What happened in Scarsdale last night just couldn't have happened."

Reluctantly, David and Heather climbed out of the dusty, rusted Gray Ghost.

Arm in arm, they walked toward the imposing forty-one-room manor house where David had grown up.

"Where's the Sousa band and welcoming committee you promised?" Heather whispered in David's ear.

"Inside." David tapped his knuckle against the house shingles. "The other side of these great, half-timbered walls. With bells on their toes, I'll bet."

Inside the grand Tudor house, the two of them were semi-prepared to meet the mainstays of David's immediate family; Strausses, Cohens, Hales, Loebs, Lehmans, Kleins.

All that, plus David's older brother Nick on NBC network TV.

On the 52nd Academy Awards—which was the ostensible reason for the party.

Just thinking about "Nick the Quick" brought a smile to David's lips. Nick was what their grandmother Elena called a *tummler*, a big, lovable clown—who maybe was going to turn into a successful "alrightnik" out in Hollywood.

The closer he got to the big house though, the more serious

second thoughts David had about the tricky evening ahead.

For one thing, some of the people inside had actually boycotted his and Heather's wedding two years before.

Some of them still hadn't even met "David's *shiksa* wife."

"Hello. Oh hi there, Mrs. S."

Heather was looking pale as the Gray Ghost as she and David stood together on the stone front porch. "Just practicing my act," she assured David, both of them looking up at the great glazed bay windows over their heads.

"O.K., let's do it." Heather took a deep breath. "Twang your magic plunker, Froggie. Bang the brass knocker, Davo. I'm as ready as I'll ever be."

David couldn't help smiling at his wife. Just then, though, the big wooden front door seemed to open by itself.

"Aahh-ha," said a flaming red mouth and fluttery blue eyes—David's great-aunt Frieda Loeb. "Everybody! Everybody! David and his girl friend are here. . . . Oops!"

"Oops is right, Aunt Frieda." David held Heather's arm real tight. "Frieda, this is my wife of two years, Heather. Heather, welcome to the North Pole."

Not unexpectedly, the exact tone of voice of the large catered party was difficult to pin down and isolate.

"It's part very sophisticated cocktail party." Heather looked around at chiffon empire gowns and tuxes; at Queen Anne side chairs; Cromwellian tables and cabinets; expensive art on every available wall space.

"And it's part New York delicatessen service-crew reunion," David smiled. "Knishes. Sour pickles. Those chocolate-chip cookies made by little Negroes in California."

"Also, it's part Irish wake, I think."

"And part Indian suttee . . . Also part United Jewish Appeal breakfast. Remind me to take you to one of *those* some time."

Technically, it was David's brother's day. Nick's day. Only in the Strauss view of the world, that made it the whole family's day, which meant that everyone attending the gala party was up for an Academy Award that night. The entire Strauss family.

After peeling off from yenta Aunt Frieda, from Uncle Milt (Colonel in the Army Reserves; ten-million-a-year salesman for Prudential), David and Heather were roadblocked by Aunt Shirley Lehman, who was a trustee of the Brooklyn Museum even though she lived in Tarrytown now, who was writing a chic-chic novel about East Side housewives called *Pure Vanilla Extract,* who sat Heather and David in front of Degas and Chagall, and kibbitzed and kibbitzed until they both felt amazingly at ease and almost welcome at the party.

In fact, after being there for half an hour or so, David began to feel a vaguely familiar glow kindling inside.

He saw that Heather *was* being accepted into the family— and that Heather herself knew it.

David Strauss found himself smiling a lot.

This was family, damnit!

They blew everything out of proportion all the time. They badgered you. They made you dance the horah. They cut you up, down, and sideways in incisive ways that went right to the bone marrow. But *somehow*—David started to laugh out loud as he thought this—*some way,* they cared for you more than anybody else ever would. They loved Heather—because *you* loved her.

At one point, loud clapping started up around the huge, warm, familiar living room. People were clapping for David and Heather. His grandmother Elena's wolfhound rolled around the carpet yowling and farting. David kissed Heather and he felt a little warm tear on her cheek.

"I'm real happy," Heather whispered. "I like them a lot."

"Nazi mystery in America!" the *London Times* would report to its long-time Nazi-hating readership.

"For this to happen so close to New York City with its large Jewish population, is its own special tragedy," the *New York*

Top left: *Elena Strauss in Berlin around 1928. The second woman is Aunt Jorja, who died in Buchenwald.*
Bottom: *Elena, Sam Strauss, and David and Nick's mother, Isabelle, at Cherrywoods.*

Daily News would say on its front page.

"Cary Grant and Grace Kelly in *To Catch a Thief*," David whispered to Heather as they crossed the upstairs hallway.

"Two of the little Japanese soldiers in *Godzilla Meets King Kong*," Heather said, suggesting another cinema image.

The two of them snuck past the ancient ruins of David's old bedroom. Past his father's ten-thousand-book study. Then David was slowly twisting the glass knob on one of the closed bedroom doors.

The polished walnut door sprung open a thin crack. A golden blade of light sliced out into the hallway.

They could both smell lavender water and sachet, and a boyhood epiphany closed around David: expensive family cars that purred like cats; old family cats that made noises like broken-down cars.

Across a long, busily furnished bedroom they saw eighty-two-year-old Elena Cohen Strauss.

David's grandmother.

Prominent in the woman's very personalized bedroom were some fifty of her original paintings and etchings; a brace of cozy ottoman chairs; bedspread, drapes, and mirror frames all done in matching flowered cotton; a wall of hard-covered books in German, English, Russian, and Hebrew—all of which Elena Strauss read and spoke.

"So come on in out of the cold." Elena's eyes grew wide and surprisingly alert.

"Your big brother is on the television any minute now. How are you, Heather dear? What a pretty blue dress. *Very* striking. *Helloo*, Davey! Come for some shmooz with your sick grandmother?"

Both David and Heather started to smile broadly.

Since the 1971 automobile crash deaths of David's parents, Elena Strauss had once again taken full control of the family's eighty-odd million dollars. That meant being chairman of the board for Samel Industries (movie theaters, real estate, diamonds); chairman of the Cherrywoods Hotel Realty and Construction Company; director of White Plains Finishing Industries; and director of the Strauss Foundation for the Arts.

Besides being entirely capable of the jobs, Elena gave the task a Volpone/Scrooge McDuck spirit that David at least found refreshing and wonderful. His grandmother had a pioneer's approach to life that was almost lost in America these days.

Even at eighty-two, David thought, she was more self-sufficient in many ways than he was.

David and Heather hadn't gotten halfway across the room when the big-time small talk began.

"The reason I'm not joining in the party, why I couldn't go out to California—I'm feeling awfully, terrible sick, Heather and David. Dizzy spells. Brain not always so connected with my muscles. What's wrong with me, Davey?"

David and Heather pulled up two of the ottoman chairs.

"A high-priced consultation," Heather kidded.

"You're eighty-two years old, Elena," David answered their patient's question.

Elena nodded in an exaggerated fashion. Her mouth made a perfect little red circle.

"Aahhh! Thank you, doctor. And how much will that be?"

"She's been working like a charwoman for seventy-one years. You see, Elena personally watches out for the health and welfare of every living Jew in the world," David advised Dr. Heather Strauss. "*Also,* she still futzes around up at our family hotel . . . because nobody else can run Cherrywoods, right? Not like you and Grandpa Sam could?" David bent closer to his grandmother. "Tell me one thing, Nana?"

"Anything, my dear, sweet *bokher.*"

"*Bokher,* Heather, is like a little brown-nose kid at yeshiva classes. Listen, Elena, are you and your dizzy spells planning to go up to the hotel for spring cleaning this year?"

Elena started to laugh. David and Heather watched smile-cracks form in her powder plaster. Intimations of a much younger woman, a *Mädchen* back in Berlin, showed in her clear brown eyes.

"Maybe. Maybe not. Who can tell about these things?"

"Listen, Nana. Seriously. Why don't you take it easy? *Don't* go to spring cleaning this year."

The elderly lady got very serious for a moment.

"Davey, Heather, in this country, everything is to be young. Have lots of money. Have a Pepsi-Cola life. Why should an old woman retire? Only to die. Don't you think so, Heather? Davey?"

"You don't have to retire," Heather said.

"Saying doesn't make it so. I *will* retire from the hotel some-day," Elena shrugged. "Do you know when? Davey knows when."

Davey knew, all right. Davey nodded. Davey knew what was coming next, too.

"I will retire if ever our enemies come back. Only if they should attack Israel or something terrible. Nineteen thirty-four," Elena said to Heather. "I was a young woman in Berlin. The whore and drunk capital of all Europe. Now? The same thing here in New York. Nineteen thirty-four. Terrible economy in Germany. Always blaming the Jews. Nazis marching in small towns, then in bigger towns, finally right in Berlin. Do you know Jabotinsky, Heather?"

"I know Jabotinsky," David nodded. "Zev Jabotinsky. Great guy. The Jewish Garibaldi."

"You should read Jabotinsky, Heather. Zev J-A-B-O-T-I-N-S-K-Y. That Jabotinsky understands the enemies of Jews like nobody ever has."

David placed his hand over Elena's on the arm of her chair.

"All right, we'll both read Jabotinsky. Now tell us how you're feeling, Nana. Seriously."

The old woman shrugged her narrow shoulders. She sagged back into her ottoman chair.

Elena stopped being playful and gave David one of her wise-old-woman looks. For the moment, his grandmother was clearly being the head of the family.

"Read Jabotinsky," she said. "Seriously."

As she spoke the words, the color television winked. The bedroom lights flickered.

"Probably Nazis up on the roof," David deadpanned, then winked at his grandmother.

"As a comedian," the old woman winked back, "you could be in serious trouble, *bokher*. Even with my incredible contacts. Even in the Catskills, which I practically own."

7

"I was taking a little walk out on Horse Guard," a local attorney named Arthur Taylor would relate to the FBI before the evening was over. "This certified maniac stepped right out of the bushes in front of me. He was wearing a Nazi armband, I swear to God. Said something in goddamn German, then he took off like a bat out of hell."

10:35 P.M.

In a terminally ill part of Scarsdale, near the ancient railroad station, Vulkan walked into Monaghle's Bar & Grill.

Monaghle's was a drab, dusty parlor that hadn't changed a drink coaster since the death of Sean Monaghle's wife.

Three men in oil-stained work clothes and a woman in a satin-doll party dress were hunched over red vinyl bar stools up in front. On a semi-regular schedule, the union bartender served up some draft beers, or a port wine for the lady, or a Robt. Burns Black Watch cigar for the man with "Witte" marked on his work shirt.

At the rear of the narrow room, Vulkan observed doors for public toilets, a tinny phone booth, a color TV that positively sparkled in the dull room.

A naive portrait of John Kennedy and his wife sat beside the cash register, presumably safeguarding Monaghle's cash from the union bartenders.

Vulkan bought a glass of brandy, then sat in an empty booth under the color TV.

He began to watch the Academy Awards.

At eleven o'clock, station identification for NBC, the strange man bundled himself into the phone booth and shut the metal-and-glass door tight.

He dialed 212-949-1234.

General information for America's largest newspaper, the *New York Daily News.*

Vulkan had some news to tell.

A young woman answered "New York News" in a subdued, businesslike speaking voice.

"You are to write down exactly what I tell you," Vulkan instructed the young woman.

Back at the *News* offices meanwhile, Mary Gargan's first thought was "Nut," then "Screwball," then, "What's a nice girl like me doing answering phones late at night in New York City?"

"Sir?" she said.

"Then you are to call Mr. Harold Ney, editor-in-chief of your newspaper. Mr. Ney can be reached at 826-0359, his mistress's number at the River Bend apartment building. This is the message you're to read to Mr. Ney."

The man called Vulkan paused, both to catch his own breath and to let what he'd said so far take effect. He then read Mary Gargan a short, prepared statement.

Slowly.

Sentence by absolutely riveting sentence.

"Today in our country there are approximately six million Jews among us. That is correct—six million Jews.

"Tonight, effective measures are being taken against the wealthy, powerful Jews living here in America. These Jews are being taken care of by proven methods once employed at Auschwitz, Buchenwald, Dachau. Jews such as the Kleins, the Strausses, the Shapiros, the Cohens, the Loebs.

"Tonight marks the beginning of an important policing action called *Dachau Zwei* . . . Dachau Two!

"Once again, the Jews have proven that they can never learn a lesson.

"The ovens are warming up.

"Heil Hitler."

On the shrill color television in Monaghle's Bar & Grill, meanwhile, on over thirty million sets across the country, Nicholas Strauss and his wife, Beri, were running straight into the wide-angle lens of an RCA TV camera.

The sun-browned, attractive couple was racing down the far right-side aisle of the glittery Dorothy Chandler Pavilion in Hollywood.

Among those who turned and clapped for them: a shaggy, bearded Jack Nicholson; Jacqueline Bisset, wonderfully back-lit by the stage lights; George Burns; Joseph Levine; Robert De Niro; hordes of opera-glass renters.

For Nicholas and Beri, the Oscar for best feature-length doc-umentary film was the well-deserved climax to two singularly uncompromising careers. The Strausses were known to work under one idealistic and therefore somewhat unrealistic show-business philosophy: *If we don't believe in it, why should we expect anybody else to?*

Their film, *The Fourth Commandment*, had taken only twenty-four days and two hundred thousand dollars to shoot and edit, but it had been in preparation and pre-production for over seven years. An unusual and unexpected tour de force, the film somehow communicated to 1970s America a "you-were-there" feeling for 1940s Germany. "*The Fourth Commandment* is a sane, surprisingly objective, and I must say, moving depiction of an intelligent, sophisticated and civ-ilized country brought to lower depths than any other in mod-ern history," the critic for the *Los Angeles Times* said at the time of the film's release. "In my mind, it is a wise and know-ing portrait of an era we ought not to forget."

Nick Strauss was shaking badly as he stood like a wooden figurine behind the stage microphone and podium; as he looked out on the faces of the most powerful show-business people in the world.

"I have an unconscionably long list of people I want to thank," the trim, long-haired filmmaker said.

"But we don't want all of you to suffer through it," his wife Beri added, brandishing their golden award proudly. "So we won't name all the names here tonight. You know who you are. You are wonderful, wonderful people. We love you a whole lot. More than I think we could do justice to right now, shivering and shaking as we are."

As Nick said a few final words, a defiantly unreal scenario began to develop at the already phantasmagoric Chandler Pa-vilion.

A convoy of powder-blue NBC cameras began to dolly to the right side of the brightly lit stage with its glassine stairway to a star-studded ceiling.

A collective shriek came from the velvet tuxedos and see-through dresses out in the audience.

A paunchy, balding man, *Siegfried*, had apparently broken through the casual, tuxedos security, and was now actually walking onto the stage. It was something that hadn't occurred at the Awards ceremony in the past few years.

The last time, the gate-crasher had streaked naked past an only slightly nonplussed David Niven.

This time the intruder was screaming angrily and incoherently. Siegfried was waving an automatic revolver that glinted steel-blue in the stage lights.

Halfway across the stage, the man began to scream at Nick and Beri Strauss. He was screaming in shrill, guttural German.

"Ich representiere die Sturm Truppe. Ich bringe diese Nachricht die Dachau Zwei!"

I come from the Storm Troop. I carry this message of Dachau Two!

The revolver's first four shots all struck thirty-nine-year-old Nick.

The fifth and sixth shots struck Beri, who pulled down the stage podium as she fell.

With the seventh and eighth shots, Siegfried succeeded in killing himself.

Three thousand miles away, the long scream began for Dr. David Strauss.

Oh my God, please no, please no.
It had begun in California, of all unlikely places.
A coast-to-coast Nazi horror spectacle.
In America this time.

Dr. David Strauss's eyes were transfixed on the gleaming Zenith console television screen.

Slowly then, David became aware of something else gone terribly wrong.

Elena was tottering forward in her stuffed chair. She was making a soft, gagging sound like a death rattle. His grandmother's wet-brown eyes were dilated and fluttering wildly.

"Oh Jesus, David. I think she's having a stroke."

Heather helped him move the feather-light old woman over to her bed.

"I'll go for my bag. Are you all right here with her?"

Heather waved him away. "Yes, go. Hurry." David had never really seen Heather in a medical emergency before. Heather was a doctor now. He left her with his grandmother.

David rushed out into the upstairs hallway. He had to get himself under control, he began to think. *He was a doctor. He'd seen every kind of terrible emergency working in New York. . . .*

Nick! Beri! Elena! Oh please God no . . .

Then David thought he heard windows breaking inside the Strauss house. Glass crashed and tinkled—like an entire cabinet of crystal. Wood split like lightning striking somewhere in the west wing. A terrible melee was in progress . . .

The upstairs lights suddenly flickered. David glanced up as the hall lights fizzled to a dim yellow-brown, almost a sepia tone.

There was hoarse shouting and unbelievable screaming downstairs at the family party. Children were beginning to cry out.

David Strauss ran toward the center-hall stairs to see what could possibly be happening.

The Soldier and the Housewife first, then the Weapons Expert and the Engineer burst into the overcrowded, expensively furnished living room.

The four came inside through beautiful French doors leading out to formal gardens and a dining terrazzo.

A single pistol shot disintegrated a gold-framed mirror over the great fieldstone fireplace.

A fair-warning shot had been fired; full attention was expected now.

In the flicker-frame lighting of the room, the Strauss family saw hooded invaders with drawn revolvers and pump-action shotguns. . . . Then they saw the worst of it.

The white-on-red Nazi armbands.

The dreaded, vile swastikas.

It was difficult, nearly impossible to believe that any of the next few minutes actually happened.

A German-accented voice was calling out commands.

"All of you people down on the floor! Down on the floor. . . . You! You there! Down on the floor."

David negotiated the last front stair just then. He heard the imcomprehensible instructions. *"No one will be harmed if you obey orders."* A black-gloved fist came out of nowhere.

David saw the huge gloved hand when it was too late to stop it. His nose smashed open like a melon struck by a hammer.

Faded wine-and-dark-blue Persian carpeting came flying up at David's face. Tiny Oriental birds flew toward him. Then there was nothing but a quick fade to black.

Heather could hear everything from Elena's bedroom. Now she had to decide what on earth to do. She had to make her important decision immediately.

"Nana, can you come with me? If I help you walk?" Heather gasped out.

"Someone wants to hurt us, Nana. Please."

Nodding weakly, dazed and horrified, Elena Strauss let herself be pulled up from the bed. She felt Heather's sure hands go around her back, up under her arms.

Elena and Heather finally pushed out into the dim upstairs hallway. Heather went to turn right and Elena Strauss had to try to speak.

The old woman tried to scream, but no sound came.

Heather finally saw the two men in the hallway. She started to push Elena the other way. She couldn't believe this terrible hide-and-seek game was happening. She didn't understand how it could possibly be. Out of frustration perhaps, Heather finally screamed at the men.

The Soldier fired just as Heather stepped in front of the older woman.

The young blond doctor crumpled down onto the hallway

runner. For a second, Heather desperately wanted David to be there. Then she wanted nothing at all.

As Elena Strauss began to fall, second and third shots rang out in the bizarrely lit hallway. Three more shots were fired. Then it was unnaturally quiet upstairs in the Strauss house.

"Outside! . . . Everyone outside. Move quickly there. Move! Move, I say!"

Downstairs, the Strauss family was being marched single file out onto the dark side lawns.

The confusion was unbelievable, surreal. Terrible memories began to come back for some of the older family members.

David Strauss was being helped to his feet. Holding his broken, bleeding nose, he was being led forward with the others.

Suddenly, the two other Nazi intruders appeared from another side of the house. *"Let's go,"* the Soldier called out. *"This way! Now!"*

The four Nazis ran north into the thickest estate woods. Dogs began to bark at all the neighboring houses. Police sirens could be heard howling in the direction of the village of Scarsdale.

Amazingly, everyone outside seemed to be unharmed. The attack appeared to be over.

The Strauss family members began to weep, to hug and kiss one another. The *wrow, wrow, wrow* of the sirens got closer. Wide-eyed neighbors were coming across North Avenue in housecoats and pajamas.

Then suddenly, unbelievably, David's Aunt Shirley was pointing back toward the gardens.

Everything became deadly quiet. Everyone just stared.

David turned and saw it, too. In front of Grandpa Sam's pear and boxwood trees. Right in front of an old gazebo brought down from the Cherrywoods Hotel.

"Rotten, pathetic, filthy bastards!" David Strauss spoke in a hoarse whisper. "Oh you rotten sons of bitches."

They'd burned a monstrous, five-foot-square swastika on the estate lawns.

Dachau Two.

10

Later that night, a sixty-eight-year-old man, former SS Colonel Hermann Rinemann, sat in his Old World décor New York City apartment and tried to be reasonably calm.

Colonel Rinemann watched the ABC television replays of first the Academy Awards slayings, then the Scarsdale attack.

Rinemann then tried to watch a movie until the next news report at 2:30.

At 2:30 he watched the last news on channel 9.

At 3:30 he watched the final news on ABC.

At 4:30, the old war criminal walked his dog out on the empty, steaming streets of upper East Side Manhattan.

He then fixed himself toast and tea with lemon—but he found he was too excited to eat once the food was prepared.

Something called "Not For Women Only" was on TV. At 7 A.M., CBS began its morning news with more Nazi clips from the previous night.

Finally, at eight New York time, Hermann Rinemann made a long-distance phone call.

The call went to La Paz, Bolivia.

A manservant answered the distant phone.

Rinemann inquired if Senor Eliazer was up at his usual hour. If Senor Eliazer was available to come to the telephone *... Yes, it was very, very important.*

The next voice Colonel Rinemann heard was that of Senor Eliazer. Senor Eliazer—who had once been known by another, much more famous and powerful-sounding name.

Martin Bormann. The former Reichsleiter. Confidant and secretary to Adolf Hitler.

In a hushed voice, Hermann Rinemann began to describe in great detail what he was watching on the "Today" show's eight o'clock news.

The American Nazi raids.
The warning.
Dachau Zwei.

That evening, former SS Colonel Rinemann went to Luchow's restaurant on East 14th Street in New York.

To celebrate with old, old friends. Old Nazi war criminals.

42

PART II

11

Henri Bendel's, New York City.

Sleek and elegant, her thick black hair blazing like the coat of an expensive horse, Alix Rothschild struck a beautiful New York *Vogue* pose beneath the rich brown-and-crème canopy of Henri Bendel's on West Fifty-seventh Street.

Behind Alix in Bendel's glossy window the arms and legs of several mannequins were strewn on top of broken light bulbs and colorful bazaar streamers. In a second window, there was much tastier display from Bailey-Huebner, one of the boutiques on the ground floor inside.

When Alix had been just ten, she remembered, her uncle Benny had bought her a white beaver topper from this very same, wonderfully screwy department store.

Now Alix was shivering in a blowsy, summery Halston gown. She was also falsely representing a cloying new women's fragrance called Tricot—(the French word for knit sweater, she hoped someone at the Madison Avenue perfume factory realized).

For three magazine ads and two television commercials, Alix Rothschild would receive two hundred fifty thousand dollars to promote Tricot, a scent very much like Rive Gauche, Charlie, Wind Song, Cachet, Babe. A touch less alcohol; a smidgen more jasmine. And Alix Rothschild!

All around the stately, dark-haired actress there were flashing mylar reflectors on aluminum tripods.

No more than an arm's-length away was an expensive troupe of make-up, fashion, and hair stylists. *Dabbing, blotting, curling. Crimping, glossing, spraying, powdering.*

45

Making certain that Alix Rothschild looked perfect.

Which Alix did.

An art director, photographer, assistant director, and account executive told her so. The crowd gathered around Alix showed it with their approving smiles and wide eyes. Even Bendel's ancient doorman, Buster, looked mildly animated or amused.

"Gorgeous, darling." "Perf, Alix." "Sexy kitten now." Alix heard the vague shop talk among the reflectors. *"Varushka got herself preggers in New Hampshire. Yes, she did too. I heard it from Kimberly over at Elite."*

Alix's mind meanwhile was drifting somewhere else altogether.

Whenever the crowds and bright kleig lights tried to suggest to Alix that she might be someone special—her own tremendous guilt, her terrible visions came rushing in to countermand any pleasant experience.

This time it was worse than it had ever been, Alix realized.

Rather than chic, expensive perfumes, she could smell the most horrible rotting decay.

Instead of the wealthy Fifth Avenue crowd, Alix saw a line of stick-limbed, terribly bent-over prisoners in striped fatigues. She saw the big yellow stars branded on their backs and chests.

Thirty-five years before, Alix Rothschild's mother had died horribly on one of those terrifying lines. At Dachau Konzentrationslager. Her father had died in Buchenwald. Alix was one of nearly a million concentration camp survivors in the United States.

Lately, she'd been obsessed.

Ever since the shocking Nazi raid in Westchester. Since the threat of some kind of uprising by the Reich, Alix had been able to think of nothing else.

On May 7, 1945, church bells, fire alarms, air-raid sirens, had tolled and pealed all through ravaged Western Europe; inside Russia; all the way to America.

The terrible war in Europe was finally over.

Winston Churchill had said: "This moment is signal for the greatest outburst of joy in the history of mankind."

What Alix Rothschild remembered was a long, grim line of German civilians. The American Army had forced them to come and visit Dachau after the liberation.

Their heads hung low, protesting their innocence, the Germans were led through the rotting barracks filled with dying Jews.

They were brought eye to eye with the walking skeletons, so frightening because "they almost resembled human beings," one American soldier later wrote.

The German civilians were shown the infamous rows of gallows, where men, women, and children had been hanged; the torture racks and laboratories; the crematoriums, still packed with human ashes, the last attempts to exterminate just a few more Jews.

It was UNRRA that eventually found shelter for some two hundred Dachau children at the Kloster-Indersdorf monastery, due north of the infamous death camp.

Among the children survivors was three-year-old Alix Rothman.

The monastery experience was a sad and unreal one, too.

Little bald children, their stomachs swollen from malnutrition, followed the UNRRA people around constantly—telling their personal stories over and over. Though there was sufficient food at Kloster-Indersdorf, the children continued to steal. The Dachau children said they couldn't help it. A few of them who broke the habit early would leave the dining refectory proudly showing the nurses that they had empty hands and pockets.

In bizarre contrast to the actual DP camps, a famous photo essay appeared in *Life* magazine in 1945. In eighteen photographs, two pretty little "Heidi-types" were shown having a "typical" camp experience; the girls were then followed across Europe as they bravely hitchhiked (with their *Life* photographer, of course) back to their homes. The pretty blond girls were shown "making friends with an American doughboy"; having a medical exam—"their hair is washed and well brushed"; being given an "extra hot chocolate" before they began their cross-country jaunt. No wonder that so many Americans came to believe that the death camp and DP camp horror stories had to be bizarre exaggerations.

When Alix was three and a half, her aunt and uncle finally came to Kloster-Indersdorf to claim her. They took the little Jewish girl to America, the land of *Life* magazine, where Alix was told "to blend into the melting pot"; where she was told "to forget all those terrible things that happened"; where she became Rothschild instead of Rothman.

"I just can't do this anymore," Alix muttered to herself, standing in front of Bendel's. Then suddenly she announced it to the large commercial crew.

"Do what, love?" The director started to walk toward her.

"I can't sell any more perfumes. Or wash-your-hair-once-an-hour shampoos. Or automobiles. Or anything. I'm sorry."

Alix began to push her way out through the film crew.

"Please excuse me. Please. Please *don't touch me.*"

With that, the beautiful actress hurried away down Fifty-seventh; she turned onto Fifth Avenue in her Halston gown.

A sweet spring wind was coming up the famous street. Alix was feeling a little better; somewhat relieved; able to breathe at least. For the moment, she tried to forget about Dachau and Buchenwald.

For the moment, Alix looked down at her feet—size 10-Bs—and she wondered why she had ever thought they looked good in white rowboats from Charles Jourdan.

Alix Rothschild wondered why people thought she was pretty at all.

12

Nestled midway between Albany and New York City, ten miles northwest of beautiful Mohonk and Minnewaska, the famous Strauss Family hotel was set high in the Shawangunk mountains. The multi-winged and turreted hotel was like somebody's fantastic idea for an American-style castle.

Over 550 rooms, Cherrywoods Mountain House was actually *two* great, sprawling hotels, one building on either side of three-hundred-foot-high shale cliffs separated by a shimmering black lake.

Because they were originally constructed in stages over sixty years' time, both "Houses" combined several conflicting styles of European and American architecture. In fact, approaching the Mountain House from the main gravel road, the near wing and livery stable looked not so much like one but rather like ten or twelve different styles, different color buildings. All interconnected like a pretty city street out of the 1890s.

Most awesome and beautiful, however, were the grounds of the resort hotel.

Over two thousand acres of gardens, grape arbors, barber-cut lawns, and virgin woods, which hotel guests were encouraged to tour on foot, or in a horse-driven buckboard.

In summer, the beautiful place was tended by college students. Skinny, shirtless boys with corkscrew belly buttons and ax-sharp shoulder blades; tidy New Paltz College and Vassar girls with friendly smiles, freckles, butterscotch thighs.

From most rooms there was a breathtaking view over evergreens and apple farms that stretched nearly to Newburgh, some thirty miles distant on a thin blue ribbon that turned out to be the Hudson River.

Rockefellers, Roosevelts, Vanderbilts, and Kennedys had had the wind knocked out of their sails by the Cherrywoods Mountain House view. "The finest view on the Atlantic coast," some travel editors raved.

"Someone really ought to make a scary movie here," Nick Strauss had always said, and once had shamelessly suggested to hotel guest Roman *Rosemary's Baby* Polanski.

Maybe someone *would* make a horror film there, Dr. David Strauss thought as he surveyed the land one overcast and particularly graphic afternoon.

Because it was at pretty Cherrywoods Mountain House where select members of the Strauss family were finally sequestered under specially arranged-for FBI protection; where they waited in relative safety; where they began to hope things would go back to normal soon.

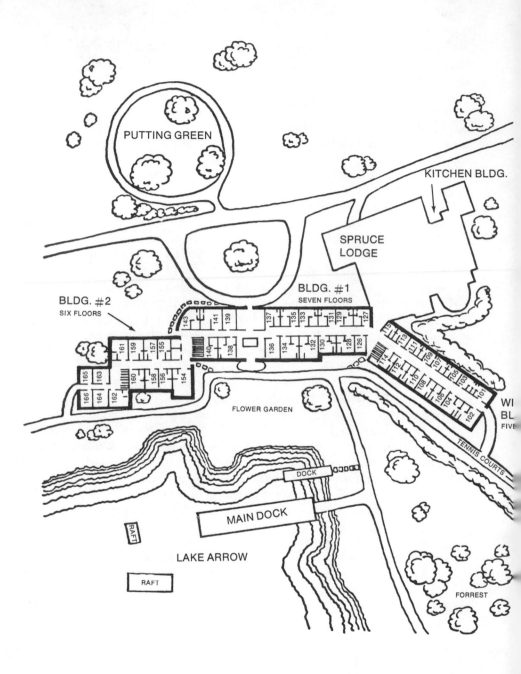

CHERRYWOODS' EAST WING has over 300 rooms. The West Wing has 250. Both wings combine several conflicting styles of European and American architecture. The tremendous grounds stretch out for over 2000 acres.

Strauss Cherrywoods hotel around 1950. The Strauss inheritance from the hotel, real estate, and motion pictures was estimated to be in excess of eighty million dollars. The status of the estate is in unbelievable turmoil.

13

First there had been two weeks under FBI guard at a more secluded "safe house" in the Adirondacks.

Then came Cherrywoods. A gradual return to sanity, to some facade of normality.

In the beginning of David's stay—the three weeks before the hotel reopened for regular guests (just a trickle of Cherrywoods's normal spring business, though)—the young doctor rarely went out of his suite of rooms on the fifth floor of West House, hanging over the storybook lake.

David Strauss was totally obsessed with his grandmother's, his brother's, and his wife's deaths. David was particularly obsessed with memories of his and Heather's life together before the evening of April twenty-fifth.

Once he began to go out on the hotel grounds, David tried to lose himself in a flurry of very physical activity.

Mornings at dawn, he would row a modified scull around and around steamy Lake Arrow. He went for long, solitary swims, and long jogs through the pine forests.

In the afternoons, David began to offer a free medical clinic for hotel workers and their families. He tacked up a very unofficial-looking sign in one of the long hallways on the ground floor. *Dr. David Strauss. Hours: 3 P.M. until I'm finished.*

More and more, though, David found himself being drawn irresistibly to the subject of modern-day Nazis. He pored over Nazi books and stared at old Nazi movies with unhealthy attention. Almost daily he tried to reach an old friend of his grandmother's, the famous German Nazi-hunter Michael Ben-Iban. Ben-Iban, however, never seemed to be at his home in Frankfurt. "I'm sorry, Ben-Iban is away in Israel"; or, "Ben-Iban is on business in England," David heard from the old man's secretary.

David had always overintellectualized and romanticized the Nazis, he decided midway through his reading and research. *So who exactly were these Nazis?* he now asked himself like a monotonous broken record.

In May of 1980, who were they?

Who was it that had attacked his family on Upper North Avenue?

Who had murdered Heather?

In a quasi-Victorian suite of hotel rooms that brought to mind the movie *Niagara*, David Strauss stockpiled some three hundred Nazi books and pamphlets, many of them generously supplied by the Ulster County Lending Library Association.

Among the Nazi books were Hugh Trevor-Roper's masterpiece, *The Last Days of Hitler*; Thomas Mann's *Order of the Day*; hefty tomes by Walter Langer, Michael Bar-Zohar, Shirer, Speer, Toland; *The Final Solution; Hitler's Twelve Apostles*.

There was also the swastika-covered, quite stupefying *Hate Book*; pornographic Nazi paperbacks imported from a drugstore in nearby Poughkeepsie—*Gestapo Prison Brothel* and *Bitch of Buchenwald; The National Socialist White People's Party Songbook* (To the tune of "Jingle Bells": "Riding through the Reich/In a big Mercedes-Benz/Killing lots of kikes/Making lots of friends").

And: the Holocaust volume of *The Jewish Encyclopedia*; the complete Lucy Rabinowitz; Samson the Nazarite; Jabotinsky.

Almost daily now too, a man named Harry Callaghan from the FBI brought David excellent new information. Like exact data from the Library of Congress on the known Nazi organizations still flourishing anywhere in the late 1970s.

From all of this information, Strauss began to compile his own composite box score on the Nazis. They certainly knew who he was; now David wanted to know all about them. Literally everything about the Nazis.

The American Nazi Party. Now calls itself the National Socialist White People's Party, David wrote in a foolscap note pad. *Based in Alexandria, Virginia, FBI guesstimates 800 to 2,000 active members.*

The National States Rights Party. Out of Marietta, Georgia. Hate sheet called Thunderbolt *distributed to 15,000 members every month. Members included Fred Cowan, New Rochelle furniture mover who went berserk in 1976, killing five people in Westchester.*

American Nazi splinter groups:

The National Socialist Party of America. Based in Chicago. Attempted Nazi march through Skokie, Illinois, on July 4, 1977.

The National Socialist Women's Organization. Chicago.

The National Socialist League (Gay Nazis). Los Angeles.

A small group in Pennsylvania called Stormtroopers, but considered "harmless" by FBI.

International Nazi groups and movements:

Die Spinne. "The Spider." Leaves no mailing address. Not considered "harmless." The same goes for Die Schleuse, L'Araignée, and ODESSA.

Day after day David Strauss rummaged through, or just stared at, the hateful stacks of Nazi papers and Nazi books.

He wondered exactly which page had killed his brother, his grandmother, his wife.

Every night when David closed his eyes, he saw after-images of the funerals.

Heather's funeral had been disturbingly peaceful. A handsome Episcopal cemetery called Evergreen. Imperial-blue skies overhead. Tall, full-boughed trees like those in Van Gogh's final paintings at Arles.

Nicholas, Elena, and Beri's service had been at Temple Emmanuel on Fifth Avenue. The large, emotional funeral was held the day after the shootings, according to Jewish Law.

As David lay in his bed at Cherrywoods, he could see himself riding to the funeral in a somber, tomblike limousine. The trees along Fifth Avenue were silently flashing by the limousine's windows. His own face was reflected on the windows: dark, dreamlike, severe.

There were nearly four thousand people at the temple.

Gray police barricades had been set up for three blocks in either direction on Fifth. Two pale-blue police buses sat at Sixty-seventh Street, which happened to be the site of the Soviet Embassy.

David held the arms of his two great-aunts as he slowly walked down the roped-off entranceway to the temple.

"Kill the Nazis now!" He heard a piercing scream come from the grieving crowd. Insane, *unreal* epithet. The whole scene impossible to sort out and understand.

Inside the temple, David's gaze fell down the long center aisle. At the sight of the three plain pine caskets his eyes filled. A deep baritone cantor began to sing. A swirling wave made up of sadness and immeasurable loss tried to turn David's stomach inside out. He felt unpleasantly light-headed.

You never know how much you're going to miss people, he understood. At that moment, David was certain he couldn't go on without them.

Dear, dear Heather; Beri; Nick; his Elena.

Not only family, his four best friends in the world; his flesh; a physical and spiritual part of David gone without any warning.

As he listened to the cantor, then to the droning chief rabbi, David was reminded of Elena most of all. And thinking of his grandmother, David remembered her one consuming hatred. Now David's hatred as well.

The depraved, unregenerate Nazis.

The unspeakable Reich.

Who came to him every night at Cherrywoods; who would come to Dr. David Strauss every night, no matter where he went.

In nightmare, after nightmare, after nightmare.

14

James Fixx suggested a hopeful premise in his *Complete Book of Running*: "People I talked with told me they felt they had benefited psychologically from running," Fixx had written.

Dr. David Strauss ran to punish his body, it seemed—*for what sin or sin of omission he wasn't exactly sure.*

Dr. Strauss ran to prepare himself—*for what Olympic task he wasn't certain either.*

Six miles a day at first.

Then eight miles.

Ten miles; plus heartbreaking quarter-mile sprints.

As many as twenty-three miles one marathon Sunday, with the sun seeming to be racing him through the pine forests— a big lemon-yellow pie-face, obviously mocking David's folly.

Probably because he was a doctor, David pretended to himself that the running was helping to lower his blood pressure; that it was decreasing his cholesterol; that it would build up his cardio-pulmonary fitness: that these were the chief reasons why he ran.

Pure folly. Just as the lemon-pie sun had suggested.

David ran for the pain.

David ran because during what he called his "ruthless runs" he had no memory; no practical necessities; no tragic past or frightening, very unsure future.

There was just the physical act of running; the cleansing pain.

There was pushing himself to his absolute limits; there was teaching his body to accept extra pain like heel spurs, runner's knee, groin pulls; there was learning to exist without oxygen before a second wind came; and learning to run hard in spite of crippling excesses of lactic acid.

One overcast afternoon, the FBI chief Harry Callaghan approached David about his running. Callaghan was short-haired, physically fit, in his mid-forties. He was tall and gauntly thin. He reminded David of a New England college professor—of Gregory Peck trying to play a college professor role. He was getting a little soft puttering around Cherry-woods, the agent said. Could he possibly work out a little with David? Might he tag along on one of the ruthless runs?

David didn't like the idea, but he didn't know how politely to say no. He recoiled from the thought of having a running partner: someone who might take his mind off the *pure physical act*.

A little before 5 P.M., Callaghan appeared in a burnt-orange-and-red USMC T-shirt, loose basketball shorts from George-town, pale white and freckled Irishman's legs.

David himself wore gray-and-red-striped snowbirds, ancient Pumas, a faded apple-green shirt and shorts, and an old ratty sweatband that had evolved from snowy white to mouse gray.

David's well-muscled body was a beautiful mahogany brown from the sunny afternoons. He was completing a hybrid combination of the Royal Canadian Air Force and the West Point fitness drills when Harry Callaghan came up to him on the Lake Porch.

"No, no, Dr. Strauss. You don't do the West Point drills before you run." The FBI agent couldn't really believe what he was seeing.

"I do a few sit-ups, squats, leg and knee raises before I go out," David said. "When I come back in I try to do another set with rocking sit-ups and isometrics."

Callaghan shook his silver-gray head from side to side. This was the first time he'd realized that Dr. Strauss was a bit more than just another fitness nut.

The two men completed the final exercises side by side on the sympathetically groaning wooden porch.

Grunting and cursing, they did squats, leg thrusts and raises, push-ups.

Acidy sweat began to waterfall into Harry Callaghan's eyes. His Tiger Corsairs sloshed as they began to fill with water. Gnats and horseflies landed and took off his glistening back as if it were the national insects' aircraft carrier.

"Do you mind if I run with this?"

It was said so low-key and matter-of-factly.

David was strapping a yellowish, cowhide pack onto his back and shoulders. The backpack was a professional training device made by Dunlap. It could hold from twenty to fifty pounds of lead weight and David had it full.

"You know what I'm going to say."

"I'm the doctor, right?"

"Or maybe, you should *see* a doctor."

"O.K. I'm ready. Run from the hips, Mr. Callaghan. Breathe from the belly." David smiled for the first time. "Let's go, partner."

They ran straight back into the tall evergreen forest. Very cool in the shade. Actually, quite nice, Harry Callaghan thought as his feet padded softly on the pine needles. Maybe the worst of it had been the exercises.

Seeming to sense the FBI agent's contentment, David turned onto one of the winding trails leading up onto Lookout Mountain.

Here, the lay of land was steep and rocky. The running of the two men became closer to mountain-climbing.

After two-and-a-half miles of mountain, Harry Callaghan began to feel an uneasy tightness in his chest. Tightening in his upper legs. A burning in his chest. Shortness of breath. At first, he guessed that Dr. Strauss was trying strongly to discourage him from tagging along again.

The Washinton, D. C., man struggled so that he ran right up beside David Strauss.

"What are you trying to do to yourself?" Callaghan asked in a puffing, grunting voice. "What are you trying to do *to me?*"

Very suddenly, though, something else struck the agent; in an intuitive flash, Callaghan knew exactly what David Strauss was doing on his "ruthless runs."

"You're getting yourself ready," Callaghan huffed, his heavy steps landing like small bombs now.

"Want to fight them, don't you?. . . . Nazis? Storm Troop?"

David Strauss began to pick up the pace. He tried to ignore the silver-haired man. "Little stitch in my side. Diaphragm spasm. Getting my second wind, though."

"You can't fight them." Callaghan was struggling to keep up with the younger man. His chest was twisting tighter and tighter; his legs felt leaden; his neck and shoulders ached.

"Fuck I can't. If I ever get the chance . . . I goddamn will. Fight the bastards. Murdering coward bastards. Not going to be marched to the camps again."

"They're not going . . . challenge you to a foot race, doctor."

David said nothing to that. The young doctor was trying to run away.

That made Harry Callaghan angry.

Damnit, he *knew* about the Reich. Callaghan knew more about the Nazis than just about any field man in the Bureau. *He could help.* That was his job. Dr. David Strauss was choosing to ignore him, though. Acting as if the agent was some kind of useless second asshole.

In a moment of anger, Harry Callaghan stuck his foot out.

He knew he shouldn't have the second he did it. Not professional, Harry. Not rational and professional at all.

David fell hard and fast. As if he'd been hit by a powerful sniper's rifle—something Harry Callaghan had seen happen to a man.

The apple-green shirt and shorts, the wheeling arms and legs, flipped, somersaulted, rolled to an exaggerated stop against a wall of scrub pines.

"You might as well learn a lesson right now." The FBI agent called down from the main trail.

"A very valuable part of your training. *The Nazis run dirty, Dr. Strauss.*"

Harry Callaghan headed back to the Cherrywoods hotel. Walking.

15

The realization that she was maybe royally screwing up her life, her acting career at least, came to Alix Rothschild slowly, over a couple of nightmarish weeks in mid-spring.

First there had been the million-dollar perfume stink in front of Henri Bendel's. Then another tempest in a teapot; this one in The Café of the Sherry Netherland, with a slick "packager" representing CBS, MFA, and apparently two million dollars.

Now there was the most uncomfortable tableau of all. At her movie company's New York offices, high over Central Park South.

Alix's agent, Mark Halperin, was there, the paradigmatic California golden boy: biting his manicured nails, sliding his sunglasses in and out of a breast pocket of his chambray Western shirt, rubbing the soles of his fashionably soiled tennis sneakers together. Of Mark it could be said: here was a man who loved lunches with models at the front table in the back room of P. J. Clarke's.

Also present in the posh business office was Arnold Manning: bald, stout, gonzo independent producer; former president of one of the few remaining large studios in Hollywood.

Plus a coterie of studio lawyers, accountants, and other vice-presidents; overindulged men who seemed to confuse themselves with their company's movie stars and best directors.

Arnold Manning was speaking to Alix in the softest voice

imaginable—as if she were a wayward but much loved daughter—which in a way, Alix was.

"Must I remind you, Alix, dear, sweet, confusing, confused, sexy-as-hell lady, that we have a three-picture arrangement, you and I. That's for *movies. Three* movies."

"That's fine, Arnold," Alix nodded. "I just haven't much liked the scripts you've been sending me."

One of the studio heads reared ugly. "Point of information, Alix. As I understand it, Jackie Bisset didn't like the script for *The Deep*. Dick Dreyfuss didn't want to do *Jaws. Facts*."

Alix stared away out the floor-to-ceiling windows that were rattling softly in their giant aluminum frames.

Outside was Columbus Circle. Lovely Central Park in late spring. Yellow sun balloon; lollipop trees; hobby-horse hansom cabs. No visions of concentration camps today. No Dachau; no Buchenwald. Not yet, anyway.

"Please listen." Alix turned back to Arnold Manning. On her face was a small child's hurt look. Crestfallen green eyes. The slightest thin-lipped moue.

"I promise to do the three pictures for you. I promise. I owe you, Arnold. I also kind of love you, dear, sweet, dark, confusing, I forget the rest, man."

Arnold Manning looked hurt now. The slightest fat-lipped moue. "You forgot *sexy as hell*."

For the first time in the meeting, Alix smiled.

"Arnold, I need a little time to be by myself . . . This terrible Nazi scare, I . . . Basically, I have to get away from being such a big deal to everyone I'm around. I need to think. I need to be a plain nobody for a while. No admirers. No catty detractors."

Alix Rothschild smiled again. "And I'm aware, Mr. Manning, that at the rate I'm going, I could be a *nobody* for a long, long time to come."

Arnold Manning began to laugh as if he was being tickled by chimps with pink feathers. The peculiar laugh grew until the stout, bald man let out an almost painful howl.

"So go away, Alix. I agree you have to relax. I agree you need some time by yourself. Everybody does. . . . I understand what this horrible Nazi business must mean to you."

Manning had waited just long enough; now he was giving Alix back her own ideas, almost her own words. They both knew what he was doing, but that was fine. That was the secret of the business relationship between Alix Rothschild and Arnold Manning.

"Where are you thinking of going, Al?" Mark Halperin was still nibbling his sunglasses. "Just in case your agent needs to get in touch."

"That's my Mark-up!" Alix put on a smile. She was trying to be like her old self again. *Leave them laughing*, Alix had long ago learned on advertising agency casting calls.

"I was thinking of going upstate for a while. In a week or so. I have an old friend up there . . . who knows how to treat me like I'm nobody. He still calls me Alice Rothman."

Alix stood up, and the whole room of suits and sunglasses rose with her. "I'll be going to a place called Cherrywoods Mountain House. But I won't be accepting any phone calls."

16

Alix Rothschild passed a final frustrating weekend in Manhattan. Arranging what seemed like a thousand unraveled loose ends. Breaking commitments such as long-scheduled fashion photography shoots. Severing overextended friendships with New York theater people and one well-known actor in particular.

On Sunday afternoon, she traveled to the farthest tip of Manhattan Island.

Battery Park.

Where the annual Solidarity Sunday rally was being held in support of Soviet Jewry.

At the large rally, Alix was scheduled to appear and speak from the main podium with other celebrities and Jewish leaders.

Bizarre thought patterns had begun to trouble Alix on Sunday morning, though. Strange, obsessive images were flashing through her mind, one after the other. Like an early Ingmar Bergman or a Jean Cocteau film, she thought. *Orpheus. Le Sang d'un Poète.* A host of morbid death-camp ideas.

When she arrived at the pretty riverside park, Alix went through the main entrance as part of the large crowd, rather than through the special VIP portal.

She was wearing oversized sunglasses, plus an unfashionable kerchief to hide her familiar face, her long black hair. She didn't identify herself to the authorities; she spoke to no one.

"Over three-hundred-thousand people will attend this year's very emotional rally," CBS had predicted on its morning news.

"Solidarity Sunday is an organizational masterpiece," the Sunday *Times* had said.

Alix's eyes traveled over the vast sea of bobbing heads. Shiny black and also colorful knitted skullcaps. Fedoras from Pitkin Avenue. Stuka-fighting kites and Israeli flags, all the way up to the very high main podium.

Behind the podium was the shimmering nexus of the East and Hudson rivers. The hundred-and-fifty-two-foot-high Statue of Liberty. A hovering WPIX helicopter.

Alix passed by assorted flag-sellers with their catchy slogans curling and flowing in the river breeze.

Save Soviet Jewry.

Their Fight Is Our Fight

If You Loved the Book, You'll Love the Country.

Stamp Out (a large black swastika).

Alix began to wonder if the leaders of Solidarity Sunday believed that the large rally would have a meaningful effect on the Russian government—even on American politicians who might in theory pressure the Soviets (as they supposedly had been doing for the past thirty years). These were very well intentioned, emotionally involved people gathered in the park, Alix was thinking. But what strange, strange ideas they had of the way tyrannies functioned.

Thousands of Jews were being MURDERED in Soviet Russia. The finest rally in the world wouldn't solve that. The most logical and intelligent speeches wouldn't stop the bloodshed, Alix considered.

Some SSSI members were waving placards with the names

of Russian Jewish POWs. Many of the students were also wearing POW wristbands.

Not POW, Alix's mind screamed out. *There are no rules of the Geneva Convention being practiced in those hideous concentration camps. Please understand that. Please understand that your placards will not stop a Fourth Reich Storm Troop!*

The folk singer Rabbi Schlomo Carlbach finally began to chant from the main platform. An old familiar rally song. Affecting.

"Amyisrael Chi! Amyisrael Chi! Amyisrael Chi!"

Alix watched the celebrities on stage gather together and begin to sing along.

Democratic leaders: Jackson from Washington; Koch; Bella; Percy Sutton. Opera singers. Israeli generals and politicians. Catholic and Protestant leaders.

Alix tried to ready herself to go up there with them.

What do I have to say to these people?

Good people! You have come all the way to the end of Manhattan this very hot afternoon. I love you very much for doing that. But can we really expect to crumble the walls of Jericho with our prayers? With our just anger and our frustration? Do we believe this will help those dying in Russian concentration camps?

The shofar, the powerful ram's horn, suddenly blared from somewhere up around the main stage.

Tekiah.

Shevarim.

Teruah.

There was so much beauty possible. So much justice, passion, power, Alix thought to herself. *If only this could work to stop the Soviet Nazis and their tyranny. If only it could work to stop the Reich. If only the Storm Troop would come now and fight us.*

"You are Aliza Rothschild. . . . Agtress . . . Why you here with us? You shouldn't be here. . . . Up on stage there!"

An old man. A small, thin man in a tattered jacket. Yellowing white shirt and teeth. Baggy, stained trousers. A Jewish man from the Old World—Germany, Austria, Poland.

He kept clutching at Alix's arm. He grabbed at her blouse. He smelled of the heaviest tobacco. Of stone chess benches and libraries in Williamsburg.

"Please go away!" Alix said.

He wouldn't leave her. Hands kept pawing.

Terrified, embarrassed, Alix finally pushed the man. An impulse. A repulse. She pushed away the specter of the death camps. She pushed away some vague unformed idea that this man had somehow permitted the Nazis to do terrible things. He had survived—and now here he was at this brassy, noisy show.

Finally, Alix fled.

She pushed her way back toward the park entryway. Back away from the main speaking stage. Away from her commitment to speak to the crowd.

"Shema Yisroel!" A chant followed her.

"Shema Yisroel!"

"Shema Yisroel!"

Alix Rothschild *walked* from the tip of Manhattan to her hotel apartment on Central Park.

Nearly six miles on the boiling hot afternoon in New York. *Like nothing at all in her growing nightmare state.*

That same Sunday afternoon, David Strauss sat on a leaf-green bench out along one of Cherrywoods's prettiest nature trails.

Sitting beside him was the FBI agent, Harry Callaghan.

"I'm sorry about the other afternoon. Our inauspicious running debut," the lean, slope-shouldered Irishman was explaining. "I was trying to help—at least to let you know that I was available. I got mad when you shut me off. I guess we were both off in our own little worlds."

"I'm sorry about what happened, too." David nodded. "You were right. What you were trying to tell me. I was being a shithead. . . . It's just that I have this unbelievable, pulsing hate building up inside of me. No outlet. It's hard to communicate exactly."

"Not so hard. I can imagine at least some of what you must feel. I *would* like to help, though. That's what I'm here for. My job. My vocation."

From their spot on the woodlands trail, David and Harry Callaghan had a perfect view west across the Roundout Valley to the sleepy Rip Van Winkle mountains.

"Hundreds of millions of years ago," David said, "all the land around here was covered by a great inland lake. My grandfather used to tell me that every time the two of us came up here." Dr. David Strauss smiled. "I guess I'm *still* off in my own world a little. Lots of family stuff floating around loose in my head."

"Yeah. Well, when you come back down to earth, don't forget what I've been trying to tell you. Please don't get me confused with any of the negative Washington bureaucrat images which you probably have. Which *I* have, for Christ sakes."

"I appreciate what you're trying to do. Really. I'm going to be fine," David Strauss promised.

After the FBI agent left, David went and sat on one of the fancy gazebos perched high over icy-blue Lake Arrow.

Looking down on the lake, the hotel, the sprawling Crayola-green grounds, David began to think about his brother Nick. How every summer, the very day school let out, they'd escape to Cherrywoods for two spectacularly glorious months.

One particular scene at Cherrywoods, David was sure he'd never forget.

At the time, David had been eleven or twelve years old. He and his best friend Mark Davidson were spending two fabulous weeks together at the hotel. During the second week, a boy they knew from yeshiva school arrived with his parents.

The boy's name was Chaim Rabisky, and like his mother and father, he was a strict Hasid.

This meant that Chaim had strange, kinky sideburns. It meant that he wore black, baggy trousers, black tie-shoes and white socks, an over-sized black hat. It meant that the boy dressed and acted in a way that brought outrageous attention to his Jewishness.

For three days, every time David and Mark saw Chaim they winced inwardly and shook their heads. In their humble opinions, Chaim was definitely a *putz*, a real jerk.

On the afternoon of the fourth day, however, Chaim Rabisky suddenly found himself walking in the pine forests with David and Mark. It made the boy feel good, much better. He knew that the other boys disapproved of his clothes, the way he acted. Sometimes Chaim had trouble with the strict religious ways himself. . . .

At any rate, they were much friendlier that day. They were actually having a good time. David and Mark even seemed to be listening when Chaim dutifully tried to teach them about the Gemara.

Far, far from the hotel, miles into the dark sunless woods, David and Mark suddenly started to run. Outfitted in sneakers and jeans, they ran much faster than Chaim Rabisky could. They completely lost Chaim within two minutes. . . . Then David and Mark ran all the way back to Mountain House— laughing uncontrollably, like mad, evil elves.

His black trousers ripped and covered with burrs, his hat lost in a rushing brook, Chaim didn't get back to the hotel until well after six. Within an hour, he and his parents were packed into their Ford Falcon, heading back to White Plains. . . .

Just before family dinner that evening, the door to David's room suddenly crashed open.

David never forgot looking up to see Nick storming across the old-fashioned bedroom.

Nick slapped David as hard as he could across the mouth. He slapped David a second time. Hard, stinging smacks that echoed in the room.

Only then did Nick Strauss sit down beside his sobbing younger brother. Very patiently, very adult-like, Nick tried to explain the anger he was feeling.

"I don't particularly like Chaim Rabisky either," Nick began. "I know exactly why you and Mark did the shitty thing you did today. Chaim makes you feel uncomfortable. What you two call 'creepy.' The Hasid's black hat makes Chaim look like a small, silly grown-up. All his talking about the Gemara is a real pain in the ass. I understand that.

"But David, you must never consciously hurt another Jew.

No matter what, David. You must never, never hurt another Jew. O.K.?" Nick had asked. "O.K.?"

There were tears in David's brother's eyes. "Davey, I did this because I love you very much," Nick finally said. "I love you, Davey."

Looking out toward the fuzzy-blue Catskill Mountains, David tried to picture his brother Nick. Nick the Quick. Nick the Eloquent. Nick the brilliant filmmaker.

David tried to remember the soothing quality of his brother's voice.

Goddamn it, he was starting to forget everything. Nick, Heather, Elena. What a *farshtinkener* business life can be, their grandfather Sam always used to say.

What a *stinking* business life can be!

A sad one, too.

18

David couldn't quite get the idea that *Heather Duff Strauss was dead* out of his mind, though. *That she was gone from his life.*

Forever and always.

Never to be heard or seen by him again.

Distractions helped, David had to admit. The more peculiar the distraction, the better.

When he'd been an undergraduate at Princeton, David had begun a curious diary/journal that he called his Crapbook.

The Crapbook now contained such questionable treasures as a visitor's pass into Olympic Village in Munich; a college letter for sculling; one of his favorite first lines from a book— "Like most men, I tell a hundred lies a day." All sorts of junk that antique people call "collectibles." The Crapbook. Something future true-crime writers would pay thousands of dollars to own.

To the more whimsical first half of the Crapbook, David now added an obsessive collection of clippings on the North Avenue Nazi attack. He faithfully pasted in news stories on other suspected Storm Troop activity: a synagogue bombing on Long Island; the grisly murder of an influential rabbi doctor in Chicago. He put in condolences on Elena and Nick's deaths from important Jewish leaders all over the world. Plus selected Naziana from his ever-expanding Nazi library.

While the scrapbook helped David maintain some balance of sanity, what seemed to help more were the medical clinics he offered every weekday afternoon.

A general practitioner for the first time in his career, David Strauss suddenly found himself treating asthma, roseola, croup, enlarged prostate, insomnia, peptic ulcers.

Most important, while he was treating one of the hotel staff, David felt almost human and useful again. Inside his office at the hotel, Dr. David Strauss could just about feel alive.

Late one afternoon while David was treating one of the gardeners' children for a raging case of poison ivy, the head of the FBI team dropped by at his make-do office.

This particular afternoon, Harry Callaghan looked like he would have fit much more comfortably into a Louis Auchincloss chronicle than a Fourth Reich neo-Nazi adventure. Other than being the tall, silent type who seem to inspire confidence when it's needed, Callaghan was all broadcloth button-downs, subdued tweeds, dark-brown cordovans.

The Washington man sat on the edge of David's examining table. He ran his index finger across the bottom of young Neal Becton's foot.

The boy started to giggle. Callaghan grinned too, and it was the first time David had seen any sign of humor coming from the FBI guards.

"We've just gotten a very strange report." Callaghan tamped down on his pipe, then lit it. "The report says that Martin Bormann may have recently entered the United States through Miami. Did your family ever have any contact with that bastard, David? In the concentration camps in Germany? Even the most remote contact?"

As he dabbed Albolene cream onto Neal Becton's inflamed legs, David began to feel slightly whimsical, a bit light-

headed. It was a feeling he hadn't experienced since the Westchester attack.

"Reichsführer Martin Bormann? Short, squat man? . . .
Yeah. Sure we knew him. He used to come to breakfast at our
house when I was just a boy. My grandmother Elena would
serve Nova and bagels and he'd get all sorts of pissed off."

Just the far corner of Harry Callaghan's mouth broke. About
half a smile showed. It was interesting hearing the young doctor beginning to joke around for a change, Harry was thinking.
Maybe Dr. Strauss was finally healing a little. Maybe he,
Harry, was breaking through a little to Dr. David Strauss.

"The other thing," Callaghan went on without giving David
the satisfaction of a real laugh. "One of the few American
Nazi-hunters has been in contact with us. Strange man. Benjamin Rabinowitz? A friend of your grandmother's."

David nodded. He'd heard quite a bit about Rabinowitz.
For years, Elena had been a contributor to Rabinowitz's ef-
forts, in fact. She'd contributed to Rabinowitz in America; to
Michael Ben-Iban's Centre for Jewish Studies in Europe,
David knew.

"Rabinowitz has some interesting theories I'd like you to
react to. The only slight catch," Callaghan began to relight his
pipe. "We'd have to leave the hotel for a few hours tomorrow.
Rabinowitz doesn't want to be seen with you. He seemed
somewhat paranoid. Frightened."

David felt a sudden chill shoot up his spine. He had an
ominous feeling that maybe something was going to happen
now. Maybe the Nazi-hunter would have some kind of new
and important information. *Something* revealing about the
Nazi Storm Troop.

"I'd like to meet Mr. Rabinowitz very much," he said.
"Tomorrow is fine with me. I'd be glad to meet him anywhere."

David Strauss didn't completely grasp it as he stood in his
doctor's office that afternoon, but his personal hunt for the
neo-Nazis had just officially begun.

19

The Sans Souci Restaurant, Washington, D.C.

The Führer and the Warrior were eating steaks and sipping wine, enjoying as amiable and light-hearted a tête-à-tête supper as was evident anywhere in the clubby, chatty Washington, D.C., dining room.

"A pleasure, as it always is here." The Warrior sipped his burgundy, letting the fine red roll on his tongue. He then wiped his crinkly, slightly puffed mouth.

The Führer smiled in agreement. "A very decent steak. Even at approximately twenty-five dollars a pound."

Their attentive black waiter, Randolph, came with two snifters of Courvoisier.

"I believe it is time now," the Warrior said. "You have wined me and dined me most graciously. Now we must talk."

For the next fifteen minutes, the Führer was alternately a graceful Diplomat, a Moralist, a harsh Military Strategist.

The complete plan for the operation known as Dachau Two was revealed to the Warrior.

The plot was then mercilessly torn to shreds. It was rebuilt from the remnants. Truly terrifying and unassailable this time.

Black coffee was ordered by the Warrior. The face and broad neck of the white-maned man had grown bright scarlet red over the intense quarter of an hour.

"Finally," the Führer said in a nerveless monotone that was quite chilling at the intimate table, "my group will strike. The effect will be like nothing ever seen. Unique. An extraordinary blitzkrieg, even in this age."

The powerful old man called Warrior answered slowly, with grave consideration showing in every deep line of his face.

"If it was anyone other than you who asked this of me—I would say *no, no, no*. The risks of your plan are almost unconscionable. Because it is *you* who ask, however, I must give my tentative approval."

The Führer started to speak, but Warrior slowly raised his hand.

"*Not* approval to proceed, my friend, approval to seek further guidance from the other Council members. You now have one negative vote. My vote is no."

The Führer's head remained bowed for several seconds. Words finally came with obvious difficulty and great emotion.

"I have to tell you a most difficult thing now. You see, I have already approached the other members of the Council. I have all five votes. Yours is the only negative vote cast."

Warrior nodded. "I must fight you then," he said. "I will use all of my resources."

Outside of the Washington, D.C., restaurant, the Warrior and Führer got into separate black limousines, one with bulletproof windows, one with DPL license plates.

As one of the limousines crossed Victory Bridge, the black car sparked suddenly, like a match being lit in a stiff wind.

There was a bright red-and-yellow flame at the center of the famous bridge. A magician's puff of smoke. Then dark metal fell on the Potomac like the largest imaginable raindrops.

Back at the Shoreham Hotel, the Führer made a single-sentence phone call.

"Begin Dachau Two."

20

Rusted, off-white farms, ripe for exposure in *National Geographic*—evidence that upstate New York is really part of the Midwest—lined either side of Route 32 South going toward Wallkill.

Stone-pocked mailboxes were designed for Browns, Grays, Halls, and the *Kingston Freeman.* An ocean of tea-green and silver leaves filtered the low late-May sky. Hay fever grew high along the roadside. Spring sang "Come Build a Maypole under My Apple Tree."

An agent named Hallahan suggested to David that traveling

under armed bodyguard was like "being a little bait fish, with some other bait fish trying to protect you from mako sharks."

"That must be comforting as hell for David to hear now," Harry Callaghan said. "Not inaccurate, though," he added, puffing on his Dunhill.

"It does have an eerie quality to it," David offered from the back seat of the government Lincoln. "It feels like, oh, when you leave a movie-theater matinee and walk out into bright sunshine. Or like the first time you go outside after a shitty flu."

David was extremely aware of the smallest details on the trip, he noticed. The different bird sounds along Route 32; some melodic; shrill; electric. The muted colors of the landscape. Shadow shapes. Fresh earth smells coming in his open window.

He began to imagine the Storm Troop behind every boulder and all the Pepsi and Ford truck billboards; inside every car that zipped by on the two-lane blacktop.

It was ridiculous, he was sure, but his heartbeat was a steady *thump thump* for the entire forty-minute trip to meet the Nazi-hunter Rabinowitz.

A village populated with New York City Puerto Ricans and Villas this and that came and went on the fly-splattered Lincoln windshield. Small apple farms shot by on either side of the road. Then the Wallkill Correctional Facility—a slate-gray building in the center of a raving-yellow cornfield.

David and the two agents each had a shot, then a second shot out of a flask filled with Dewars.

Then came the unincorporated village of Wallkill, New York.

Pimply teen-age boys and girls stood around Main Street in Wallkill Central jackets and engineering boots.

The Lincoln cruised past Fescoe's Feed & Grain. Frank's Beauty Salon for Women. Western Auto. State Farm.

Nazi-hunters, David thought in a mild haze daydream. *Dachau Two. Total insanity. And I am a big part of the mess.*

Halfway down the main dragstrip, the Lincoln slipped into a diagonal space in front of Robt. Hatfield's Wallkill Inn. "Good food and grog," it said on a wooden sign. "My beer is Rheingold."

A strange thought occurred to David—at least something hit

him the wrong way as he got out of the car in the haggard, peculiar farm town.

Inside this little bar was America's *premier Nazi-hunter*.

21

This much is documented everywhere.

Through the late 1960s and '70s, the man most responsible for bringing Nazi war criminals living in America to justice wasn't a sharp U.S. federal attorney or FBI department head.

The man was a shy, skinny U.S. postal worker named Benjamin Paul Rabinowitz, a survivor of Auschwitz *Konzentrationslager*.

Working nights and weekends out of his Secaucus, New Jersey, studio apartment, it was Rabinowitz who had uncovered the fact that the U.S. Immigration and Naturalization Service had actually been protecting former Nazis for over twenty-five years; that the State Department had refused to turn Nazi mass-murderers over to the Justice Department for prosecution; that high-ranking Congressmen, the CIA, maybe even a U.S. President had used special influence to get important Nazi files transferred around The System so fast and so frequently that they never seemed to be in one place, and thus were effectively closed to public scrutiny.

Benjamin Paul Rabinowitz. Postal worker. Chasing the Nazis through rain and sleet and snow.

Inside the Wallkill Inn, David, Rabinowitz, and the government agents huddled around a splintery pine table. They drank Rheingold beer so cold it might as well have been carbonated water.

Watching Rabinowitz in the flesh, it was difficult for David to imagine much more than one of those pale, balding men who shuffle around the back rooms of every post office in America, quietly sorting the mail.

The government pensioner was under five feet, five inches, with mottled, mush-yellow teeth. His wrinkled cheeks and turkey neck were covered with dark gray stubble. He wore a stained gabardine suit bought in 1960 at the latest. Benjamin Rabinowitz also had a great drooping wen on the right side of his nose; that plus the disconcerting habit of saying *"bullchit"* every fourth or fifth word out of a slightly collapsed, somewhat feminine-looking mouth.

Rabinowitz certainly knew his Nazis, though.

At the time of the Wallkill meeting, he was hard at work on a manuscript that was already some twenty-one hundred type-written pages long. Titled *Leading American Nazis*, it traced, among other things, four hundred of the seven hundred fifty companies set up by Martin Bormann to protect the Third Reich. The book tracked several of these companies right to the heart of some of America's richest and most prestigious corporations: a major oil company—one of the "Six Sisters"; a noted cereal maker; a corporation which owned one of the big TV networks.

If Rabinowitz was correct, David figured, business fortunes, major stocks, and impeccable reputations would tumble like dominoes come publication time for *Leading American Nazis*. Was that a clue to consider, David suddenly began to wonder? Could that possibly be connected with the Storm Troop? Or was his imagination simply getting out of hand?

"Let me ask you a rather strange, leading question, Dr. Strauss," the Nazi-hunter rasped soon after all the general introductions were over.

David Strauss found himself shifting uneasily on the wooden bench. He had no idea what to expect from a man whose obsession, hobby, whatever, was Third- and Fourth-Reich Nazis.

"What do you know about the Jews and President Franklin Roosevelt? This is during World War II I'm talking about. What do you think?"

David was noticing that he kept adjusting his gold wedding band as he sat at the slightly surreal barroom table. He found it especially hard to look into Rabinowitz's rheumy, blood-flecked eyes.

"Not an awful lot. A little bit," David started to answer the strange little Jew's question. "Roosevelt, Cordell Hull, Harry Hopkins. They all must have known about the German and Austrian concentration camps, say, from 1939 on. They waited until 1943 to do something substantial or meaningful about the Holocaust. That's fairly well documented, I think. Arthur Morse wrote a popular book, right?"

Benjamin Rabinowitz nodded indifferently. He bit off half of a hard-boiled egg brought with the beers. Yolk crumbled down the front of his white shirt.

"Now why in God's name do you think President Roosevelt and Secretary of State Hull acted like that toward the Jews? Sort of a peculiar way to act, eh? I mean, you and I wouldn't have acted like that, waiting four years to do something about the ovens."

David thought that he had no goddamn idea why President Franklin Roosevelt had done *anything. Ever.*

"Well, I would imagine Roosevelt was getting unbelievable pressure to stay out of the war in Europe. Isolationists. The 1940 election and his promises to 'keep our boys home.' I also believe that some large American companies were still supplying and secretly arming Germany at that time."

"And?"

And what? Dr. David Strauss suddenly felt as if he were taking orals in Modern World History. The little mailman manqué was watching him like some sort of madman professor emeritus.

"I guess . . . Uh . . . Well, shit." David finally had to laugh. "If the American people had known about the Nazi death camps, they would have forced this country into World War II sooner. Let's hope so anyway."

The Nazi-hunter now had his liver-spotted hands together, Christian prayer style.

"No bullchit now," he said. "All right, Dr. Strauss. David, if you believe that I'm a sane man—and I am. If you believe I am a relatively intelligent man to have tracked down all of these Nazi bastards, what do you make of this statement?" Rabinowitz made a small dramatic pause. "No bullchit now, David. This is important with respect to understanding the killings in your family. Tell me what you think of this idea: *President Franklin Delano Roosevelt was a Nazi."*

The agent Hallahan spit out a mouthful of beer.

David's mind whirled off into blank, empty space for a few seconds.

Rabinowitz just stared at the young, dark-haired doctor. He was perfectly serious, David was certain.

David realized that his face and neck had gone all red. He'd begun to feel slightly paranoid, foolish. He answered with a statement that didn't make a whole lot of sense to him.

"Well, I'd have to take it that you were . . . using the word *Nazi* metaphorically. Like—Richard Nixon was a prick."

At that, David thought Rabinowitz's face lit up with the most wonderful Halloween-pumpkin smile.

"Good. Wonderful." He began to praise David like a proud yeshiva instructor. "Mr. Callaghan. Mr. Hallahan, are you still with us?"

Harry Callaghan nodded his head slowly. "Yes. Sure. Only in addition to being a *prick*, Nixon was a *Nazi*."

Which came so unexpectedly from the serious-faced agent that it got all of them laughing for the first time. Benjamin Rabinowitz especially, laughed until tears were rolling down his mottled cheeks.

"O.K. then," he finally said to David, his eyes suddenly shiny and alive. "O.K. Let's make up a theory about the Strauss family. You see, it's stupid to try and think with one, two, three, four logic, because we don't have all the one, two, three, four facts yet. Let's suppose, just suppose that someone in your family—your grandmother, your brother—had seriously, perhaps inadvertently, threatened the Nazis.

"Yes, yes. *Maybe*, it's Die Spinne. ODESSA . . . This is a very complicated matter, though. Many possibilities, given what's happened so far. We have to move one step at a time."

David was literally on the edge of his seat; he was watching the Nazi-hunter with quiet amazement. He was beginning to understand certain new things about being a survivor; about being a Strauss. David also got the feeling that Benjamin Rabinowitz was being cautious with him. Bringing him along slowly.

"For the moment, I think two things." Rabinowitz finally clasped his hands once again. "*One*. Someone in the Strauss family has seriously frightened the Nazis. Somehow. I don't know exactly how yet. That part confuses me. O.K.? O.K.

"*Two*. We mustn't limit our thinking to the old-time Nazis,

David. Remember Franklin Roosevelt. Nazis take many odd shapes and forms today. As many shapes as evil itself. I mean that last, very seriously.

"And Mr. Callaghan. If I was to take a guess, I would say that what is involved here could bring a serious war to entire countries. Big, big doings. Bigger than anyone might think to guess right now. A very interesting combination of things at work here."

Benjamin Rabinowitz suddenly thrust his skinny hand across the table. He shook David's hand with surprising strength.

"You're a nice man, David. I wanted to meet you. This is a good start. This is terrific. Maybe we're going to hunt Nazis, young man."

22

Benjamin Rabinowitz took a deep breath.

"Now I have to tell you a few things about your grandmother and myself."

For the next hour, Rabinowitz patiently told David about the old days: some good; some not so good.

Rabinowitz told David all about himself, about Michael Ben-Iban, and Elena; about the Stern Gang in Israel; about the *Surviving Remnant* from the DP camps.

Rabinowitz even gave David the very vaguest details about the secret Jewish group that had been formed to ensure against another Holocaust. He told David about the meeting of Jerusalem—where David's grandmother had underestimated the Fourth Reich.

At the same time, Benjamin Rabinowitz began to get the feeling that David knew almost nothing about the Jewish defense group.

Elena Strauss had kept her grandson David out of it. She

had shielded the young doctor from any involvement whatsoever.

"In Jerusalem, we had wanted to try and stop the Reich once and for all, David. One final time and then it would all be over. We wanted one last confrontation with the swine," Rabinowitz rasped.

David Strauss couldn't have agreed more.

Just one final battle with the Nazis would be perfect.

When they finally left the Wallkill Inn, it was minutes after nine on the beer sign glowing in the front window.

The village of Wallkill was hidden behind a dark gray-blue stage curtain.

A bright green stoplight at the four corners shivered on a steel necklace hung across Main Street.

Maybe it was his imagination, but David felt a chill crawling up his back. His mind was racing wildly with all the new possibilities. Extreme pressure was pushing in on his skull from all sides.

Actually, though, he felt pretty damn good, David thought. Better anyway. He was suitably excited about working with Rabinowitz. He wanted to meet Michael Ben-Iban, too. The night was buzzing with possibilities and prospects.

"It will be interesting to see," he heard the Nazi-hunter say in a dream voice. He felt the skinny hand on his arm. "I wouldn't even discount Arabs. Black September. Even Arabs have to be a possibility at this point."

Arabs. Franklin Roosevelt. Nazi conspiracies high up in the United States government.

The important Nazis would have to be truly frightened to come out in the open after all these years.

The Reich moving once again. For whatever reasons . . .

David was actually beginning to think something like a Nazi-hunter. It was a fait accompli, then. He was going to become involved. Amazing as it all seemed right at that moment.

"You must be careful now," he heard Rabinowitz warn. "The Strauss heir must be careful, David. I begin to wonder if I shouldn't respect your grandmother's wish to keep you out of all this. . . ." Rabinowitz's voice trailed off.

As he got into the Lincoln, David noticed a tiny silver light flash across the darkness of Main Street.

A harmless cigarette lighter, he thought after his initial start.

So this is how the paranoia feels. So this is how it's going to be from now on, David Strauss realized with a shiver.

Just then, David heard a distinct *thhhppp* noise outside the open car door. A sickening, crunching sound.

David's eyes opened wide. His nervous system clicked on as if an unseen hand had thrown a full-power switch.

The next forty seconds were impossible to comprehend.

Both of Benjamin Rabinowitz's hands flew up to clutch his forehead. The old man groaned loudly; he looked at David, utter disbelief and shock stamped onto his face.

"They shot him!" David screamed out.

"Oh, my good God!"

A second wild bullet ripped through the car's side roof. David threw his arms up to protect his head.

He went crashing down into the narrow space between the front and back seats.

The Lincoln suddenly jolted, it screeched away from the curb.

David was lying across the floor and the Lincoln's back door was swinging wide open. David could feel the road bumps coming hard and fast against his cheekbone. The floor, the pile carpeting, was bouncing up and clubbing him repeatedly.

It was all a terrible, unreal nightmare. It had to be.

"They killed Rabinowitz!" David could hear himself yelling. "They shot him! They killed him!"

As the Lincoln swerved and turned, David began to throw up.

So this is how it's going to be from now on.

23

Stranger events transpired later that same week. Much stranger events. On Fifth Avenue in New York of all places.

Frizzy Wyatt Earp mustache drooping, six-gun banging off his meaty hip, twenty-five-year-old New York City patrolman Michael Rosenberg finally had to stop and sit and vomit.

Rosenberg plopped down on the dusty curb at Fifth Avenue and Forty-eighth Street. In front of a Pan Am ticket office. Across from Scribner's bookstore.

He took his visored cap off, hung his head between dark-blue trouser legs, and out it came: a viscous orange-yellow river running down over the gutter litter.

Rosenberg then unbuttoned his police tunic down to the third gold button. Perspiration was pouring down onto his V-neck T-shirt. It dripped from his thick mustache.

The young New York policeman simply *could not believe* what he was witnessing on Fifth Avenue.

The morning before, a gawky zombie in a Fleet messenger service hat and "Let It Bleed" T-shirt had arrived bright and early at 1330 Avenue of the Americas, the executive offices of ABC-TV.

He had hand-delivered a reel of film in a flat silver can. Taped to the can was a paid invoice, plus a two-page cover letter addressed to the executive board of America's most successful TV network.

Less than fifteen minutes later, four New York City policemen descended on Fleet headquarters on the Lower Level of Grand Central Station. The letter and film delivered by one of their messengers contained the first substantial news from the Storm Troop since the Strauss family murders thirty-three days earlier in Westchester.

". . . Unless the accompanying educational filmstrip is shown on all network news programs tonight," the cover letter instructed, "one of the Jewish families listed on page two will be extracted within twenty-four hours. There will be no deadline extensions. None."

Listed first among the names on page two was an obvious choice: the powerful Jewish family that owned a controlling interest in ABC. *Mr. & Mrs. Charles Samuelson; United Nations Plaza; children: Robert, Louis, Rachel; grandchildren— thirteen.* Listed #2, 3, and 4 were the Jewish stars of ABC's top-rated TV shows.

At 7 P.M. New York time, the anchorman for ABC "Evening News" came on the air looking particularly pale and tense. The newsman recited a short preface to the special film ABC

News was about to present, citing the extraordinary circumstances behind the film's showing, apologizing for the film's content beforehand. The eleven-minute clip was then shown without interruption.

The first five minutes of the film consisted of old black-and-white news and Nazi propaganda footage.

The 1940s-style film presented the usual straight-arming, jackbooted marching scenes through Munich and Berlin. Then Hitler Youth and little *Deutsches Jungvolk* in Frankfurt, singsonging *Sieg Heil! Sieg Heil! Sieg Heil!* It panned across crowds of German people screaming approval like Stuka dive bombers. It flashed a sign on a Munich street lamp: *ACHTUNG JUDEN!*

Then the Führer appeared, the famous manic stare making him look more like Charlie Chaplin than Adolf Hitler. The Führer was shown driving a new black VW convertible through a crowd of 200,000 cheering Nazis. He was pictured after just having made monkeys of Daladier and Chamberlain.

Most chilling of all, a brand-new, original piece of marching music had been composed and scored for the film.

After the black-and-white segment, a tall, blond man, a recognizable film actor named Owen Landers, appeared on screen.

This portion of the film was in slickly shot 35mm color. No expense seemed to have been spared in its filming.

The pleasant-looking actor wore a charcoal business suit, starchy white shirt, striped rep necktie. He looked very much like the president of some large, very successful company. On his right arm, the actor wore a red-and-white Nazi brassard.

Very calm and reasonable, with the intensity and polish of a regular news commentator, the actor explained how misguided Jews now living throughout America were a major cause of the country's social, economic, and especially moral problems. The Jews were America's pornographers; its slumlords; its dissidents. The Jews were the money-hoarders on one hand, the moneylenders on the other. The contentious Jews were the chief reason America had made enemies all over Europe and in the Middle East, of course. Because of their vast wealth, the Jews had unequal representation in Washington.

The camera slowly crept in on the impressive-looking actor.

"The time has come for all of us to look closely at the Jewish element in America. To carefully consider some fundamental questions about our country.

"This does not mean any kind of violence directed against Jews. It simply means examination. Careful examination of the priorities of this country—and the reasons behind our priorities.

"Those of you who agree, those of you who believe we should reexamine important issues at this time, I ask you to do one thing only. A simple, harmless gesture," the actor said.

A gesture.

Almost too small a gesture it seemed.

Curious.

"Tomorrow at noon . . . Simply honk your automobile horns. Tomorrow at exactly noon."

All along Fifth Avenue, every other car, or third car, or fourth or fifth car was honking its horn.

Cars down near Forty-second Street and the library honked. Cars and trucks opposite Korvette's, Brentano's. Right in the heart of America's most sophisticated city they honked. Right in the middle of the city with the largest Jewish population in the world.

Up near Saks and St. Patrick's Cathedral cars honked, and a fist fight had begun in the street. Past Central Park and the Plaza, on way up into Harlem—the shrill symphony of horns seemed even louder, more horrifying, and unbelievable.

At about three minutes after twelve noon, the din began to lessen.

A false silence came. Then a few late beeps. Angry personal statements.

Then an eerie calm fell over New York, over Los Angeles, Chicago, Miami, over any little highway where there were cars, and horns, and Nazis.

On Fifth Avenue, a pretty, short-haired businesswoman wandered out of a soup shop called La Potagerie. The dazed woman sat down on the curb next to New York patrolman Michael Rosenberg.

A complete stranger. Another Jew.

The two young people held one another for a long, tender moment. They just held on and looked into the dark, passing automobiles.

24

Automobile horns.

Bleating against the thin skin of her eardrums. The hammer, anvil, stirrup, vibrating. Making Alix Rothschild feel nauseated and afraid.

That evening the actress wandered south on Fifth Avenue from the Sherry Netherland, where she had her New York apartment. Down toward a violet shroud of smog and night which lay over the area of Manhattan known as Gramercy Park.

11:15 P.M.

Dark suits and long gowns were arriving home at the Plaza from *A Chorus Line* and *Deathtrap;* from expensive suppers at Sardi's, Caravelle, Gallagher's. A few late-night lights blinked off in the GM Building: Hispanic cleaning ladies; investment house and advertising agency workaholics. Doubleday's was just closing on the block between Fifty-sixth and Fifty-seventh. A shopping-bag lady slept peacefully in the alcove of Elizabeth Arden.

Automobile horns.

Simply honk your horn, the Reich had commanded.

The new Nazis. Countless thousands of them in New York; in Southern California; in Maine, Arizona, Georgia, Florida, Texas.

A cab honked in front of the St. Regis and Alix nearly flew out of her skin! "God damn you stupid! . . ."

Her long legs felt tired and rubbery all of a sudden. Her mind was bogged in a swamp of the blackest, foulest images. Her stomach was twisted into a tight, impossibly hard knot.

Alix heard distant New York police sirens; she could almost hear the Gestapo cars wailing through the streets of Berlin, Frankfurt, Munich. The overhead street lamps might have been the searchlights on the dark towers surrounding Dachau *Konzentrationslager.*

The Nazis were marching again.

The Nazis had never actually stopped marching.

Alix Rothschild was struck by a severe blood-sugar rush on her walk down Fifth Avenue. A slight ringing in her ears grew into a shrill, head-splitting whistle. She gasped out loud for air, more oxygen.

Finally, she had to stop walking altogether.

The tall, slender, dark-haired woman leaned against the hood of a parked car. Her movements were like those of a drunk about to be sick. Out of the corner of her eye, Saks's front canopy sign appeared to be *spinning* across the Avenue.

A familiar series of pictures went flashing through her mind. Out of control as they flew at her optic nerve. An old favorite nightmare album.

A scarlet, a blood-red dawn shone across acres and acres of gray, muddy fields. The rising sun seemed to sit like a squashed red egg on top of a line of ghostly ash trees.

Dark wooden walls interceded. Blackwashed turrets. High barbed-wire fences.

A very early morning parade in a bleak, smoking prison yard.

A young woman seen from the waist up. Naked, emaciated, Nina Rothman.

Alix's mother.

A German soldier, an SS Captain, telling nineteen-year-old Nina Rothman to kneel down on the muddy, smoking ground. A smell that is a hundred times worse than the worst decaying smell of fish and uncleaned animals thick in the air. A heavy odor of human sweat, excrement, dysentery, spotted typhoid all over everything. Nina seeming not to notice. Thinking in her fear-crazed mind that this is such a waste— such an incredible, stupid, horrible twist of fate.

The erect SS Captain sauntering away from the young Jewish woman. Down a long line of young women and teen-age girls. The prettiest ones this morning—a few of the elite German Jews, the wealthy ones. Sixty-seven of them. Most past guessing what the Nazis wanted this time.

This SS Captain turned out to be their friend. A Nazi of unusual compassion. Almost no taunting and cruel delays. His right arm flashed quickly behind the sixty-seven backs.

The squad of prison guards fired for less than a minute.

The kneeling women toppled over into a three-foot-deep gulley dug just in front of them. Young mothers and teenagers obliterated in a matter of seconds. Nearly buried as well.

*Some ragged camp children ran and peered into the long,
gaping trench. Alix Rothman saw! The large, bloody hole in
Nina Rothman's back.*

Her mother's murder.

Alix screamed out on Fifth Avenue. She couldn't remember
her vision: just the feeling of terror. She screamed words she
wouldn't remember a minute afterward. *The horns. The
death-camp visions.* A few late-night strollers stopped. No one
came to help.

Two New York City policemen finally came on the run.

Two heavy, Bronx- or Brooklyn-accented voices. Gruff. Very
male and scary.

"What's going on here?"

"What's the matter with you?"

Alix was suddenly alert and embarrassed. She was trembling uncontrollably. She understood what had happened.
What was about to happen now.

"I'm all right now," she managed. Her mouth was incredibly parched, sticky dry.

A lucky circumstance then. One of the policemen recognized who she was. Talking to his partner. "Hey! Do you
know who this is?" Suddenly a high soprano voice as he spoke
to Alix. "Are you all right? . . . Miss Rothschild? Are you on
any drugs, Miss Rothschild?"

Alix shook her head. She tried to stand away from the
parked car. . . . *If they take me to Bellevue,* she began to
panic.

"Today was very bad, I am a Jew. The horns . . . I'm sorry
that I screamed out. I was just very afraid."

She didn't know how much she was going to have to explain. Thank God, they seemed to understand.

The two policemen brought Alix back to Fifty-ninth Street
in their cruiser. They were gentle and they tried hard to be
understanding. One of them was Kevin Stapleton, a St. John's
graduate. The other was Howie Cohen, a young fallen-away
Jew from Brooklyn. They had both seen *Sara, Sara* and they
told Alix that she was a tremendous actress. *An artist. The
American Liv Ullmann.* In the car with them, Alix slowly
came back into control. . . . She was thinking that she couldn't
allow herself to get this out of control again. She promised
herself she wouldn't let it happen again. No matter what.

The officers brought Alix inside the gold-and-Italian-marble lobby of the Sherry Netherland. They escorted her up to the lacquered birdcage elevator bank. Doormen, bellmen, deskmen, wealthy European and Texan hotel guests stared a bit. Impossible not to.

Their strange images reflected off the nearby windows of Le Petit Café, Patrolman Cohen made her promise to see a doctor.

Alix promised.

PART III

25

"The new, super ROTHSCHILD look. How you can have it, too!" proclaimed the current front cover of *Vogue*.

"The ROTHSCHILD Only Her Masseur Knows," squealed a cutesy subhead on *Cosmo*.

ROTHSCHILD AND REDFORD bellowed a hundred-foot-long movie poster over Broadway and Forty-fifth Street just north of festering Times Square.

There had been a time when *five-foot two, eyes of blue* was the American dream. No more. Now the dream had grown up to five-feet nine, eyes of Ming green, ensemble by St. Laurent, Gucci, Halston, and Levi.

That year, Alix Rothschild was the living legend in America. At least Alix was as close as she wanted to being a legend.

It had begun when she was twenty-one years old, 1964, with Alix quietly establishing herself as one of the world's more successful commercial models. In the next few years, Alix Rothschild had done everything from the latest shampoo to Burger King to Russian Crown fur. Both men and women seemed to like her very sensual face, her figure, the way she moved, especially her down-to-earth smile.

Then Alix had segued into film acting. One of the more successful model-to-actress transitions since Grace Kelly's, it turned out. ("Imagine a Marisa Berenson who can actually *speak*," a particularly acerbic New York critic had said.)

Alix had subsequently been nominated for Critic's Circle awards for her first two films. She'd won an Oscar for her fifth film. Alix already had her own bronze star on Hollywood Boulevard.

Film No. 6 had been a hugely successful nine-part television movie tracing Jewish Arab roots in Palestine. Number 7 had grossed in excess of ninety million dollars. So far, there had been no eighth film—just an endless stream of gossip broadcast from Chasen's and the Polo Lounge. No matter though, ROTHSCHILD was on the verge of joining KEATON and STREISAND as Hollywood's Three Leading Ladies. For that year, anyway.

Curious at first hearing, but the film star and David Strauss had three important connecting points in their pasts.

First—Alix and David were either third or fourth cousins, both of them always forgot which. From the time they were six or seven years old, they had been thrown together at a variety of card parties, bar mitzvahs, weddings, and funerals. David, in fact, had been one of the first children Alix had been able to successfully relate to after she'd come to America.

Secondly—Alix and David had been teen-age lovers at Scarsdale High School. They'd suffered through the traditional ring and letter-sweater transferrals; the mutual loss of virginity at fifteen inside the Pound Ridge Reservation; the awful nicknames for one another—Franny and Zooey, after the J. D. Salinger novella.

Third—they had been lovers in college as well. David at Princeton. Alix, a two-hour car ride away at Vassar.

Then Alix had mysteriously left Vassar in the middle of her senior year. She'd gone to the Ford Agency in New York; then to Wilhelmina during the bloodletting "Model Wars"; and finally to William Morris as she launched off into moving pictures.

Alix admitted to interviewers again and again that she was

neurotically driven; that she was obsessively motivated to be one of the best actresses in the world. Most of all, Alix revealed in the interviews, she had to feel that *her life had purpose*. . . . Otherwise, she might as well have died with the others back in Germany.

David, meanwhile, had decided that he wanted to be a doctor. He was also fairly certain that he was over Alix Rothschild, or Alix Rothman as he'd known her back in Westchester.

Every so often one of them sent off a letter or telegram—TO FRANNY . . . TO ZOOEY (usually when one or the other of them was in trouble; when they needed a sympathetic shoulder), but that was the extent of it.

THE END, in movie terms.

26

Nearly sixteen years later, David thought he spotted Alix from high up on his creaking fifth-floor sun porch at Cherrywoods.

It was late on a sparkling, blue-skied Saturday, less than a week after the tragic and mysterious death of Benjamin Rabinowitz.

Alix was walking down in front of the Sunset Lounge. She had on a pink alligator shirt; perfectly faded and fitted jeans; sandals hanging from a beaded Indian belt. Her shiny black hair was longer than ever, and dazzling.

ROTHSCHILD!

Even from that distance and perspective, David could see why she'd had such enormous success everywhere. Somehow Alix managed to fuse the *haut monde* and the everyday one. She could be strikingly beautiful or down-to-earth—sometimes with just a turn of her head.

After watching her slender, long-legged walk for a few minutes, David retreated off the creaky wooden porch. He walked back inside his bedroom.

He put on a fresh shirt, and he reviewed the dim, distant past in his mind.

Then David stopped and sat down hard on the edge of his bed.

He stared at the collection of Nazi books and papers. He gazed out the porch screen door at blue skies and puffy white clouds.

Very slowly, David wandered back out on the wooden porch again. Alix was gone.

David's eye drifted along with a tiny green canoe down on Lake Arrow. He saw two little boys in red rubber swim masks and matching nose plugs playing on the diving float. Across the lake, an FBI agent sat in a high-perched gazebo casually watching East and West Houses through binoculars.

David raised an arm to the man. The agent seemed to wave back. *"Cozy as hell,"* David muttered. Why the hell hadn't he just gone downstairs and said hello to Alix like a normal human being? Damn it!

David stepped inside again and looked at the face in the clever mirror over his sink. Familiar enough. David smiled at the well-meaning jerkass in the mirror. Frowned. Shook his head of curly black hair.

"Ass.

"What the hell do you think you're doing, anyway?

"*Ass.*

"Oh, Jesus. Talking to mirrors now. Talking to yourself about talking to mirrors."

There was a soft knock on the door and David could feel his face and neck turning the deepest crimson red. Of course! Alix had come up to say hello *to him.* David started to laugh at himself. He *had* to laugh.

"Shee-oot, David. You better snap to soon, son."

He pulled open the bedroom door.

Only it turned out not to be Alix after all.

It was one of the hotel porters.

A black man named Johnny Williams, who lived over in Poughkeepsie; who used to take David and Nick to the big YMCA basketball tourney on Market Street in Poughkeepsie every spring.

David succeeded in blowing his opening lines anyway.

That particularly pleased the young doctor.

"Oh! . . . Yes? . . . Uh, er, hi, John," David managed.

To which Johnny Williams said something like: "Oh, uhm, Dr. Strauss. Excuse me, Dr. Strauss. Uhm, er, uh . . ."

Which finally forced Alix to step into the dark oak door frame herself.

Her hands were nervously smoothing down her jeans. Her beautiful face seemed almost terrified.

She pushed a lock of hair away from her eyes. Little sunglass marks on the bridge of her nose were the only obvious imperfections.

"Oh, damn it. I'm sorry. I was just afraid to come up alone, David. John sort of volunteered. I sort of volunteered John."

Then the two of them were hugging.

Johnny Williams was patting them both on their backs—as if to say that whatever they were doing was just fine. Alix was crying a little. She was trying to give her condolences about Upper North Street, Elena, Nick, and everything.

Then Alix was stepping back and looking at David.

"How are you doing?" Alix Rothschild started to laugh. "I couldn't just write this time. I had to come."

"How are you?" David was smiling like a Japanese beaver.

And looking at Alix this close up, he was suddenly remembering something he'd partly forgotten, partly put out of his mind for a long time.

Alix Rothschild, or Rothman, or whatever she wanted to call herself, was the most beautiful and desirable woman he had ever seen.

27

That evening, Cherrywoods's famous Lake Lounge smelled of pine resin and wild flowers—also faintly of wood ducks and brown trout. Outside on the lake, a flotilla of colorful sailboats looked like patchwork Indian teepees on the horizon.

Right away, the few heads at the bar began to turn and look at Alix and David.

At first, the two of them talked about how Cherrywoods hadn't changed since they'd been teen-agers coming up there every summer. They retold old Scarsdale stories and family and school tales. Nothing too seriously revealing or boat-shaking. Just nice-man-meets-nice-girl talk. Just two young Jews trying to remain sane during a particularly bad time. A time worse than either of them wanted to let on in the Lake Lounge.

At eight-thirty, the two of them hiked back to the hotel's summer kitchen.

That hectic 80-by-60-foot food emporium was a chef's wildest dream in the flesh. To be more exact, the kitchen was everything a French Jew named Jules Stein could dream about, read in *Gourmet* magazine, hear on "The French Chef," or outright steal on his annual six-week pilgrimage back to Provence.

Alix's eye traveled along wooden pegboards with cutting and spooning utensils; down past a fleet of stainless-steel pots and skillets.

Even with the hotel less than a third full, at least forty loaves of brick-oven white, caraway rye, pumpernickel, and sourdough bred sat like adobe houses on marbled butcher-block tables.

New York-cut steaks, as thick as the Ulster County phone directory, were stacked on another table.

Roast beefs, ribs, roasting chickens were in abundance.

So were delicious apples, pears, Kadota figs; tins of cocoa; David's old childhood nemesis, Postum. There were cold pantries and vegetable bins; a walk-in freezer with separate butter and milk refrigerators; nine flat-black gas stoves, each with sixteen burners.

"Since we've been displaced persons here, I've been cooking," David said as he conducted the cook's tour. "If you're hungry, Alix, and brave, we could maybe cook something tonight."

Alix broke into her most comfortable and natural smile of the day. Her first real smile in weeks, she thought to herself.

"I can't tell you how much I like that idea. I might even cook for you," she said. "If *you're* brave."

David fetched a bottle of Lafitte-Rothschild from the bar,

and, drinking immoderately as they went, they fashioned boned chicken breasts, tomatoes, little pommes frites, cherries, sausage, and *beaucoup de* garlic into a spectacular feast for two.

After which, they ate like pampered royalty in the Sunset Lounge.

All 125 by 200 feet of it.

With Tommy Thompson's Four playing "Feelings" and "Tie a Yellow Ribbon" for forty to fifty ballroom-dancing couples. With two FBI agents taking shifts sitting at one of the banquette tables, guarding David and eyeing Alix.

David ordered a third bottle of wine, and they began to listen more closely to Tommy Thompson. Sax, drums, trumpet, piano. Slightly staccato and not always together; shmaltzy as hell. "Wonderful as leafing through old *Life* magazines," Alix said.

A young bearded man was dancing with his wife and five-year-old daughter. Very touching and nice. Two eighty-year-olds performed a tango hustle.

Finally, David and Alix got up and danced themselves. They danced to "Fascinating Rhythm," then a fox-trot to "There's a Small Hotel."

The band shifted into a slow number, "Moonlight and Roses," and David and Alix could suddenly hear the floorboards of the Lounge creaking like a gymnasium underfoot.

They danced one more slow song, the band's finale, "Stars Fell on Alabama," which segued into "Too Marvelous for Words," and "Good Night, Irene."

They left the moonlit Lounge through French doors leading into the even more moonlit gardens. Owls were hooting way off in the woods. Nearby cicadas sounded like a softly blown whistle. Very disturbing to David, though; he began to get obsessively paranoid as soon as they walked out into the darkness and night noises. At the same time, Alix loosely took his arm. David was terribly aware of her perfume; a light, flowery, subtle smell. Her soft hip was just barely touching his. There was the faintest *swish* of nylon.

"Three bottles of vino. Whew!" Alix shot her eyebrows up. "We should go in now, David," she finally said. "I'm a little frightened being out here in the dark, too."

"You're a wonderful host," Alix said as the two of them walked the long corridor to her room. "And you're the best French cook in New Paltz, Dr. Strauss."

"Maybe next to my mentor, Jules," David said. "You're the best schmaltzy waltzer around," he added.

David then bent slightly and kissed Alix. He tasted a sweet, faint fruit he couldn't quite identify. He felt slightly dizzy all of a sudden.

The two of them stood in the hallway for another uncomfortable moment. Alix switched her weight from one foot to the other. David brushed his hair back with his fingers.

"I'll see you in the morning?" Alix finally said.

As he climbed the remaining two flights to his room, David caught himself whistling "Feelings," a song he didn't particularly like, but which seemed pretty fantastic that night.

Inside his room, he sat on his big Victorian couch and felt a little horny.

He doodled on a page in his Crapbook. He listened to the crickets and owls.

David then sketched out a fake *New York Times* front page, and wrote a whimsical headline.

NOTHING BAD HAPPENED TODAY, it said.

28

Bucks County, Pennsylvania.

Something quite nice; then something not so nice.

First, two bicycles, their riders in perfect control, letting their machines glide through the woods like electric-blue hawks.

Coming up behind the bikes, the Führer. Cruising along a Rockwellian country road in a black, late-model Mercedes sedan . . . A classic German automobile, the Engineer observed. A wealthy and powerful German's pleasure car.

Stepping out of the automobile, the Führer was formally

introduced to SS Captain Oscar Kaltenmaus, supervisor of Auschwitz crematorium No. 1, smuggled out of Germany in 1945 by HIAG, the organization of SS veterans set up by Martin Bormann.

Kaltenmaus had been living in Pennsylvania for almost thirty years now. He was known as Sven Hetling; a good neighbor; a very good citizen. Had anyone accused Mr. Hetling of the mass-murder of innocent men, women, and children, his neighbors would have defended him staunchly.

When the Engineer had revealed to Hetling that he was once again needed by the Reich, however, Captain Oscar Kaltenmaus had returned to his old form with the snap of a crisp salute. It almost seemed as if the slightly gawky-looking farmer missed the excitement of the old days.

Captain Kaltenmaus would do whatever was necessary to further the plan of Dachau Two and the Fourth Reich.

Later that afternoon, the Führer and the Engineer sat on the warm hood of the shiny, hand-tooled Mercedes.

Four hundred yards down a rutted dirt turnoff, Otto Kaltenmaus's ramshackle house seemed to be leaning up against a great old elm tree.

On the opposite side of the farmhouse stood the much more impressive living quarters of his prizewinning Wyandotte, Rock Island, and White Leghorn chickens.

A very necessary, a potentially devastating pre-Dachau Two experiment was in progress on the earnest-looking farm.

The Engineer was already well along in his final countdown. His work of the past two and a half years was on the line right now.

The Engineer's voice was measured and tranquil: a metronome, an emotionless sound that was frightning in itself.

"One hundred forty-six . . . one hundred forty-seven . . . one hundred forty-eight. . ."

"This little chicken house," the Führer said. "It is something like the barracks that once stood at Auschwitz. Also, you know that Reichsführer Himmler owned a chicken farm?"

The gaunt, scholarly-looking Engineer nodded. His flat gray eyes never once left the chicken house.

"Look there." The slightest octave change in the man's voice. "Do you see it?"

Bright white sparks were jumping off the shack's roof. There was evidence of extreme heat or electricity at work.

Inside the building, Sven Hetling's chickens had begun to screech and buck. Their blood was boiling, the Engineer computed. Compounded microwaves were penetrating their bodies at an extraordinarily high rate.

Then came a low-register buzzing noise. As if a nearby high-tension tower had shorted out or fallen.

"One eighty-nine." The Engineer solemnly checked his five-minute stopwatch. "A little over three minutes. This is exceptionally good. It's better than we should have hoped for."

The eerie white sparks were flying over the chicken house like silver rain, like shiny white moths. The low sky was filled with black clouds and it was the weirdest natural sight imaginable.

"Well, let's go see," the Engineer finally said, something like sadness or concern coming into his voice.

The Führer and Engineer began to walk in measured deliberate strides toward the glowing farm.

The weaving ruts were ankle deep from the tires of heavy delivery trucks. The crabgrass on the strip between the tracks had grown nearly a foot high; it was full of rotting green apples.

The Engineer had to use a wet rag to open the steaming door of the blistered, peeling shack.

The splintery door finally swung open with a loud yawn.

Terrible heat and a sharp, unpleasant odor escaped in a blast like that from a furnace. Tiny sparks were flying around the dark room like lightning bugs. Little droplets of silver rain seemed to cling to the rafters and overhead beams.

As they stepped farther into the smoking building, the Führer and Engineer saw cage after mesh-wire cage filled with burned, nearly blackened chickens.

In one corner, Captain Otto Kaltenmaus lay on a bed of shredded sawdust. The German man had been burned to death as well.

"The Captain served Dachau Two well." The Führer quietly shook his head. "No need for unnecessary witnesses, I suppose. No need for an old man who might accidentally share a secret with one of his American friends or neighbors."

On a closer look now, the upper layer of cages drew the Engineer's attention.

Inside these cages, slightly gray hens and capons with deep, red-rimmed eyes were stumbling from wall to wall. The birds walked something like barroom drunks. As they touched the sides of their cages, the chickens sizzled and appeared to dance a bizarre step or two.

"This is not acceptable!" The Engineer spoke in a disturbed whisper. "Some of the birds are still alive!"

The Führer, meanwhile, had already turned away and was walking down the rutted dirt road. . . .

Not the least bit displeased with the work of his brilliant Engineer. Quite awestruck and shaken, in fact.

The ovens were ready.

29

Las Flores, Brazil.

Making for the beautiful island of Las Flores, two hundred fifty miles north of São Paolo, Brazil, there was: an expensive, blue-and-white Corniche sedan; a golden Cessna Skyhawk; a sleek Chris-Craft Corinthian yacht.

From the dazzling white yacht, the unsettled Brazilian coast appeared to be lush, impossible jungle.

From the sun-splashed airplane, it was jungle plus a thin ribbon of virgin beach winding monotonously alongside the sea.

From the sports car, the crystal white sand, rather than the jungle, was the thing: the creamy beach itself was the only road to Las Flores and the exotic Hotel Mercedes Bleu.

By four that afternoon—tea time—the occupants of the sports car, the plane, and the yacht were seated on a palm-

and-umbrella-shaded terrazzo at the spectacular resort hotel.

On the rattan table in front of them were spread several newspapers outlining the curious events of the past few days. The *New York Times.* The *Washington Post.* London's *Daily Mail* and *Times. Le Monde. Suddeutsche Zeitung,* which came all the way from Munich. In the background, a big-band version of 1923's "Yes, We Have No Bananas" played from stereo speakers hidden in the palm trees.

"Well, so what does anyone make of all this sudden madness?" asked Dr. Ludwig Hahn, former chief of the Warsaw Gestapo, now a retired banker in São Paolo. "Wealthy Jewish families terrorized in America. Adolf Hitler on American television."

"I have no idea myself. Shall we contact any of the others?" The second speaker was Richard Glucks, former SS General of all German concentration camps, a respected financier in Rio since 1947.

"Perhaps a meeting of 'The Spider' is in order?"

"What about Martin Bormann? Back in America, I hear?" asked Hahn. "Or Mengele?"

"Bormann is sick. Bormann is going to die soon. Mengele is senile. He's always been senile."

"No. You're wrong there. Mengele has made a career out of being a creative child. Mengele is no fool, though."

Walter Rauff, No. 2 man in the Fourth Reich's Latin arm, La Arana, was speaking now. At Nuremberg, this same Rauff had been charged with the premeditated murder of 106,000 human beings.

"Bormann seems to get sick and die every three years or so." Ludwig Hahn laughed into his glass of gin. "Every time Mossad or Michael Ben-Iban comes sniffing around."

Gold teeth sparkled all around the table. Glasses of whiskey and Strega were tipped.

"Well, what do we think about this?" Rauff pointed at the pile of foreign newspapers. There were Storm Troop or neo-Nazi headlines on every one of them.

The No. 1 man in La Arana, the yachtsman, calmly and thoughtfully answered the question posed by Walter Rauff.

"Personally, I propose that we drink a toast to them," said Heinrich Muller, former chief of the Gestapo, the most wanted Nazi of all. *"Whoever they are!"*

30

Her third or fourth afternoon at Cherrywoods, Alix Rothschild sat on a sun-drenched boulder half-submerged in softly
rippling, silver-blue Lake Arrow.

She thought that the Ansel Adams setting would be just
right for a sappy Tricot perfume commercial. The lake was
covered with glinting stars and sun spirals. Her hair was
gleaming like polished chestnuts.

Alix's other, almost simultaneous idea was that her life had
gotten much too confusing and out of control in the past several weeks. Out of control even beyond her nightmares about
the Nazis.

For one thing, there were heavy, lingering thoughts about
the terrible murders of Nick and Elena Strauss. Especially
Elena, who had been a patient adviser to Alix since she'd
been a little girl; who had understood the special problems
of being a survivor better than anybody else.

For another thing, though—Alix had begun to fall in like
with Dr. David Strauss.

Very strong like, she had to admit to herself. More tenderness and concern than she had *ever* felt for David before.

And that wasn't providential or even possible, she was
thinking to herself.

She and David had made love one afternoon at the hotel.
Then another afternoon and night. The lovemaking had been
unexpected, an accident of time and place. *All right,* Alix
thought to herself. *Fine. Fantastic, to be honest.* David had
a very strong, healthy body; she was attracted to him in other
ways as well. His mind was quick; he had a sense of humor;
a gentleness that was rare in good-looking men.

But that wasn't for right now. Not under all the unhappy
circumstances twisting and turning around the two of them.
Not when her mind was so perilously close to overloading.

Alix took her size 10s out of the rippling lake water. She
shook them off, then tied on leather thongs from the Stitching
Horse in Manhattan. Ninety-five dollar thongs, Alix thought
in passing.

Anyway. So what exactly was going on now? What exactly was her heart's point of view on this matter? Alix jumped ship to shore from her rock. She ducked down and disappeared into low-hanging pine and spruce branches.

She had come to Cherrywoods for three reasons, she thought: 1) she had *badly needed* to get away—both from theater people and from herself; 2) she'd been in California during Elena's funeral and she wanted to pay her personal condolences to the family; 3) she'd simply wanted, she *needed* to be with David for a while during the Nazi terror—her old friend for over thirty years, and a *survivor* now himself.

Instead of leaving Cherrywoods after a day or two, she'd stayed on with David, though. Unfortunate mistake No. 1. Just for a few more days, right? Just until they both could think straight? Until she could come to grips with the neo-Nazi trauma and danger.

She'd subjected herself to the Peeping Tom-ish media— who were choreographing the Fourth Reich story with a flair for melodrama not seen in America since the kidnapping of Charles Augustus Lindbergh, Jr.; who were already composing those wonderfully familiar tabloid headlines: DR. STRAUSS AND ALIX TOGETHER; ALIX A SURVIVOR; NAZIS IN STRAUSS AND ROTHSCHILD PAST.

Well, she didn't see how she could stay on with David, Alix decided for the third or fourth time that afternoon.

It was too complicated; too messy, and emotionally loaded. It was difficult to see how it could possibly work out for the best. *Maybe it's because I've stopped working that I've become so vulnerable to my emotions. That must be it! An idle mind. . . .*

On her way back from the lake, she did pick some Queen Anne's lace for David. . . .

Damnit all! How could this be happening now? "Out of my way, little gray squirrel! Out of my way, tree branches. Ouch. *Shee-oot.*"

Somehow Alix had the idea that things were going to get a lot worse before they got better. There were things she wanted to say to David. She didn't know if she knew how. She wasn't sure if she could *ever* tell David all her secrets.

She purposely dropped the little bunch of Queen Anne's lace at the edge of the woods.

A minute later she came back and snatched them up again. *Shee-oot.*

That evening, Alix and David had a light supper served on the porch of Alix's suite.

After the meal they talked. They talked in a way that they hadn't since they'd been back together again.

The two of them sat over the scant evidence of their dinner. Outside the screened porch, an orchestra of half a million crickets and cicadas was tuning up. Inside Alix's bedroom, the *Eroica* played softly on WQXR.

"When I was out on the lake before, I was thinking about everything that's happened," Alix said. "The very strange, very awful last few months."

"I went for a walk up in back with Harry Callaghan," David's fingers were drumming the lip of his coffee cup. "I guess I was doing pretty much the same thing that you were. Reviewing everything. I'm not sure exactly what I figured out. . . . Other than that I like Harry Callaghan quite a lot. A very nice, quiet gentleman."

They listened to the radio music for a few minutes. They listened to a combination of the mountain noises and Beethoven. David and Alix held hands lightly and each waited for the other to speak.

"I've been having . . . these awful dreams, David. . . . I mean, I've had them since I was a little girl. I see these very horrible scenes from the death camps. Very, very vivid scenes."

Alix looked over to make sure David wanted to listen. She didn't usually talk about her nightmares. People never seemed to understand, which Alix supposed was natural. *How could anyone but a survivor comprehend a death-camp nightmare?*

"When I used to ride the New York Central into the city, when we were kids, I always pretended that the train was going to Dachau. . . ." Alix stopped. She looked away from David. "I'm sorry, David. I don't usually talk about it. I don't know what's gotten into me lately."

"This friend of mine from New York," David said in a soft voice. "He's a surgeon over at Flower Fifth Avenue. His family was lost at Buchenwald. He says that he's always had this terrifying fantasy. . . . In his fantasy, he's dying of some incurable disease. So he goes back to Germany. He kills as many Germans as he can in the streets. This is the straightest, meekest man. Terrific doctor. Good friend. He's partially ashamed of the fantasy, but he has no control over it. It's a fact of his life as a survivor. Every time he walks up in Yorkville, it comes down on him like the Furies. Lately, I'm beginning to understand the feeling myself.

"Remember I told you about meeting with Benjamin Rabinowitz," David continued. "I don't know everything there is to know—far from it—but my grandmother was a contributor to a secretive Jewish group. Benjamin Rabinowitz was one of the group's leaders. They were heavily involved in the search for Nazi criminals after the war. Elena was always a little vague with me about it. The group's methods weren't exactly orthodox or legal. That much I know about."

David stood up and stretched out his arms. He was feeling terribly uncomfortable. He was saying everything *but* what he actually wanted to say. The words that were right on the tip of his tongue. Had been for about ten minutes.

They were both feeling uncomfortable now.

"My grandmother was also very close to a man named Michael Ben-Iban. Ben-Iban is in the secret Jewish group. He's one of the Nazi-hunters still working inside Germany."

Alix nodded. She was listening—intently listening to every word.

"Right now, Ben-Iban is apparently trying to stop whatever it is the Nazis are up to. Ben-Iban is in England at the moment. In London, his people told me."

Finally, David felt he had to blurt the rest out. Get it over with. Say what had to be said.

"Now that Elena is dead, I think I'd like to help the Jewish group if I can." David self-consciously lit up a cigarette. "Of course, I don't know how much help I can be. Maybe it's just money." He clicked his lighter shut.

"There's also a little unsolved mystery attached to my brother Nick's film. Nick made about half of *The Fourth Commandment* in Europe. Germany, England, Paris. I've been reading through some of his production notes. He'd made contact with some of the old Nazis. Some wealthy men and women. Respectable European business people. It all sounds a little like Alfred Hitchcock right now, but—" David stopped in the middle of the sentence. He had to smile.

"I'm babbling. Why do you let me babble like this?"

"You're also trying to tell me something," Alix whispered. "So tell me. What are you trying to say, David?"

David nodded. "All right. *I have to go to Europe.*" He finally said it. "I'd like to do ... to be honest, I don't know exactly what. I just have to go. I have to see Michael Ben-Iban. Talk with him in London. Hear what he thinks. For Nick, Elena, Heather. For myself, I guess. I have to try to find out more about the Nazis. I *have to* try and help."

Alix swayed gently in one of the antique porch rockers. Horowitz was playing a Chopin sonata inside now. Alix's heart was beating faster than the great pianist's fingers.

She didn't have time to stop and logically figure everything out. What made sense; what didn't. Alix let her emotional side make the decision.

"David, if you're going to ask me to stay with you, to go with you, I will." she finally said.

"If you're not asking me, then I'd like to ask you. Please?"

Alix Rothschild stood up. She walked over to David. For a moment they were both very quiet.

"I'm asking you to go with me," David finally said.

They were holding hands again.

This time a little more tightly.

Alix was thinking that her own problems could wait. They could wait until she was certain David was ready to understand her nightmares, if such a time could ever come.

The following evening they were in London together.

Nazi-hunting.

PART IV

31

Nice, the French Riviera.

The Storm Troop began to march again during the final days of June.

In the most curious manner; in some of the strangest locations.

The Soldier knifed his way through the snobby, tacky, zany crowd mobbing Côte d'Azur Airport in the glittery, the still very fashionable French Riviera.

This particular sick-gray day, the military man looked like a gangly Mediterranean playboy. He wore lemon-yellow aviator sunglasses; Cardin accessories; a white silk shirt open down to his trim thirty-two-inch waist.

Not on each arm, but close enough to look like it, were two, bosomy, long-legged women in their late twenties.

These two were the *Nurse* and the *Legal Secretary*, both of them important weapons experts in the burgeoning plan for Dachau Two.

From the crowded little airport they went by "Acapulco jeep" to a pink stucco villa a few kilometers up the Riviera coast at Menton.

The appointed house was a mile or more from the nearest neighbor, a two-star, four-crossed knife-and-fork restaurant. The pink villa itself belonged to the restaurant owner, a wealthy businessman from Paris. The *Banker*.

The pretty house was visible only for an instant as Renaults and Citroëns, headed for Italy, made a long sweeping turn around the spectacular Moyenne Corniche.

The *Engineer*, the *Accountant*, the *Newspaperman*, and

the *Lawyer* were already unpacked and waiting inside the villa when Colonel Essmann and the two attractive women arrived.

By Wednesday, June 28, all those who were coming had settled in at the curious Riviera villa. The fun and games, the eating at Le Bec Rouge and Colombe d'Or were ended abruptly. A very serious meeting was called among the conspirators.

"Because of the need for complete secrecy, because of the extreme importance of this project," the Soldier, a surprisingly dramatic speaker in front of the Storm Troop group, said, "none of you knows precisely why he's here sunbathing, playing baccarat with someone else's money, getting fat on rich French food down in Monaco and environs."

There was scattered laughter from the group.

"I say that you don't know the precise reason . . . because I'm certain all of you know or suspect the general reasons.

"To begin at the beginning, an extraordinary commando attack has been authorized . . . on Olympic Village in Moscow."

The Soldier paused to let the statement take its full crashing effect. Very suddenly the villa living room was completely still.

"This plan—Dachau Two—has been conceived to produce maximum effects through the use of the very best people. *Yourselves.* You and a few other experts have been carefully chosen to execute the military portions of this important plan."

Once again the Soldier paused for effect.

"First of all, my sincere congratulations. This is history you are partaking in, I can assure you. Secondly, though, my condolences, because the chances of this turning into a costly, unprecedented disaster are very high indeed."

Suddenly there was cheering in the fancy villa's living room. There was loud clapping and shouting. The conspirators embraced and kissed one another. Bottles of French wine were popped open. The important meeting then went on through most of the night.

The Storm Troop was preparing a coup that would astound the world.

32

A sweet *frisson* carried the smell of sea and pines up from the royal-blue Mediterranean.

At 6:30 the next morning, a *joie de vivre* sort of Frenchman—a simple farm-implements salesman from Lyon—got to watch a most bizarre and unexpected spectacle from high up on the Moyenne Corniche.

As the middle-aged Frenchman paused for a casual roadside relief stop, he gazed down at a luxurious villa.

First, a band of sun-tanned men and women in bikinis converged on the villa from out of the nearby woods.

The salesman squinted his eyes and bent for a closer look.

They were all running fast. Some of them carried long pine or olive branches, which reminded the French salesman—of what? Make-believe rifles? African spears?

The salesman wiped his brow with a red handkerchief.

Inside the villa, the salesman could then catch glimpses of the people racing from room to room. Working their way upstairs, quickly and efficiently.

Finally, they all came out on the sun roof, which was covered with candy-striped lounge chairs and bright beach towels. They started to laugh and slap palms like athletes from America.

The French salesman didn't understand. Not at all.

What an amazing life to be able to play King of the Castle at six-thirty on a Thursday morning, he thought. No wonder he had to pay more than thirty thousand francs for his piggy little Renault. These silly rich bastards were probably part of the idiot government of that pretender to the throne, Valéry Giscard d'Estaing.

Merde.

Double merde.

As he zipped up, however, the salesman no longer had to worry about or understand the travails of modern France.

An Italian stiletto was inserted between his shoulder blades. It was then twisted hard; driven forward until it nearly came out of the Frenchman's burly chest; pulled back out in the manner of a corkscrew. The salesman went into shock and convulsions and was dead in a few seconds.

What the poor man had accidentally witnessed had been the first rough rehearsal for Dachau Two.

The Frenchman's killer, Colonel Ben Essmann, had very closely watched the first draft maneuver as well.

Very soon, nearly two billion people around the world would get to watch it.

Greatly polished, of course.

With frightening Kolnikov and Dragunov assault rifles instead of scrub pine branches; with formal business suits and swastika armbands instead of bikini bathing suits.

Dachau Two.

33

London, June 29, 1980.

"From May through October," David wrote in his diary during the BWIA flight, *"London is, first of all, marginally more expensive than New York. Secondly, it's absolutely mobbed with tourists and terrorists from the four corners of the former Empire. All come to pay their proper respects, of course.*

"Blame William Shakespeare, Churchill, the Beatles, Monty Python. Blame those wonderful double-decker buses. Blame the London-towners themselves, for maintaining some small standard of grace and civility in this graceless, uncivil century of ours."

At midnight on June 29, David and Alix Rothschild bumped along in one of two funereal Austin cabs toodling down Knightsbridge.

A quick night tour, as it were.

The cabs beetled past Harrods department store and Hyde Park. Under a few unfortunate billboards: *Beenz means*

Heinz; Drink your daily pinta! Past the perdurable Claridges, and the Edwardian Connaught on sleepy Carlton Square.

Finally, the cabs stopped in a Chelsea square, very much like New York's Gramercy Park.

They stopped in front of a gilded hotel awning that said "Rosecraft Gardens Inn." "A sort of an elegant English safe-house," Harry Callaghan called it.

Inside the Rosecraft Gardens, David and Alix observed a certain majesty to the high-ceilinged, chandeliered lobby. Yet there was intimacy as well.

A log-burning fireplace. Comfy sitting chairs filled with comfy-looking Britishers. Floor-to-ceiling windows looking out on the square and nearby Thames.

Grace. Standards. Civilization. And a few neo-Nazis, of course.

Because the Nazi-hunter Michael Ben-Iban couldn't be located that first weekend (his Frankfurt secretary confirmed that Ben-Iban was on business in England), David and Alix thought they would uncoil in London.

With no Fourth-Reich Nazis.

No nerve-racking interviews.

No nothing.

Silly, romantic touch, but each day they stayed on in London they bought one another a present.

On Friday it was a riding jacket from Sterling Cooper for Alix; a silly bowler from Harrods for David. Then a bottle of port from Berry Brothers and Rudd; and dinner and a night on the town. Then a stick pin from Hatton Garden, tied to a clip of heather from a Chelsea gypsy ("Good luck, Dearie," she'd promised David); and an enormous Winston Churchill cigar.

Also on Sunday afternoon, Alix and David received a surprise present of sorts from Harry Callaghan & Co.

Harry let them go for a day trip around London. Without any bodyguards.

34

"Relax," they told one another.

Try not to think about the Nazis right now.

London was in marvelous full bloom.

David and Alix's feelings for one another were blossoming as well.

It was all idyllic for a few very special hours that Sunday afternoon.

"It feels so strange to be out here alone," David said as they roamed the handsomely landscaped streets between Chelsea and Knightsbridge. "It feels very good, doesn't it!"

Two tall, very impressive Yanks.

Alix wearing a bluestocking disguise: long skirt, sweater, scarf, Chelsea Cobbler pumps, dark glasses, sheer blue stockings. David in charcoal slacks and a loose, preppy, crew-necked sweater.

The loose sweater neatly covering a .38 Smith & Wesson.

Pretty much, they stuck to the great, mindlessly funky sights of the city.

Buckingham Palace with its red-brick road, Coldstream Guards, large, safe crowds. Westminster—where a colorful busker tap-danced and mimicked the Queen of Sheba to elbow taps and music from his portable record player. Madame Toussaud's, where Alix found herself fashioned in wax and gruesome dyes.

"In my heart of hearts, I know that Harry's secretly sent some of his men along." Alix looked at David over the tops of her dark glasses. "But just not seeing them is great. Isn't this the strangest sensation, David? We're actually being tailed by the FBI, aren't we?"

David suddenly stopped walking along the crowded London sidewalk. He nearly created a twenty-pedestrian chain-reaction accident.

He waved to the front of him and Alix; he waved to any of Callaghan's pavement artists lurking behind.

"Now I feel a little silly." David began to blush as they

continued to walk. "I wonder if they *are* watching us."

Alix jumped up and tried to click her heels.

"Oh I hope they are. I hope they're taking photographs for their sacrosanct files in Washington, too."

Trundling down Albemarle Street off Piccadilly, his arm protectively around Alix's shoulder, David caught himself sneaking looks at the way her breasts were rolling against the soft front of her black cashmere sweater.

The nicely rounded points lifted and fell with great independence and spirit. Exactly like Alix's swift model's walk. In front of The Bird's Nest Pub David started to get an erection, and he found that slightly embarrassing and funny on the very proper London avenue.

Halfway down the street of expensive galleries, tobacconists, and sandwich shops, Alix suddenly burst into hysterical laughter.

"Typical gynecologist." She grinned.

She'd caught David ogling her like an involuntarily celibate schoolboy. Then she pulled him, very suddenly, inside a handy, swinging brass, glass, and oak door.

"DUNS" was all David could make out on the door sign before it closed on him.

Moments later the two of them were padding down the fourth-floor hallway of the very proper and sedate hotel.

Then Alix was pushing an overly solicitous hotel bellman back out of their room. Handing the efficient little man a pound note to get rid of him.

She closed the hotel door with her hip.

Suddenly they were all alone inside a cozy spot full of tasteful Regency furniture, fresh-cut flowers, a big, brass-railed double bed. The famous Duns—on Albemarle Street.

Tall and slim, Alix leaned back against the door, standing on one heel of her pumps.

"Now you can look at me all you like."

"Can I?"

David started with the dazzling black hair and exquisitely sculptured face. High cheekbones, of course. Full red lips. Sparkling green eyes that added the right touch of playfulness.

She was both Alix Rothman and ROTHSCHILD, he couldn't help thinking. His eyes fell down to her breasts, flat stomach, hips, long legs in their sheer blue stockings.

"I think we've lost Callaghan's people at least. That's a positive start."

Alix balanced carefully on the sides of her shoes. Something like an ice skater with weak, beautiful ankles.

"For just a little time, I'd like us to be alone. Nobody but us."

David felt as if he had a boxing glove lodged in his throat.

"I'd like that," he managed. "Very much."

Alix's cashmere sweater started to come off. Kilowatts of crackling static electricity, which seemed like a good sound for the moment.

Alix actually blushed.

David pulled the hotel room shades all the way and they were left in half-light from the tiny bathroom.

David kicked off his scuffed loafers. He unbuckled his belt and the .38 automatic strapped on as if he were Bullitt or somebody dangerous.

A pepper-gray skirt from Brown's dropped around Alix's ankles. She began to skim off the silk stockings.

Then suddenly David and Alix were rolling on hills of crisp, fresh-smelling Duns bed sheets.

Alix's long hair was flying everywhere. She flashed a faraway scene of the two of them in another hotel room somewhere. Long ago, when they were in college, or maybe it was even high school. There had been a special song, she remembered—"So Rare."

The two of them began to arch up over the bed. David reached out and caressed her face and hair. He was locked in a soft bracelet of Alix's legs.

She whispered to him so softly that it almost sounded like an apology.

"Please wait for me," Alix said.

He did.

They waited for one another.

It was the best thing that had happened to either of them in a decade.

When they eventually arrived back at the Rosecraft Gardens, David and Alix were hit with another surprise—this one not nearly so pleasant as their freewheeling afternoon alone in London.

Michael Ben-Iban had contacted his secretary in Frankfurt. Ben-Iban was changing his itinerary, his immediate plans. Ben-Iban had a personal stopover to make, then he was reportedly heading back to West Germany.

Something was happening now; something was going on.

David even started to wonder if Michael Ben-Iban might be avoiding them.

Then he and Alix began to pack for Germany.

Clothing, maps, books. The .38 Smith & Wesson. Two pocket-sized Berettas.

The abrupt and unexpected shift of locales, the idea of going into Germany, was enough to make both of them sick with apprehension.

Something was happening now. Dachau Two seemed so very close.

Frankfurt, Germany.

My own goddamn, terrific brother dead. David found himself growing morbid again.

Nick the Quick, the Marvelous, the Eloquent.

Heather and Elena dead.

Fourth Reich Nazis operating again. Why? What in the name of God was going to happen? How could whatever it was be stopped? Where was Ben-Iban?

Alix meanwhile spotted the sign they'd been scanning the stainless-steel horizon for.

AUSGANG! it proclaimed.

A sparkling clean, white-on-royal-blue sign. Posted over a flank of stainless-steel escalators. Right next to a German security guard with a nasty-looking machine gun.

"*Ausgang!* That's Nazi for exit," Alix whispered cautiously over the airport noise. "This way to the ovens, David."

"It isn't exactly wonderful to be in Germany, is it? Smiling faces. Pretty little blond children there. How can those little kids be making me shiver, Alix?"

That very morning, they'd flown out of London's Heathrow Airport on a Lufthansa 747. Harry Callaghan. Harris Tanana. David and Alix.

Now perhaps they'd find out if Nick and Beri might have uncovered something while making *The Fourth Commandment*. Hopefully, David would finally get to meet the Nazi-hunter, Michael Ben-Iban.

Hopefully, too, Ben-Iban wouldn't wind up like the last Nazi-hunter David had managed to contact. Hopefully, Ben-Iban would be able to help them somehow.

KINDER SCHOCOLADE? asked an almost edible candy poster inside Frankfurt am Main International Airport.

Then, MARLBORO DIE ZIGARETTES?

HERTZ DAS AUTO?

"And so, the American doctor and the American actress returned to the Fatherland," Alix whispered. "They were *Jüden* again."

At Hertz, David rented a handsome, efficient BMW 2002.

Moments later, the group was out on a wide, swift autobahn—trapped among speed-crazed West Germans averaging nearly a hundred kilometers an hour in their spit-shined sedans. They were off to the Schlosshotel Kronberg, a combination thousand-year-old German castle and mansion ten miles or so outside of Frankfurt.

Seated at the lovely turned ankle of the Teuton mountains, the famous Schlosshotel (Prince Philip had supposedly come there for a few of his celebrated trysts away from Elizabeth) was to become their headquarters on what Callaghan and Tanana called "the Nazi Front." With its stout towers and a few fortified rampart walls, the German hotel looked the part, too.

The Schlosshotel Kronberg was also where Nick and Beri Strauss had stayed while they were making *The Fourth Commandment*.

Until Michael Ben-Iban arrived back at his home base in Germany, David and Alix decided they would try to contact some of Nick's film connections. They also began to retrace Nick's steps while he was prepping and shooting the film in West Germany.

They began to pore over original source material both on the concentration camps and on the 1972 German Olympics.

Cramped together in a six-by-nine-foot bunker that was packed to the ceiling with yellowing papers, David and Alix closely studied the old Nazi records that clogged the Ludwigsburg Center for the Investigation of Nazi War Crimes.

They used Nick's actual prep notes, and soon found that the German Nazis were becoming an obsession with them, too. The grand abomination, the mass extermination, was becoming so real they could feel it all around them.

Daily, they received courtesy pouches from the Berlin Document Center.

And they also studied New Nazis, whose criminal records were kept in slapdash order by the otherwise neurotically efficient *Polizei* of the State of Hessen.

David was certain they were getting close to some kind of explanation in Germany. The answer was so close, it was frustrating to think about.

From all the Nazi records and files (and with the expert technical help of three handsomely paid researchers from the German magazine *Der Spiegel*), David and Alix settled on five promising suspects for the Storm Troop leadership.

David wrote the names in half-inch-thick dust on one of the Ludwigsburg reading tables.

"Just look at this unbelievable shit."

"Martin Bormann. Animal.

"Klaus Barbie. Butchering pig.

"Walter Rauff. Murderer of a hundred thousand Jews.

"Heinrich Muller. Gestapo head. Still walking free.

"Josef Heine. A twenty-nine-year-old neo-Nazi terrorist who was born right here in Frankfurt. Who Nick actually interviewed."

They were all very old men except for Heine. All proven dead at one time or another. (Bormann, it was claimed, was buried in Frankfurt itself—a flagrant violation of the Nuremberg War Crimes regulations—which clearly stipulated that *Nazi war criminal remains be burned and distributed to the wind.)*

"Ah, that old Nazi magic," David said as he, Alix, and the researchers sat among the dusty Nazi records. "How unbelievably absurd it all seems when you get close enough to really observe the sleight-of-hand. Some terrible Fourth-Reich coup in the offing. *The Strausses connected somehow.* Why can't we figure any of it out?"

Peter Ostraeur of *Der Spiegel* then constructed an interesting hypothesis.

"Please, David, don't discount the possibility that all these bastards are involved. All of the ones still alive, anyway.

"Die Spinne, The Spider, has been threatening to go public for years," the researcher said. "Of course, most of these Nazi bastards are very old now. But *because* of that fact, they must be suspected and feared more than ever before.

"Do not forget, young people, *the Fourth Reich will die, literally die, if the living Nazis don't act very soon.* You see what I'm getting at? It is difficult for young people to grasp this. Young people don't believe that there ever really existed Nazis."

David and Alix understood the German researcher's point. . . . A little, they understood it. . . .

Very soon, though, they would understand it a lot.

More perhaps than either of them wanted to.

36

London, July 6.

As he stepped from a funereal Austin cab to the grassy apron of St. James's Park, the Führer knew that he had to prepare quickly to match wits with the *Ambassador,* the *General,* and the *Chancellor.*

The three important Council members were awaiting him in the agreeably disarming park. They sat in a neat row on a green bench centered among waves of chrome-yellow tulips. At their backs, very art-directed nannies pushed baby trams along the crisscrossing sidewalks.

Across the way, a gentleman with a tightly rolled umbrella

and a bowler read the pink *Financial Times.*

It was all very London, thought the Führer.

"The murder of Warrior has created an unfortunate international situation." As expected, the portly Chancellor had the first word.

"The Americans especially are incensed. They're all over the Middle East searching out answers. In their own inimitable manner, they'll probably stumble upon some things they shouldn't."

"If Warrior had lived, Dachau would not have survived." The Führer spoke in a soft whisper. "He told me as much himself. Warrior was more of a threat to us than the Strausses. If you three don't agree, I will be glad to step aside now. I'd be more than happy."

The tall thin man, the Ambassador, spoke now. This council member had a somewhat silky, patrician look. He wore Dunhill suits; had his silver hair styled twice a week at Smile in Knightsbridge. "The Strauss boy is poking about in Germany now. He's trying to contact the Nazi-hunter Michael Ben-Iban."

The Führer shrugged.

"You have to leave all of the incidental details to me now. After this afternoon, we won't be able to meet again. Probably, we shall never meet again. Watch your television sets in the middle of July."

The General and the Chancellor exchanged concerned looks.

"Good luck then," the Ambassador finally said. "You're very correct in reminding us there is no turning back now. Just *refining,* extreme *carefulness, intelligence.* As has always been the case, we place our full trust in your judgment."

The Ambassador reached out and took the Führer's hand. The other two then shook the Führer's hand as well.

As expected, the portly Chancellor had the final word.

"The black case is for you."

The Führer walked off with the black leather satchel that had been brought by one of the three powerful Council members.

Once out of their sight in the park, the Führer rudely thrust open the case.

Inside, were fourteen stacks of hundred-dollar American bills. Nearly seven hundred thousand dollars.

They were getting so very close now. Nothing could be allowed to stop Dachau Two.

Now all that remained, the Führer began to think, were those few incidental details he'd promised to take care of.

Like Dr. David Strauss and Alix Rothschild.

37

Odessa, Russia.

When the Cessna 172 began its strange evening flight, a lemon-yellow and burnt-orange sunset stained the low, gentle waves of the Black Sea.

Even the stuporous Turkish pilot was impressed enough to animate his slack face; to whistle between blackened, roughly serrated teeth.

The beginning of the Final Solution, the second Holocaust, now lay just across the flat, navy-blue waterway. A five-hundred-kilometer ride from Zonguldak in Turkey to Kolesnoye, southeast of Odessa in Soviet Russia. Then a Russian truck north to Moscow, site of the twenty-second Olympiad.

The rain and stiff winds came with pitch-black darkness out over the sea.

The two engines of the tired old Cessna began to bitch and moan like a squadron of Waring electric blenders. The plane's wings looked like they were held on by piano wire. Somewhere in the fuselage, metal scraped against metal, making a high-pitched squeak that was worse than five hundred pieces of chalk scraping blackboards.

In the cramped rear seats, a man and woman from West Germany sat in cranky silence.

This was the Nurse and the Teacher. Both in pinching-tight wire-rimmed eyeglasses; in corduroy jackets and slacks. Impressively convincing as the taciturn married couple—Olympic tourists—they would soon portray in the streets of Moscow.

These two made up the advance team for Dachau Two.

They were slickly trained professionals who would be able to buy the necessary small arms and rifles in Moscow's black market; who would take care of safe hotels and cars for the remainder of the strike team; who would arrange the final escape back out of Russia. It was a difficult task, one that the two of them had previously succeeded at in Paris, in Baghdad, in Madrid.

Sitting beside the beret-wearing pilot meanwhile, the Soldier tried to concentrate all of his attention on small details inside the cramped cockpit.

An ancient twelve-gauge instrument dial. *Fuel pump on. Speed: 150 knots.* (The plane didn't seem to be moving at all.) The Turkish pilot's habit of spitting into a small can, his motorman's companion.

Colonel Essmann finally turned his attention outside.

Drops of rain were catching onto the plastic window, holding, then suddenly sliding down into the crack. The airplane's propellers were a vague gray blur out of the window.

"Before we see the coast," he said, turning to the Nurse and the Teacher. "*If* we see the coast in this terrible rattletrap. . . . We should make one final review of everything."

He turned back to the front windshield and could feel the young people's eyes burning into his neck. How many times did they have to review this plan? he knew they must be thinking. Well, the Soldier considered, it wasn't just a matter of how many times. Obviously, they would review, they *should* review, right until the time when the real thing occurred.

Otherwise, somewhere along the way, someone would make the mistake that would kill them all. It was that basic and simple.

"Who wishes to begin?" The military expert spoke without looking back at them again. "In Odessa, there is a man named Andrei Sergeevich Pavlov."

"*Pavlov is one of us,*" the Nurse and Teacher said in unison. "*Pavlov will be wearing a black hat and a red jacket,*" two young people said in a singsong.

Yes, and Pavlov may very well save both of your lives.
The Soldier sat up front with a deep frown over his face.

Ten miles or so from the Russian coast, the intrepid Turk brought the sobbing two-engine plane down below Soviet radar; down extremely close to the black water with its thin headdress of whitecaps.

The sea winds continued to whip the Cessna around without mercy. The little plane constantly thumped and bumped, as if chunks of flying debris were ripping apart its tail and fuselage.

Somewhere very near to the coast the plane seemed to be losing even more altitude. It was as if the plane were being pushed down by a great flat hand. The Soldier could feel the same large palm pushing down on the back of his neck.

Down below them, the sea was a great black hole.

Paper-thin clouds were shredding and falling away before their eyes. The Cessna's wing lights were like toy flashlights in the storm.

The tough young German girl finally threw up all over her back window. Spitting and coughing, she cursed the plane, pilot, Teacher, Soldier, and herself.

"Is this the normal way in?" the Teacher complained loudly, snapping off his wire-rimmed glasses.

"No much trouble. No much trouble," the pilot kept yelling over the plane and wind noise. In truth, the dark little man had made the illegal and very dangerous trip many times, even in the dead of Russian winter.

This time, though, dark unidentifiable shapes were flashing past the cockpit.

"Birds!" the pilot screamed out.

"You've passed the coast!" Colonel Essmann shouted suddenly. "You're flying straight into Soviet Russia, you damn fool. We'll be shot down!"

Just then, the Soldier thought he saw jagged rock not two feet from his window.

Suddenly, rocks and trees outside were all tilted crazily, almost sideways.

"My God, no!"

The Cessna was clotheslined by a long, strong pine limb.

The plane's tail fell off and sailed away under the cockpit.

124

A bright red fire exploded all over the second engine. The Cessna made a strange scraping sound like automobiles skidding in gravel.

Then it was plowing through a forest of Russian birch and fir trees.

The Turkish pilot was screaming and steering insanely, as though the dark trees made up some strange landing field.

A fir tree exploded through the cockpit as if it had been thrown at them.

An enormous black shape flew over the plane passengers like a steel blanket. A loud rumbling noise was everywhere and deafening. The entire cockpit was twisted savagely to the extreme left.

The pilot screamed in terrible agony as airplane metal and tree passed through his chest and stomach. The young Nurse was decapitated by a window stanchion. There was a booming, roaring explosion that must have sounded like the end of the world.

The Soldier was desperately trying to throw himself out of a burning flat door.

Suddenly he was stumbling over a smoking, burning wing.

He thudded onto the ground and he was forcing himself to run.

He ran past the Teacher, thrown up into a tree somehow. Very gruesomely dead. Eyes gray and bulging like a fish on newspaper.

A third, tremendously loud explosion came as wet leaves began to slap his face.

A plume of bright flame shot up at least thirty feet high, lighting the treetops and the low Russian sky. The precious explosives they had been smuggling in had blown the plane into bits and pieces.

Then there was only the crackling sound of water falling on a small fire in the dark, deep forest.

There was the lonely sound of the Soldier's ammunition boots on the wet leaves and twigs.

The strangely driven Soldier forced himself to look back.

He stood still and dripping, and stared into the insignificant-looking blaze.

The work of thirty-five years, he whispered.

The advance team is dead, he told himself, trying to sort

out information and understand. *You are now your own advance team. Do you understand, Colonel?*

Do you understand?

Answer if you understand. . . .

"In Odessa," the shocked, wounded man began to chant, "there is a man named Andrei Sergeevich Pavlov. Pavlov is one of us. . . .

The Soldier began to walk out of the forest.

38

Munich. July 8.

Where in the name of God was Michael Ben-Iban?

Both David and Alix had begun to worry about the old Nazi-fighter. Three times they'd actually gone to Ben-Iban's Jewish Studies Centre in Frankfurt. Even Ben-Iban's secretary was rightfully concerned now.

Could they have gotten Ben-Iban, too?

Killed the Nazi-hunter the way they'd murdered Benjamin Rabinowitz and Elena?

Still more questions were added to the nasty bulging catalogue of mysteries and catastrophes.

For the time being, David and Alix decided to spend one last day with Nick's movie. The two of them flew to Munich, where the final scenes of the documentary feature had actually been shot.

David and Alix went to the location where the single most affecting scene in *The Fourth Commandment* had been filmed.

A long-forgotten chant that David and Alix had sung as smart-aleck twelve-year-olds popped into both of their heads as they rode from Munich Airport.

"Hitler had only one big ball," they'd once upon a time

harmonized on public buses, in schoolyards, outside the mock-Tudor railroad station in Scarsdale.

"Goering had two but they were small
"Himmler had something simmler
"But Goebbels had no balls at all."

It was all flashing back to them now. Hateful, sinister floods of it. A villainous Christmas when someone had thrown gift-wrapped bags of manure against the Strausses' front door. A time when David and Nick had gone as guests to the country club, then been told they had to leave by the club president. "You're the two Strauss boys, aren't you? You're Jewish. You boys aren't allowed here." A bad, bad rush of old persecution nightmares.

At noon on July 8, David and Alix stared up at the pocked and nicked gray stone walls of a one-time World War I munitions factory. They were at their final destination outside Munich.

A bright yellow sun was peeking half its smiley face around the dark, heavy building blocks and watchtowers.

"It's unbelievable," Alix mumbled under her breath. Her whole body was shaking.

"One thousand by nineteen hundred eighty feet of pure hell," David surveyed the blackened walls and said. "It's almost indistinguishable from the ordinary world now."

David and Alix had come to Dachau One.

WILKOMMEN said the sign.

Because the former scene of flogging, pole-hanging, gassing, infecting women and children with malaria, whooping cough, and cholera was such a popular summer tourist attraction—nearly a million visitors a year—Alix had chosen dark glasses and a peasant's kerchief to disguise her looks.

Because he too was beginning to be recognized at times, David wore drugstore sunglasses, a floppy white hat, a puffy navy Windbreaker.

As a result of this, the two well-known Americans felt relatively anonymous as they hiked down Dachau's infamous Turnpike to Hell.

Inside the infernal walls, they went through various chapels and sterile memorial museums. They walked into gas chambers, and alongside the ghastly shooting ranges. They were looking for the resting place of Alix's mother—the Grave of Ashes—among other morbid things to do.

Contrary to Eisenhower's orders to leave the camp exactly as it was when liberated, the West Germans had made the former *Konzentrationslager* much too pretty.

At least David and Alix thought so.

That day in particular, Dachau brought to mind well-intentioned but phony Memorial Day parades in America.

There were all sorts of brassy commemorative plaques. Crisp scrolls. Hundreds of bright-colored flags. Willow trees grew all around the outer walls.

David and Alix stopped at a museum where the History of the Rise of Anti-Semitism was supposedly captured in artsy black-and-white photographs. They visited the Christ in Agony chapel. Then a nondenominational chapel marked for meditation.

A large plaque in German, English, and Russian said:

THOUSANDS OF OUR BROTHERS, SISTERS, AND PARENTS WERE KILLED WHERE YOU ARE NOW STANDING. THIS HAPPENED BETWEEN 1933 AND 1945. BY THE MURDEROUS NAZIS.

Reading the sign, David Strauss shivered involuntarily.

"Right now. As I stand right here, I'm finally out of touch with the idea that I was ever a medical doctor. A simpleminded, somewhat old-fashioned American doctor in New York. Will you please explain to me what I'm doing here at Dachau? What the hell is happening to us?"

Alix shook her head. She seemed to be in mild shock. A glassy-eyed daze had come over her.

"I don't know, David. I don't know."

Feeling an overwhelming sense of physical unreality suddenly, the American couple finally walked to the brickwalled, ivy-covered gas chambers and ovens.

"This building doesn't feel right," Alix said as they approached it along a low-fenced gravel walk. "It's too pretty. All this ivy. I feel like I'm visiting some college English department."

Right inside the front doorway, they were immediately confronted with six ovens directly across a deep, wide room. The ovens were all neatly shined. Clean as whistles. Lined up against red-brick walls that smelled of household disinfectant.

"It's like a little Arnold's Bakery," Alix said.

Then something terrifying about the spick-and-span, efficient little room began to affect both of them.

Over a brown side door they read: THINK ABOUT WHO DIED HERE.

Alix and David thought about it. They thought about the Jews, and about the Nazis.

On a ceiling beam: PRISONERS WERE ACTUALLY HANGED FROM HERE.

On one of the brick walls: PRISONERS WERE FLOGGED HERE.

Under the shiny ovens that looked a little like resuscitation chambers: THE ACTUAL OVENS USED AT DACHAU.

David was finding it difficult to breathe. Vicious waves of nausea came over him. So did body chills.

A black family from America was posing for a photograph in front of one of the ovens. All the neatly groomed family members were smiling for the instant camera. They have no idea what happened here, David thought. None. They couldn't have any idea.

"I don't know why, but I can feel the whole thing now, Alix. I think I finally understand what happened in Germany forty years ago."

Tears were rolling down Alix's face. The black father was carefully directing his photograph session. David and Alix both felt a terrible need to be in some private place for a few moments.

Arm in arm, holding one another tightly, they walked outside next to some gray administration buildings. George Santayana was quoted in German and English: *"Those who cannot remember the past are condemned to repeat it."*

Remember was an odd, maybe even a poor choice of words, David was thinking. . . . *Was the quotation true though*, he couldn't help wondering—partially feeling like some fool who takes secret messages from songs on the radio. *Could the whole thing happen again? Could it repeat itself all over again? What did the Storm Troop want?*

Alix, meanwhile, was beginning to question whether she could ever tell David all the things whirling around in her mind. *God, it was all so complicated. All her past experience told her that only other concentration-camp survivors truly understood the nightmares, the hatred.*

David's private thoughts, Alix's thoughts, were suddenly interrupted by a strangely familiar *whirring, buzzing, clicking* sound.

39

A very ugly, long-haired man with a sloth's body and ferret's face was responsible for the noise.

Whirring, buzzing, clicking.

Whirring, buzzing, clicking.

The human mole was shooting professional 35mm photographs of them.

"Hey, Rothschild." The man growled as Alix tried to shield her face. "Give me one for *Komet.* I've come all the way from Frankfurt, doll."

From out of the gray prison-camp walls and shrubs, other people with cameras now began to appear. An old, slop-bellied burgher. A young woman with a telescope-nosed Nikon.

"Please don't," David said into the long lens of an expensive Rolliflex. "Please, not here."

"*Kuchemal da!* Alix Rothschild!" A middle-aged German man shouted and pointed at them.

"*Das ist Rothschild?*" David and Alix heard from the rear. They began to walk at a fast clip. Then they actually ran.

Across the promenade and into Dachau's formal gardens. Down a path surrounded by more ceremonial plaques. More waving Memorial Day flags. Dachau's only sign actually written in Hebrew:

HERE IS THE GRAVE OF THE THOUSANDS UNKNOWN.
HERE IS THE GRAVE OF ASHES.

Alix's mother was there somewhere.

Nick had filmed powerful interviews there with young, bitter survivors.

Alix herself was choking back sobs and tears as she ran past the memorial signpost. Her nineteen-year-old mother. Always and forever nineteen years old. She couldn't even stop to visit now . . . to say some prayer.

She and David streaked past THE PISTOL RANGE FOR EXECUTION.

THE EXECUTION RANGE WITH BLOOD DITCH.

"*Strauss und Rothschild sind dauber!*" It was like trying to escape from the prison itself. It was as if there were guards and terrible dogs coming up from behind.

Finally, they arrived at the front gates.

The black door of a car was thrown open for them. A groan went up from the crowd.

Cameras flashed in unison. Alix suddenly thought she could remember the Dachau tower searchlights. So much horrible detail was flooding back. She was feeling the way she'd felt in New York City. Before Cherrywoods and David.

"*Nehmen wir . . . bitte . . . nach Flughaven.*" David struggled with his German.

"*Take us to Munich Airport, please.*"

Suddenly, one of the taxi's doors flew open again.

"*David!*" Alix screamed. "*Get him out of here, please.*"

The troll.

The terrible inhuman photographer was there with his ratty vinyl jacket, with his Nikon aimed for one last, dramatic shot.

"Nooo." Alix was sobbing. "Nooo, David."

Then David Strauss was leaping out across the taxi's back seat.

Before he knew what he was doing, he had the photographer crushed underneath his body on the parking-lot gravel. David punched the German man in the chest. A hard, crunching blow. Somehow he avoided the temptation to keep hitting the troll. He got up and smashed the camera against a metal signpost. All the while, David Strauss was repeating a single word over and over.

"Nazi. Nazi. Nazi. Nazi."

Shaking all over, David fell back into the taxi. Alix pressed into him and held on tight. The cab then bolted away from the terrible, confused scene at the pickup depot.

In the rush and confusion, neither David nor Alix seemed to notice a second Munich taxi.

The black car left the gates of Dachau just behind them. It too went straight to Munich Airport.

The Führer had just paid a visit to Dachau One also.

40

That same afternoon, a beautiful one during which the temperature reached a dramatic eighty-four degrees all over Germany, agent Harry Callaghan coolly waded through assorted *Herren* and *Fräulein* mobbing the *botikish* Sachenhausen district of Frankfurt am Main.

Harry was chomping on a greenish Dutch cigar.

The tall, distinguished-looking man was feeling pretty good as the rich tobacco and aromas of local German cooking mixed in his lungs. He was feeling a little like Gregory Peck, whom people occasionally said he looked like.

The Sachenhausen part of Frankfurt consisted of old restored buildings crowding narrow streets. Harry observed cafes, bakeries, dress shops, chic pied-à-terres—all apparently built on a slant with the cobbled road.

No autos were permitted here. (No poor people seemed to be permitted anywhere in Frankfurt.) There were plenty of Coca-Cola culture Germans, soldiers, and well-to-do tourists, though. Eating lots of kuchen; buying strudel and sausages; selecting cuckoo clocks and women's clothing.

As he wandered the pretty streets, Harry began to be reminded of Georgetown in Washington. . . . His divorce six years ago from Betsy. His son Martin, now a senior at Pitt. God, how it all was flying by. A life. How very much he'd given up to be *a good investigator*. "One of our very best. I mean that," the Director had once said to Harry's face, knowing the praise would drive the proud Irishman more than any amount of criticism.

Callaghan forced himself to think about the job only. Only David Strauss and Alix Rothschild.

Something about the way the two of them seemed to belong with one another made Harry suddenly smile on the crowded streets of Frankfurt.

There was something special about David Strauss and Alix Rothschild. *Something.* That was one reason they'd made front-page news right from the start. There was just *something* about David and Alix together, Harry was thinking as he walked.

A big, blond Viking—James Bacon Burns—was sitting at a small wrought-iron table in one of the buzzing outdoor cafes. The Schlag.

The agent was doing his best to look like an American tourist, Harry noticed as he turned into the cafe. A very handsome, Robert Redfordish sort of American tourist. One who might easily pick up an unattached *Fräulein*, or perhaps even a *Herren.*

Harry vaguely remembered Burns from an earlier encounter in New York. Burns still wore the same patent-leather shoes with cute little gold buckles; a light gray diplomat's suit; one of those dumb blue dress shirts with the stark-white collars. J. B. Burns: also known as Casper the Friendly Ghost.

"J. B., you brought me here to show me how good you have it. Nice, cushy assignment in Europe." Harry offered Burns a broad smile and friendly handshake.

"So. They finally have something on the Strauss thing." Harry sat down, finger-combing back his own slightly thinning brown hair. "It's about time. Wouldn't you say it's about time?"

J. B. Burns laughed a little too loudly. He then took a big dripping bite of blue-plum kuchen.

"Yeah, mmmm, they have something, Harry." The agent licked the tips of his long piano-player fingers.

"Wait until you hear what it is they have. On a scale of ten— an eleven. Possibly a twelve."

A cafe waiter appeared at their table, a red cloth draped over his arm. Harry ordered Calvados and a big piece of apple-and-raisin kuchen.

"Big, big piece," he made a moon-and-the-stars motion with his hands. "If the pieces are small, bring two of them."

As soon as the waiter walked away, J. B. Burns produced a packet of black-and-white photographs. Burns's family home photos, they looked like. With a yellow Kodak mailer-envelope and everything.

"Take a look at this beauty. A definite photo-contest winner."

The first dog-eared picture was of a society-type woman. Brunette. Thirty-eight or so. She seemed to be at some sort of ball or ritzy dinner-dance.

"All right, I give up. Who is she?"

"Believe it or not, she's one of the Storm Troop operators. Her name is Rachel Davidson. She's a New York City lawyer with the code name Housewife."

Burns's tanned, manicured hand dealt out another photograph.

Harry was beginning to feel a little bit like Ross Macdonald's Lew Archer. What was he supposed to do now? Find the missing oil painting of the sister of the brunette Rachel Davidson?

The second photograph showed the same woman.

This time she was standing beside an older man whom Callaghan recognized immediately. In fact, seeing this particular man in the photograph sent Harry Callaghan's mind reeling. His presence was almost as disconcerting as that of the third person in the photograph: Mrs. Elena Strauss.

"This one was taken at Cherrywoods Mountain House. That's Mrs. Elena Strauss. And you'll probably recognize General Yagaal Ben-Zurev."

"Oh shit!" Callaghan set the photo down.

"You bet 'oh shit.' You see, Mrs. Davidson, the Housewife, is Ben-Zurev's niece."

Stroking his Dutch cigar, Harry stared down at the photo. *Cherrywoods; Grandmother Strauss; Rachel Davidson; the Israeli general, Ben-Zurev.*

Callaghan's mind was already working on a few dicey little scenarios involving the mysterious Storm Troop.

Blue smoke signals rose from the table as the German waiter, Calvados, and kuchen arrived.

"Anything else, J. B.?"

"Besides being a respected and successful lawyer, Rachel Davidson is an orthodox Jew. She was very close to her uncle, General Ben-Zurev . . . until he was found dead in Washington late this spring."

"Yes? I'm liking this story less and less as it gathers steam."

"We're getting reports that Ben-Zurev was helping to control the Storm Troop from Israel. His code name was Warrior. There was some kind of rift among their top leadership. Apparently the group had a vow of secrecy, which they took very seriously. Ben-Zurev was killed. The Arabs have known about it for about a month. The pricks sat on it.

"We think Mossad leaked the information to Washington. Whatever the hell Dachau Two is, they don't want it to come off. *Very, very* bad stuff. Like major war vibrations in the air. Everybody is very, very edgy, Harry."

"Is this the Agency's up-to-the-moment evaluation?"

Burns smiled. He pursed his pretty blueish lips.

"Those cagey bastards haven't made an evaluation yet. Like to hear mine? It's all in this little folder."

Harry Callaghan crushed out his cigar into his kuchen. "The Storm Troop is a very elaborately conceived, very dangerous Jewish terrorist group," Harry said.

"Or Israeli," Burns added. "An Israeli Black September, that has its roots way, way back. Maybe as far back as the forties. There was a commando group back then known as ZIN. ZIN attempted to poison a million Germans as *partial* retribution for the Holocaust."

"And this group carries on, they masquerade, as neo-Nazis."

"Because *everybody* goes haywire when they hear about Nazis. Because *nobody* can evaluate Nazi data properly. There has to be loads more to it. That's a start I can live with, though."

"The Jews are going to avenge the six million?"

"I don't know. I'm guessing something on that order."

Harry stared off at an office building across the cobblestone street. The late-afternoon sun was making stars and little lilac-blue rings around a flagpole from a third-floor window. Harry could feel a sharp pain starting to spread behind his eyes.

"Harry," J. B. Burns said. "Doesn't one thing strike you as a little odd? That Dr. David Strauss has somehow escaped two shooting attempts now?"

Callaghan looked back from across the street.

"I guess it does. A lot of things strike me as odd right now. Listen, I have a few things I'd like you to check for me. In a big, big hurry. Can you do me a few favors, J. B.?"

"For sure," the blond man smiled. "Hey, why do you think I wore my roller skates today?"

"I was wondering about that," Harry Callaghan shook his head and laughed. "Guccis, too, I noticed."

James Burns's office was a modishly furnished two-room walk-up in the West End business district of Frankfurt.

The entire office consisted of Burns and a nineteen-year-old German girl named Sigi. It was he and Sigi against the world, James Burns liked to say whenever he was feeling put upon by Washington—which was often.

Like now.

Like the way they'd suddenly dumped all this terrorist crap in his lap, then fled for the hills themselves.

As he climbed to the third floor of the prewar building, Burns heard loud music coming from above.

Goddamn Sigi was a Beethoven nut.

Once he got inside the office though, he saw that the long-haired blond girl (James Burns liked to call Sigi his "very own California surfer in the Fozzerland") wasn't anywhere around.

A "While You Were Out" note was pinned to the telephone. A single word—"wife."

Mildly annoyed, the American man carefully folded his suit jacket. He dialed his home phone number and then lit up a cigar.

While he waited for someone to answer, he stared at Cary Grant, Ingrid Bergman, and Humphrey Bogart on the office walls. Goddamn Sigi was an American movie nut also.

"Who dis?" Burns heard.

"Vee-gates, it's the midget!" James Burns laughed into the telephone. "Is your mother home, midget?"

"Who dis?"

As he spoke on the phone, Burns also began to write out the things he had to do for Harry Callaghan before his workday was over.

"Dis ist Herr Burns, midget. The good-looking fellow mitt the blond hair. *Daddy.*"

Patricia Burns giggled. "Daddy? You're silly."

James Burns didn't speak back to his little daughter. The door to the second room of the office had suddenly swung open.

Burns was looking at Sigi, neatly tied to a leather wing chair inside.

A man with a small Luger stepped into the doorway. Very suddenly James Burns understood why Beethoven's Ninth was playing so loudly.

"Wait a minute," James Burns said to the intruder. At the same time, Burns pulled out his own Smith & Wesson.

The Luger fired three shots into the handsome blond agent's chest.

Shaking his head over the unfortunate shooting, the Weapons Expert quickly went through J. B. Burns's papers.

He tucked two manila folders into his own briefcase. The folders contained the preliminary intelligence findings on the Storm Troop; they contained a Mossad report on the probable identity of the secret group's leader. Just as the group's secret Washington contact had informed them it would.

The only problem was that the Weapons Expert had come for the folders about an hour too late.

The Weapons Expert left the West End walk-up with the Telefunken stereo blaring Beethoven at 9++.

"Who dis?" the telephone receiver continued to ask.

42

HERE IS THE GRAVE OF THE THOUSANDS UNKNOWN. . . .
HERE IS THE GRAVE OF ASHES. . . .

Alix's mother was there somewhere.

Nina Rothman.

Alix was choking back hard sobs and tears as she ran past the memorial signposts.

Her nineteen-year-old mother. Kneeling before the gaping ditch with sixty-six others. Unthinkable mass murder. . . . Alix couldn't even stop to visit now. She couldn't say a brief prayer.

She and David ran past THE PISTOL RANGE FOR EXECUTION. THE EXECUTION RANGE WITH BLOOD DITCH.

Alix stopped running.

Oh my God! This was where! This was the place where it had happened! Suddenly Alix remembered so very much of it!

Then she was awake. She was inside an unfamiliar room. Where was she?

Alix screamed out in the darkness.

"I'm here, Alix. I'm right here with you. I'm here."

Her eyes blinked open wider. At first she could not focus on anything.

Then the fuzzy black shadow of a man sitting beside her in bed.

David.

The Schlosshotel.

David reached for her and held her tightly.

He had never seen a nightmare like this before. The excruciating, unbelievable terror and anguish. The screaming; loud cries; the thrashing—as if people had been trying to grab hold of Alix in her dreams.

Suddenly David was terribly afraid for her. He understood that there were real Nazi demons in her head. He pressed his body closer to hers. Very warm breasts and stomach. Heaving chest. He kissed Alix as gently as he could.

"I saw my mother's murder," she whispered. "I witnessed it. I was there.

"I remembered *everything* just now. A thousand small details I'd partly forgotten.

"I've had the dream before, David. I always wake up crying, but I could never remember everything about the dream. *Tonight I remembered.*"

"I'm here,"David whispered as Alix's voice rose higher.

"My mother is killed with other Jewish prisoners, David. All young, pretty women.

"They fall over into a three-foot-deep ditch. Like the Blood Ditch that we saw today."

David wanted to soothe her somehow. To do something to stop the pain. He could think of nothing to say. Everything he thought of was so trivial by any measure of comparison.

Alix began to hug him. Tightly. She clutched his arm until it hurt.

Shadows of the moon through an old oak tree were playing on the bedspread. Moonbeams making a hanging man. A fast polka among stick figures.

"My aunt had photographs. Sepia photographs of my mother.

"My mother had long, dark hair. She let it fall, flow down onto her shoulders. She always wore either a colorful ribbon or a kind of ivory barrette. To set her hair off.

"The barrette always made me sad. I could imagine something of what my mother was like because of the barrette. I knew she liked to be pretty for other people. How sad to think of."

David's mouth was quivering, his teeth hitting together. He had never felt so tender toward Alix, so afraid for her. He had never understood the camp experience, he realized. Not even that afternoon at Dachau—where he thought he'd reached a new level of understanding.

"They cut all her hair off before they could kill her, David.

"I always believed that no one would have been able to kill my mother with her long hair and the barrette.

"That was always my thought as a little girl. I would daydream about that when we were in school back in Scarsdale. Whenever the teachers made us lay our heads down.

"She weighed less than seventy pounds when they killed her. How could anyone do that, David?" Alix began to sob uncontrollably. She was crying just like a little girl, David thought. "How could they kill my mother like that, David?"

David couldn't answer Alix. He felt tears coming. Rage building. He had finally *begun* to understand the insidious damage that had been done to Alix Rothschild.

As he lay there holding her, David thought that the nightmares *were* Alix; the *dreams* were who Alix was, really. The beautiful actress that the world knew was a front, a counterfeit woman. The *actress Alix Rothschild* was a Hollywood fantasy.

David was holding the real Alix, and holding her made him very afraid.

Paris's *L'Express* would later call the relationship "one of the strangest, the most haunting of love stories."

The morning of July 9, Alix and David packed a haversack with cheeses; apple wine from Sachenhausen; the fussy local *Schweinemetzeger's* best wursts, pork sausage, and *Kalbs* medallion. After too many days chronicling and experiencing Nazi atrocities, they'd promised one another a very necessary day off.

They began their *Wanderjahr* around ten-thirty, heading up into the cool Hansel-and-Gretel forests directly behind the Schlosshotel.

Don't think about Nazis, they kept reminding one another. *You're allowed one day without the camps, without war criminals, or blitzkriegs.*

As they walked into the foothills, there was nothing but tall cedar trees and the most beautiful blue-spruce and poplar saplings. Under their footsteps, rusty-looking fir needles and duff made up a smooth carpet for the entire forest. It was like stepping into one of the Goblein tapestries off the walls of the Schlosshotel.

Beyond a steep, pretty brush slope, David and Alix discovered a silver-blue stream. The stream curled up the mountain like a tricky icicle, and they followed it.

Several kilometers deeper into the woods, the stream's source appeared quite magically at the top of a steep hill.

It was a small, sparkling pond, closed in by tightly packed cedars. With the clean smell of fresh mint everywhere.

Jagged forest reflections from either shore stretched to meet at the center of the gorgeous water mirror. A single gray-and-brown mallard sat on the shadow-fault like a fat little emperor of the lake.

David and Alix stopped walking, threw down their backpacks, and cheered and bowed for the duck.

On the near shore, a great grandfather oak had fallen half-way out into the pond. It lay stretched out over the water for seventy feet or more; long limbs and leafless boughs held the tree up like a dozen strong-armed Volga boatmen.

Alix pointed toward the fallen tree.

"All this beautifulness, Donald Duck, plus a perfect diving board. Our luck must be changing a little, Herr Hansel. *Maybe* a little?"

For just a few hours it was going to be 1959 again. They were both younger; it was like the feeling children get skipping dreary school classes for a day.

They sat on sloping granite boulders and began to take off their clothes. Unlacing hiking boots; tugging at wide leather belts; kicking off trousers and woolen socks. David set his .38 on top of their pile of clothes.

"No Nazis today," Alix said. A reminder.

Then she was suddenly gracefully tightrope-walking out on the fallen tree trunk.

For a moment, David just sat and watched her. Tight athletic legs and back muscles. Full breasts jutting straight ahead as she ran toward a smoky summer sun winking across the water at them. Leonard Cohen's "Suzanne" drifted through David's mind.

"C'mon you!" Alix had turned and was calling back to him. "Mr. All-American hotshot water sportsman."

Then David was up on the fallen tree trunk as well. His toes were gripping old slippery oak bark. The hot sun was beating on his neck and well-muscled shoulders.

"I don't believe how beautiful this is. I feel like shouting. I *will* shout. Hooray for us!"

Three-quarters of the way out on the tree trunk, Alix executed a sudden impromptu cannonball dive.

She saw David upside down just before her head pierced the black ripples of the lake.

Alix heard David yell, "*No!*"

Then, year of surprises!

The lake water was actually a livable temperature. At least sixty-eight degrees. Bottle green and clear down ten feet to eelgrass waving gently on a mud bottom.

"*Wunderbar!*"

Alix was shouting as her shiny black hair broke the surface again. She found that David was now in the water, too.

They held one another gently. Their long legs tangled and rubbed together like sticks trying to make heat. They began to make love in the water.

Every so often, David found it hard to believe that he was back with Alix again ... Alix Rothman ... "Franny" ... ROTHSCHILD. . . . It was like being with Lauren Hutton, or Margaux Hemingway, or somebody else clearly unattainable. Sometimes it made David feel a little unreal himself. As if everything was going to appear in a movie or *Cosmopolitan* one day, and then it would all be over.

"I love Dr. David Strauss," Alix whispered as they floated with the lake current. She couldn't quite believe that she'd said it. The words had just slipped out.

David found himself just staring into her eyes—beautiful green eyes.

"Say something." Alix managed an embarrassed smile. She wanted to make it all a joke now.

"You're O.K. Not bad." David grinned.

It was so damn good for them to be on top of the pretty lake. Just floating like air bubbles. Being alone together.

Just then, David spotted a man watching them from the woods. The man was standing just over Alix's left shoulder, in a clump of evergreens.

"Uh-oh."

"What?"

When he saw David catch sight of him, the man did nothing to conceal himself. He lit up a cigarette, reached down and picked up a rifle, and started to come forward.

David and Alix could do nothing but watch him come.

The lake current rippled under their chins as they watched his slow walk. Their bodies were covered with large goose pimples. Suddenly they were aware of a chill breeze blowing across the water.

Tall and dark, wearing a checked hacking jacket, the man walked right out along the fallen oak tree. Finally, the man spoke to them.

"You look surprised."

"Yes. We *feel* surprised, too. Who the hell are you?"

"I thought Harry would have told you. You're back under

142

surveillance, Dr. Strauss. I'm Ray Cosgrove. Hey, how's the water?"

43

The forest-green BMW sounded the way one of Dr. Diehl's famed German watches sound. All precise little *ticks*, no disconcerting *tocks*.

As Alix piloted the purring sports car through the countryside, the late-afternoon sun threw crimson streaks and gold coins of light onto the BMW's windshield.

It was just like expensively shot Panavision movie scenes she'd appeared in.

Nestled in the snug driver's chair, Alix listened to the beautiful engine; to the sound of four-and-twenty blackbirds chirping outside; to Otto Klemperer conducting *Finlandia* on the AFN radio network.

Alix could barely feel the autobahn beneath her.

Not even when the gold-rimmed speedometer tipped 140, then 150 kilometers.

Over a hundred miles an hour.

Taking solitary automobile rides was something Alix had found herself doing more and more since she had first moved out to California. San Diego Freeway rides late at night. Pacific Coast Highway rides. Also, long jogging sessions. Around and around the lovely, secluded roads of Bel Air where she had lived for nearly six years.

The running sessions were very California actressy, Alix had realized, and felt self-conscious. Yet the hectic movement had seemed necessary whenever she'd begun to think about the camps at Dachau and Buchenwald. About being a survivor. About any of a hundred different Hollywood lifestyle frustrations.

Near a natural-wood exercise *Plotzen* along the roadside, Alix pulled the BMW over onto the apron.

She rolled all four windows down to take advantage of the

clean, fresh-smelling air. She let her dark hair fall out of a flower-print kerchief.

The terrible daydreams were coming on a regular basis now. Quite uncontrollable. All of a sudden she would be watching naked mothers and children being marched to the showers. She could smell the scorched flesh, the stench of disease.

In the rear-view mirror there was a young German man in a trendy jumpsuit, washing his precious convertible out of a single red pail. It was a semi-humorous phenomenon Alix saw constantly while traveling around Frankfurt.

Something else, though. . . .

While the BMW was stopped, Alix felt that she was being followed.

Right palm lightly touching the shift stick, she gunned the sports car and it popped out in front of a speedy clique of oncoming cars.

Alix turned up AFN. *"Horst Wessel"* was playing now. *Boom, rah, rah, boom. Sis, rah, rah, boom.*

She glanced up into the rear-view mirror and saw nothing to alarm her.

A big black truck marked *Sturn.* A plum-red Audi full of German mothers and school-age children.

Then the great, gray city of Frankfurt began to replace overhanging fir trees in the BMW's front windshield.

Powerful, shimmering new office buildings stood above shorter, older ones. Commerzbank, Dredner Bank, Deutsche Bank, she read on the skyscrapers. Construction sites were everywhere. Cranes—like giant giraffes running loose in the middle of the city. Billboards for Nivea Milch suntan products, for Mercedes-Benz.

The German and American dreams were fusing together, it seemed to Alix. Strange . . . and then, not so strange, when you thought for a second. An era of multinational businesses and governments was dawning on a half-asleep world.

The German radio was starting to get a little irritating now. *"Achtung! A sale is now going on at—"* Alix twisted the thing off.

Driving alongside the gray-blue Main, which was crowded with colorful pleasure boats that balmy afternoon, Alix began

144

to think about David and herself. She tried to review what had happened to them so far that summer. Alix tried to understand exactly what was going on in the arena of her heart. How much was schoolgirl excitement? How much was atmospheric pressure? How much was something else altogether?

Her attention was temporarily diverted to city-driving problems. Like how to park the damn car in downtown Frankfurt.

A city policeman in a pigeon-gray uniform was waving and whistling, looking like a piece in a cuckoo clock. . . .

Are you waving at me? Aah-ha! A long parking space in front of a narrow bakery.

Alix put two wheels of the BMW up on the curb, the way everybody seemed to park in Frankfurt. Then once again she felt that someone was following her.

Maybe someone had recognized Alix Rothschild the actress? Maybe someone had recognized Alix Rothschild the Jew?

Alix spun around quickly.

No one unusual was to be seen anywhere. Silly, paranoid squirrel, she thought. God!

It was 5:47 on a grimy Bavarian clock over a Deutsche Bank branch.

Alix got out of the sports car, fluffed her long black hair and flipped on sunglasses. Then she walked straight ahead in the direction of the Main.

Drawing stares and a few wolf whistles, she sat on a bench with a pleasant view of the towering Henninger Turm. Then, on impulse it seemed, Alix hopped aboard one of the dull-yellow Strassenbahn trams that stopped at the street corner.

She heard the whistle and screech of the overhead tram cables as the trolley pulled away, and she thought, *There, stupid, no one got on the damn train with you, did they?*

Train rides in general were poison for Alix, though. She began to think of the concentration camps almost immediately.

She imagined bumping trains going to Dachau, Treblinka, Belsen. She saw her mother again. Then her father. She saw human legs and rib cages strewn in a field. . . . *Stop!*

STOP!

HALT! A big blue sign alongside the tracks had caught her attention. In a flash, Alix jumped off the tram—just before it crossed the barge-cluttered Main.

The young woman hesitated on the high wooden platform over the river. She seemed to change her mind about something.

Then Alix jumped back on the same train—and hurried to her seat past the somewhat befuddled conductor.

She continued the ride all the way to the Hauptbahnhof, Frankfurt's large, distinctive railroad station.

Outside the station, Alix walked along the famous Münchner Strasse.

As she turned away from the Bahnhof, the frenetic Münchner district began to look something like Times Square back around 1960. Frankfurt itself was getting fuzzy—mephitic yellow—as the sun set over local three- and four-story buildings. A crazy-sounding flügelhorn was blowing somewhere.

As she walked, Alix stared at American soldiers from the Rhine-Main base. She saw German prostitutes hanging like racks of cheap dresses in front of red- and blue-lit doorways.

At precisely seven, the paraffin street lamps on Münchner Strasse switched on. They spun out their golden strands of light like delicate spider webs.

A black American soldier seemed mesmerized by the neon lights from a dance club reflected in the street. A parrot-green building that Alix passed housed a maternity shop; a sex shop; a birth-control center.

Alix finally turned down a more pleasant side street heading toward the West End business sector. She looked back over her shoulder once, glanced at her wristwatch, then stepped inside a small restaurant called Kleine-Garten.

"Liebchen?"

Vulkan, Rabbi Doctor Michael Ben-Iban, lifted his tired eyes from one of the small dining tables.

"I'm sorry for being late," Alix apologized. She suddenly realized that she was shaking all over. She could barely speak.

"I think they had someone acting as my bodyguard. Someone was following me while I was driving out in the countryside."

"We don't have much time to talk."

Vulkan motioned for Alix to sit down.

44

Harry Callaghan and James Burns had come remarkably close with their seat-of-the-pants guesswork at the Schlag Cafe in Sachenhausen.

The Storm Troop was indeed a Jewish group: it was a well-financed, well-organized, a very intense and intelligent terrorist cell of fewer than a hundred soldiers. It was an offshoot of the original secret defense group formed by survivors in 1945.

To this point it had existed to counterbalance and discourage violently anti-Semitic groups: disparate, evil organizations such as ODESSA, Die Spinne, the PLO, Black September.

Now the Jewish group was apparently ready to move against all its dangerous enemies. One spectacular coup de grace.

The group's brilliant realpolitik Nazi ruse in America had not only succeeded in raising anti-Nazi sentiment among influential non-Jews; it had simultaneously galvanized the defense group's regular supporters to proffer their largest contributions ever.

As the summer of 1980 began, concerned Jews everywhere, even those previously uncommitted to radical action, were seriously talking about stopping the Nazi renascence once and for all time.

Which was exactly what the dedicated leaders of the Dachau Two group had in mind.

It had been their obsession, in fact, for thirty-five long and difficult years.

For the moment, though, on July 10 in Frankfurt, the problem facing Michael Ben-Iban—Vulkan, and the dilemma confronting the Führer, was how best to deal with Alix Rothschild. The Actress.

More precisely, the problem was how the sensitive and intelligent American woman might react once the neo-Nazi ploy was finally revealed to her.

Even worse, the problem was how Alix would view the unfortunate killing of Elena and Nicholas Strauss—a sad but necessary development once the Strausses had made their final decision to reveal the Dachau Two plot; to break the defense group's strict vow of secrecy.

"So, here we are at another difficult decision juncture. We need Alix Rothschild rather badly," the Führer had been saying before the actress arrived at the Kleine-Garten. "Alix *has* to be with us in Moscow. We need our beautiful film star. When she speaks, the world has eyes and ears."

"What would you have me do?" Michael Ben-Iban leaned across the small restaurant table. His thin hands were spread in a helpless, floundering gesture. "Are you asking me to lie to Alix Rothschild now? What is it exactly that you want?"

The chief of Dachau Two rubbed out a cigarette stub. There didn't seem to be a need to answer Michael Ben-Iban's question. The answer was obvious—at least it should have been.

"I just want you to make certain we don't lose the young woman's trust. To see to it that she is with us in Moscow. The method is entirely up to you."

The mysterious Führer left the Kleine-Garten moments before Alix arrived. The success or failure of the difficult meeting was now in the hands of Michael Ben-Iban.

It was entirely up to Vulkan.

Alix found herself beginning to smile as she sat across from the famed Nazi-hater.

What brought on the smile was Ben-Iban's baggy tweed jacket, a faded brown overshirt, an ancient gray felt hat that made him resemble a Thomas Mann character.

Besides that, it was just tremendously good to see Michael Ben-Iban again, Alix thought to herself. After all that had happened in the past few weeks it was especially good.

Alix felt wonderfully safe for a fleeting moment; she was happy to see Ben-Iban alive. At the same time, she was feeling very bad about David. She wished there had been a way she could have told him everything—but the risks of exposing Moscow had been too great. That had been the decision passed on to her by the secret group leaders.

So many questions and feelings rushed into Alix's mind that she didn't know exactly where to begin.

"You look a little tired. But good, *habibi*," Ben-Iban whispered to Alix. The old man began to smile as any harmless grandfather might. He liked Alix Rothschild. He liked the young American woman a great deal.

"You will be glad to hear that everything is moving on schedule," Ben-Iban went on with an expansive gesture. "Our brave people are safely in Moscow. There was a small airplane mishap as we tried to bring in some weapons. . . . Moscow is nearly ready for us now."

As Ben-Iban spoke to her, Alix sat and quietly examined the old man's face. *Survivor of Auschwitz*, she was thinking. *Nazi-hunter par excellence.* "Talmudic adventurer," as Michael Ben-Iban preferred to call himself. A good man, Alix was certain. His face was a wonderfully aged, brown leather wallet. With eyes so clear, so alert.

They began to talk about the ultimate plan in Moscow. Details Alix had to know beforehand. They spoke about David Strauss. Whether it was entirely wise for Ben-Iban to meet with David now. Whether David could have any role in what was to come.

Then Alix asked the question that had been tearing at her insides since the spring. Did Ben-Iban have any idea what had happened to Elena and Nicholas Strauss? How could that terrible thing have happened? How?

Ben-Iban groaned inwardly. The old man had been hoping to slip into this dangerous subject in his own time and manner.

He found that he didn't want to lie to the young woman. He was certain that he was about to ruin everything.

"Alix. Aliza," he finally whispered. "Elena was my dear friend. For over thirty-five years she was my friend. . . . *The Reich*," he stumbled. "Somehow . . ." He groaned again. This wasn't working out. His usually quick mind was short-circuiting, showing blank spaces. He was tripping over his own words.

"The Reich must have learned that Elena was one of the great contributors to our group," Ben-Iban finally managed. "The only thing that makes sense to me, Alix. . . ."

Ben-Iban's ability to lie wasn't very good. His lying was in fact *terrible*, he was thinking. The murder of Elena and her grandson! Necessary. Yet so very painful. *Still* painful enough to bring on tears. The group itself had been dangerously split. Ben-Iban had voted *against*. Yet, he had gone along with the decision. Maybe it *was* better if Alix Rothschild *didn't* know everything. Maybe that was the only way now.

"Alix."

Ben-Iban's eyes suddenly brightened. His eyes probed deeply into Alix's.

"*Nothing* can be allowed to stop what we are setting out to do," Ben-Iban rasped. "Not the deaths of Elena or Nicholas Strauss. Not my death, or your death. You must try to understand that very clearly now."

Alix shook her head. "I think I understand it. I'm prepared to make sacrifices if that's what you mean."

"In a few days, Alix, the most important statement from the Jewish people since 1948.

"The secret truth about the wealthy Nazis who still go unpunished will finally be told. The truth about Russian Jews who suffer and die in slave-labor camps. The truth about Israel's dangerous plight. The vicious and immoral Soviet and American arming of Syria, Iran, Egypt. To the point where they now have *more tanks and guns* than the United States itself! *Nothing* can be allowed to distract us from the importance of our message!"

Alix found that she was moved as much by Ben-Iban's fervor, the inspired gleam in his eyes, as by what he had said. Alix was frightened, troubled, but she was also convinced they were doing the best thing. Her realization didn't make the rest easy, but it made it *possible* at least. *Strange, unreal ideas. Everything so strange now. A whole new set of rules operating.*

"Alix, you must be prepared to leave at a moment's notice. To go to Moscow. To begin this final act."

Suddenly Ben-Iban's attention drifted to the front of the crowded Kleine-Garten.

A German policeman had stepped inside the front door. Now he was peering around the room of busy diners.

The German police officer's eyes seemed to pause at their table, then he continued his scan of the room. Finally though, he left.

Alix let out her breath. "For a moment, I thought . . ."

Ben-Iban put his hand inside the baggy tweed jacket. Alix

saw a large black handgun. A PK Walther. Her heart jumped again.

"Our enemies are everywhere. Especially among the German police," Ben-Iban said. "Nothing can be allowed to stop us now. Promise me."

Alix had thought she was immune to inspirational moments, to pep talks of any kind. She was wrong, she understood now.

"I promise you, Rabbi," the American woman whispered. "I promise you as I've promised my murdered mother and father. Nothing will stop us."

Ben-Iban looked to the front of the restaurant again.

This time he took out his gun.

The American and German policemen began to surround the small, ornate family restaurant like angry bees around a fallen hive.

Kleine-Garten.

The name was destined to become famous in German newspaper annals.

The bizarre Kleine-Garten incident in Frankfurt!

Neighborhood people were peeking through frilly window curtains. Whole families were rushing in off nearby front porches.

Pedestrians began to race up the street to get far away from the shiny black riot shields, the pith helmets, the submachine guns.

"What is happening here?" An old burgher tugged at a policeman's leather jacket sleeve. "Someone is going to be hurt here? No?"

David was feeling as disconnected from reality as he had at any single moment in his life.

At first, all he could do was watch.

A shiny swarm of black Opels noiselessly spilling down the

peaceful, tree-lined West End cul-de-sac.

Right behind the Opels, a scary parade of white Frankfurt police cruisers. Bugs and Volkswagen station wagons with their sirens off, their dome lights rotating silently. *Broken toys*, David thought.

Inside the front sedan, Harry, David, Harris Tanana, and Raymond Cosgrove sat like a crack team of catatonics. Like the plastic dummies they use in automobile company test crashes.

Something truly awful was about to happen, David understood in every electrified bone and muscle of his body.

His heartbeat was so loud—cavernous church bells throbbing inside his chest—that he could hear it clearly as he stepped out of the police cruiser. Crunching pebbles underfoot seemed like small explosions. David's aorta was pumping blood so fast and furiously that it threatened to blow precious vessels and arteries all over downtown Frankfurt.

Harry and his people were behaving like genuine policemen now.

They were very professional and very scary with their sawed-off shotguns, their drawn cowboy pistols, their crouched shooting poses.

Raymond Cosgrove and Harris Tanana ran into dark alleyways on either side of the vine-and-trellis-covered restaurant.

Kleine-Garten!

Harry Callaghan, meanwhile, was leading David right up to the front door.

In German, the front door said: "Hello again!"

"What's going to happen?" David finally whispered.

46

Harry Callaghan pushed open the pinewood front door as any customer might.

There was a thick smell of wursts, vinegar, and sauerkraut.

A heavy, sickening odor.

The freckled *Hausfrau* inside the doorway should have been a *Hummel* on some other *Hausfrau*'s shelf. She was posted in front of a dessert case full of *Nusse, Trüffel*, and *Sacher tortes*.

The blond woman had on a ruffled blue-and-white doll's outfit. She was smiling, and holding out large, colorful dinner menus, as if David and Harry Callaghan had come in to eat with their .38 Smith & Wessons drawn.

"Was passiert hier?" The *Fräulein* finally got her nose out of her breasts and noticed the guns.

"Vhat is dis Amerikaners?"

Startled diners stopped in the middle of tiny *Sulze* and *Ochsen-maul* salad bird-bites.

Forks and brimming soupspoons all around the restaurant paused under trembling lips.

David's eyes ran wildly around the room searching for Alix.

"This is the police!" he heard at the same time.

Back near the exit sign, David finally saw a frightened-looking old man. The man was pointing a big, black pistol across the crowded dining room.

"Watch the rear door!" David heard. *"Fire!"*

The bizarre *Police Gazette* illustration suddenly came to life.

The old man in back fired his gun. Someone else in the restaurant shot off a small cannon. The pretty front window shattered, the restaurant lettering slowly collapsing into the street.

David saw Alix. *"Get down!"* she screamed at him, a target herself.

The poor old people at the twenty or more dining tables began a slow-motion dance toward the spotless linoleum. Silverware clattered loudly.

Plates full of veal shank, *Rippchen, Leber Klose* fell and splattered. *"Polizei! Polizei!"* some of the disoriented patrons were shouting.

The little family restaurant was turned into an insane carnival shooting gallery.

Crouched behind the far end of the restaurant's bar, David saw a German policeman fall, clutching his shoulder. Another shot kicked bric-a-brac off a side wall.

An old man was holding his face, one side stained with blood. A policeman yelled "*Scheiss!*" at the top of his lungs. Another crashed through a wide screen door and was wounded in the leg.

A million police and ambulance sirens could be heard approaching outside. David found that he was holding on to the rosewood bar as if it was a life buoy.

Standing up, he saw that the back door was open. Suddenly, he was following Harry Callaghan.

Outside the open door there was an alley full of wooden Henninger beer crates. There were greasy, banged-up garbage cans. And a cat, it's shiny eyes catching and releasing light from the alley lamps.

"Oh son-of-a-bitch! Son-of-a-bitch!" Harry was cursing for the first time that David could remember.

Not far from the door, a middle-aged German detective lay spread-eagled on the pavement, one of his knees bent upward, slowly tilting from side to side.

"She comes by here." The wounded German man's tongue was coated with blood. "Woman . . . I don't know why . . . I hesitate."

A little way farther down the alleyway, the agent who had followed David and Alix to their mountain lake retreat lay wounded also. Raymond Cosgrove had been shot twice. He was staring vacantly at the dark gray sky held between mottled, black-as-night building walls.

Oh goddamnit!

David Strauss chose one of the open alleyways and he simply began to run. David just goddamn ran. Sprinted. Screamed in his brain.

"*David!*" He heard an echoing voice trailing behind him. Harry Callaghan was screaming at the top of his lungs.

"*Strauss! Stop! David!*"

Then there was nothing except David's own labored breathing going down the narrow passageways. The *splat-splat* of his loafers hitting the dark cement. A mind-splitting vision of Alix flying out ahead of him like a phantom he could never catch.

The alley he'd chosen got wider and wider. Old World houses with puny backyards began to show up on either side.

David raced by clotheslines sagging with underwear and work clothes. A yard full of green apple trees. A chained-up police dog trying to chomp into his passing, pumping legs.

He was just going by some sort of shed or garage when a shadow fell. A dark shadow suddenly came hurtling down on top of him.

David yelled out, and at the same time fired the Smith & Wesson. A wild, poorly aimed shot at the flying, frightening bat shape.

Then the heavy body crashed into him.

David was thrown down hard onto his stomach and left shoulder. He shuddered and tried with all his strength to push the body away.

The body was choking him with wire.

David shivered and gasped.

He could feel blood oozing where the wire was digging into his throat.

He had the .38 out and he got to fire it once. Straight back past his own face. The heavy body on top of him shivered and went stiff. Then the body fell away.

David looked down on the horrible dying face of the old man from the German restaurant. Calvaria broken, he thought automatically. The old man's skullcap had been shattered.

He'd killed one of them, David thought vacantly. *Killed a man*, he thought.

The moment they found David, the German police identified the man he'd been able to shoot in the alleyway. News bulletins would be soon going out all around the world.

The man was Michael Ben-Iban, the Jewish Nazi-hunter David had been trying to reach in Frankfurt.

Vulkan was dead.

47

The most technically efficient roadblocks, dragnets, and airport checks were set up to capture Alix Rothschild before she could get out of West Germany.

As of July 11, then July 12, then the unlucky 13th, none of

the clever, very professional traps had succeeded.

Somehow, the American actress had escaped.

The German police suggested that she must have had help; that she had clearly been taken out of the country by professionals. The West Germans were especially sensitive to any suggestion that their apparatus for dealing with terrorists was anything less than the best in Europe.

Early on the morning of the 13th, a mystifying telex came to the Schlosshotel Kronberg.

It was read by Harry Callaghan and his people first.

Then David was given the note.

David read the message as he walked alone down the hotel's long, pine-tree-lined front driveway. He then read the telex several times in the privacy of his hotel room. David's reaction was always the same. *Confusion. Depression.*

DAVID:
PLEASE. YOU'RE SAFE NOW. STAY OUT OF THE REST OF THIS. GO HOME TO NEW YORK. SOON, YOU'LL UNDERSTAND EVERYTHING. I HONESTLY BELIEVE YOU'LL UNDERSTAND.

WITH LOVE,
ALIX ROTHMAN

It was going to get worse, David understood now. It was going to get much, much worse.

48

Southwestern Moscow, Russia.

Across Marx Plaza, an amazing flag waved like a graceful dancer in the breeze rushing up from the Moskva River.

Five wheels twisted against nacreous Siberian-winter white.

The flag of the 22nd Olympiad was whipping about, proud as any of the great athletes who would participate in the upcoming sixteen-day event.

In the plaza itself, the Architect, Engineer, and Soldier sat together in one of the drab Russian Intourist cafes. The cafe was just wooden tables and cafeteria chairs set out on a section of wide Moscow sidewalk.

The other two were listening quietly to Colonel Essmann's version of the air crash near Odessa. Of his finding Andrei Pavlova; and his journey in a cucumber truck up through the famous black-soil land between Odessa and Moscow. All typically Essmannesque heroics. All so very much like the Soldier—legendary Israeli commando and Intelligence operator, though still under thirty years of age.

"Odessa was one way to get the advance team and some weapons into Russia. So now we have no one to buy guns and explosives for us," Ben Essmann complained. "No one to get us safe hotel rooms. Or to arrange for our escape. At least we don't have our best people. We're forced to double up."

The Russian Architect eyed a cafe table crowded with local men, summer versions of Nanook of the North. A waiter came, nodded a few times, then trundled off toward the kitchen like a sleepy, easily distracted yak.

"So Colonel Essmann," the Architect said in a low voice. "Tell us, tell me, what do you think of our Mother Russia? Of Moscow? The city of something or other glorious or sacred, Pushkin or someone else once said."

Colonel Essmann usually had no time for such banter and small talk—such *testing*. He stopped to answer this question, however. The Soldier badly needed the help of the Engineer and Architect now. With the advance team dead, he needed the others committed body and soul to him.

"Who was the poet who said," his deep brown eyes searched the eyes of the two other men, "what a strange, wonderful pleasure there is sometimes . . . seeing exactly what one had expected."

The other two men smiled. There was truth in what the surprising military man had said. Moscow *was* exactly what one expected. Huge; either solemn or insane in its architecture; forever on the verge of a winter blizzard, it seemed, even in July. Rude, shabby crowds everywhere. The happiest, most loved children you would find anywhere in the world.

"It's said that we Soviets matriculate three million engineers a year," the Architect smiled. "Intelligent country, eh?"

Now the Israeli Soldier smiled. "With all those engineers it's lucky that a dunce cap like you could find work in the Olympic Village."

"Not really. The Party bureaucracy makes forgery and other forms of paper deceit easy. If you're willing to take a few elementary risks. . . . Like death by exsanguination in the cellars of Lubyenko prison."

As a toast to the dark jest, the three conspirators touched their glasses together.

They drank up, and then the Engineer unrolled a pen-and-ink diagram. The drawing was of a twelve-story section of a building somewhere inside Olympic Village.

The map showed the building's plumbing, air-conditioning, and electrical systems. It was all wonderfully elaborate, with at least a thousand minuscule numbers on a single page.

"This will truly be something," the Soldier said as he looked down at the drawing. "I have goose bumps all over my body just seeing your diagram. Simply with the knowledge of what we have to do here. Of all the care and preparation that have gone into making this work."

The three men all grew strangely quiet. They began to stare solemnly into the flashing faces of the crowd passing through Olympic Village.

Everything was finally coming together. Now it would begin. At the 22nd Olympiad.

BOOK
2 Alix Rothschild

PART V

49

Russia, July 14

The swaying, bumping Russian passenger train was a dull, proletarian moss green; the train had a big, Pompeian red star on its mammoth locomotive forehead; it had smoky, oyster-white portraits of Nikolai Lenin and Karl Marx painted on its caboose.

Inside a cramped passenger compartment, Alix let the splendid palette of the Latvian countryside filter through tight-fitting wire-rimmed eyeglasses.

The silver-rimmed glasses, a brown stage-actress's wig, and small amounts of bulk putty in her cheeks made Alix much older and much different, though not necessarily less attractive.

Especially among the squat, broad-faced Russian woman riding the train.

The best description Alix could think of for her journey thus far—the only description that made any emotional sense—was petrifying. Petrifying, and unreal. As if she were once-removed from her own body, able to observe herself from an uncomfortable distance.

The interior of Soviet Russia! Alix's mind drifted with the scenes flashing past her window. Grand, dust-brown bowls and plains; herculean blond boys and bulky girls riding tractors and looking like Nebraska circa 1932. Two hundred and sixty million people, one-sixth of the world's landmass. A hundred and forty thousand kilometers of Soviet railroad track, for God's sake!

The spectacular, endless birch and pine forests were now falling under a heavy four o'clock shadow. Great eagles were soaring overhead like small golden airplanes. The clumsy train itself burrowed onward like a wood mole in tall grass.

Once again, Alix couldn't help wondering to herself exactly what she was doing in the middle of all this.

She wondered if her murdered parents would have understood and approved.

She wondered what David was thinking of her—then quickly pushed that thought completely from her mind.

If someone had asked her, if an interviewer had been able to ask Alix how it had all come to be, she wasn't certain that she could have given a satisfactory answer.

Three and a half years earlier, Alix remembered as the train jounced along, she had indeed been the Actress. "The great American bosom and perfume saleswoman," Colonel Ben Essmann had called her when they'd first met in Jerusalem's Hilton Hotel.

At that time, the spring of 1976, Colonel Ben Essmann had been a noisy, living legend all throughout Israel. At twenty-three a war hero and saboteur. Embarrassingly blustery and cocky, he'd informed Alix of a top-secret Mossad GAQ plot during their first casual meeting in the Hilton.

The secret was that he was about to lead a crack search-and-destroy team into Europe where they would track down one of the Black September technicians who had engineered the Olympic massacre at Munich. Ben Essmann would then execute the *fellah* himself, he said. Perhaps right on Paris's Faubourg Saint-Honoré. More likely in the Marais though, where the bastard lived with his Arab whore.

"It is a prohibitively dangerous mission," Essmann told the American actress. "Probably I'll be shot. Would you be so sympathetic as to go to bed with me tonight before I leave?"

Instead Alix had slapped the Israeli hard across his sunburned face.

"Why have you told me all of these secrets? You should be taken out on the street and shot for your brazen behavior. Or is it simply animal stupidity in your case? Too much exposure to the desert heat! Too much sleeping with camels and asses!"

At that, Ben Essmann gave forth a rare, good-natured, and somewhat winning laugh.

164

Alix Rothschild, the year she made the motion picture Sara, Sara. The movie crossed over a hundred million dollars and Alix was very convincing as Sara, an Irish beauty who comes to America to make her fortune. One critic said, "Imagine a Marisa Berenson who can actually speak. That is Alix Rothschild."

Alix Rothman. Alix Rothschild's real name had been Rothman. Her mother and father had died at Dachau and Buchenwald, respectively. Alix herself had been born at Dachau and brought to America by aunts and uncles. The famous actress was one of over a million camp survivors in the U.S.

"Actually, my dear, sexy-eyed Alix Rothschild—my mission is just yesterday finished." The commando's smile grew even wider. "Actually, my dear girl, Ali Jahir has just been shot eleven times in his head and black heart. By myself and a few others. Now what shall we staunch Israeli patriots do to celebrate such a feat of daring, eh?"

Alix took her purse off the bar. "I think I'll go upstairs, and go to bed. Alone," she emphasized. "I believe a hero such as yourself will surely pick up some other *patriot* to go to bed with tonight. After all, isn't that what Jewish women have been put on this earth for? To bed down with great heroes and providers such as yourself. I'm very happy that the *fellah* is dead. I wish the same luck for you very soon."

Not that evening, but shortly afterward, Colonel Ben Essmann began to pursue Alix fervently.

Eventually, Alix allowed Colonel Essmann a single "date"—chaperoned by a Jewish hero of another sort—her friend Michael Ben-Iban; who had met Alix at a conference of Jewish survivors in 1973; who had first convinced Alix to help solicit funds for the continuing effort against Nazi war criminals.

When Ben-Iban had eventually suggested to Colonel Essmann an idea for a modern, expanded, Jewish counter-terrorist group—*a modernized successor to the Jewish Avengers and DIN*—the Israeli military man had jumped in the air to show his enthusiasm. It had been exactly the kind of bold stroke Ben Essmann had been trying to sell to Mossad since he'd first come to Intelligence from the Israeli Army. It was a necessary deterrent both to the Arabs and the still-influential Reich. Very soon, in fact, Colonel Essmann was calling the radical group his own idea.

Ben-Iban had subsequently established necessary connections with the larger, older Council, the world-wide Jewish association which closely watched over the globe with an eye to *any* situation potentially dangerous to the Jewish nation; which had for its sacred pledge—*to remember the terrible Holocaust, every last detail of it; to protect against another unholy conflagration with their lives if need be.*

The important financiers, the select Israeli generals and politicians who controlled the Council very reluctantly agreed that the radical counter-terrorist group was needed during these dangerous times. The Council thus began to help underwrite the subgroup's activities.

For her part, Alix Rothschild had become (since 1973—the year of the Yom Kippur War) one of the Council's very best money-raisers. Not only did Alix contribute from her own considerable earnings, she also had entree and credibility at the homes of wealthy and important Jews all over the world.

At an emotion-packed meeting of the Council in the fall of 1978, a new leader was appointed to head up the previously defense-minded subgroup. Soon afterward, this new leader—Führer—had conceived the idea for a controversial and dramatic strike that would prove to be one of the most important statements ever made about Nazis and Jews.

A cataclysmic action that would finally reveal secrets about the Nazis even the most paranoid Zionist had never dreamed of; terrible old Nazi secrets that pertained to life and death in the 1980s.

Dachau Two.

The long-awaited revenge for the Holocaust.

50

Walking on almost any main Moscow boulevard made the Soldier feel physically small; painfully insignificant in the grand scheme of Russia's past and present.

The mauve, gray, and gold buildings were as large as czarist palaces; the heroic Communist Party statues reached up as high as two thousand feet into the skyline; the ten- and twelve-lane main thoroughfares made Fifth Avenue and Oxford Street seem like side streets in comparison.

Now the Soldier ambled along Razin Street. He walked at a leisurely pace, appropriate for a tourist.

He took notice of a big-breasted Russian teen-ager reading her *Soviet Life* on a patch of lawn. He noted a clique of roaring-drunk Russian naval officers, and couldn't help thinking that the Soviets were ripe to be taken. He was aware of Volgas,

Fiats, a few outdated trucks and taxis skidding by on the greasy street.

A large Intourist group, either British or American, passed by; the Russian tour leader was speaking comically stilted, noncolloquial English: "The wondrous construction of this our present Communist society . . . The gentle peace-loving nature of these, our good Soviet people."

It was such preposterous nonsense, the Soldier didn't know how the Russian guide could possibly keep a straight face. The peace-loving nature of the Soviet people was like the peace-loving nature of the wolverine.

Within sight of the behemoth Rossiya Hotel, over 3,200 rooms, the largest hotel in Europe, Colonel Ben Essmann finally stopped at a convenient sidewalk stand. He bought a tiny cup of champagne, sold on the Razin Street curb like pretzels or hot dogs.

Surrounded by touches of old Moscow, large, onion-domed churches, gold Korsun crosses, the Kremlin and such, Ben Essmann then sat on a bench and sipped his drink.

As he'd been instructed, he sat directly under a glaring red sign crammed full of Cyrillic letters.

The Soldier was acting as his own advance team now.

In the past few days, he'd arranged for thirteen hotel or apartment-building rooms within commuting distance of Olympic Village; he'd arranged for costumes to get his people inside the Village; he'd personally scouted the VIP hotels and the major sports complexes.

Two Russian men dressed in absurdly dowdy street clothes finally sat down on either side of Ben Essmann. The Russian men smelled of cabbage and raw fish; they each wore floppy refugee hats and baggy suits with excess shoulder stuffing.

In very poor English, they began to explain the conditions under which they would sell the Soldier Soviet Army rifles, pistols, *plastique* explosives. The details of the sale and final exchange of goods were worked out. Another very public site was selected for the important transfer of goods.

Before he would give the Russians half of the agreed-upon sum, however, the Soldier insisted on the early delivery of a single firearm. After more debate and haggling, a second agreement was reached.

Before he left Moscow that afternoon, the Soldier would

have one Soviet Army Dragunov sniper's rifle in his possession.

As the tall, muscular Soldier retraced his steps back down Razin Street, he was feeling much larger and important. He was thinking that the Russian capital wasn't so impressive after all.

51

Shortly after 4 P.M., Alix's train from Moscow lurched into the busy railroad depot in the Latvian city of Riga; birthplace of the ballet master Mikhail Baryshnikov; an unlikely place to imagine dancers, Alix thought.

The afternoon sky had already lost its bright, silver-blue polish, Alix noticed as she got off the huffing, puffing train. Heavy chunks of gray cloud were sliding over the city like dirty ice on wheels.

In the Russian train square itself, Alix was met by a stern-faced chauffeur; by a woman cook named Maria, who was holding a bouquet of flowers for her; by a puffy Chaika automobile that looked something like an American Packard out of the 1940s.

The couple hugged Alix convincingly, as if she were a young woman returning from a year away at university.

Her ride in the Chaika lasted less than twenty minutes through the salt-cured, resort part of the seaport city.

There were boathouses everywhere, and squawking seagulls overhead. Little dinky cottages, *isbas*, with gingerbread facades and great, overgrown vegetable gardens. The Russians apparently went on vacation, Alix thought to herself, and planted little cabbages and turnips for their relaxation.

Then Alix found herself standing outside the imposing and quite beautiful dacha of the Soviet writer Lev Ginzburg. She was, in fact, being greeted like Catherine the Great by the sparkly eyed, eighty-five-year-old genius.

In their high-spirited conversation in the front yard, standing in the shadow of sixty-foot pine and birch trees, Alix was told that the large czarist estate, as well as the servants, the Chaika, and a snowplow, were provided to Lev Ginzburg by the Soviet Writers Union.

In return for the largesse, Ginzburg told her, all he had to do was concoct mesmerizing fairy tale collections of TV scenarios for the beloved children all over the Soviet Union.

"And now you're willing to give all this up?" Alix stared into the eyes of the diminutive, almost pretty white-haired man.

The Russian seemed a little surprised by the question. "Oh yes. Of course. Come inside now. You'll be staying in the very same room where I work. *Used to work,* eh? You see, I've absolutely run out of fairy tales, anyway."

The Russian writer's workroom was unusually large for a dacha. "It's as tall as one of my stories." Lev Ginzburg grinned at Alix. His little cherry-red eyes were sparkling rubies.

Alix looked all around the magical room. She was feeling magical herself.

Ten-foot-high bookshelves took up two of the workroom walls completely. There was a cluttered table. A miniature four-poster bed.

There was a clutter of Russian folk art: icons and primitive Siberian wood carvings. A Bokhara carpet. A samovar, brewing dark, fragrant tea.

Large French doors on the far wall led to a veranda that looked down on a gray, deserted Baltic Sea beach.

The cook, Maria, brought Cognac, sour bread, and hot hors d'oeuvres for Alix. She built a small fire.

Shortly after Maria left Alix, the Newspaperman and the Lawyer came; both of them well-known and successful in their fields. After much hugging and a few tears, they began to read over the demands that had been prepared for their day at the 22nd Olympiad in Moscow.

Alix herself typed the demands out, changing phrases that struck them as inexact, or melodramatic, or undramatic. The important message had to be *exact;* people had to understand once and for all.

Just reading the accusations, charges, and proposals aloud made Alix's entire body shake. There was horrifying truth written down; justice was the cry from every page. The demands formed an important document about who the Nazis had been—and *who they were now.*

At seven o'clock in the evening, the chauffeur came upstairs with a pair of thick-bladed, all-purpose Russian scissors. While Alix and the others continued to talk, the Russian unceremoniously chopped off her black hair, the Rothschild trademark. The man clipped and chopped until Alix looked like a pretty boy.

"Let me look, please," she asked.

Alix stared into a little hand mirror, and she had to laugh to keep herself from silly crying.

Her hair had been cut off. Just like her mother's.

Just past eight, there was another *tap, tap* on the heavy pine door. The maid was speaking the most terrible, yeshiva-student Hebrew from outside.

"Madame! Madame! The others finally arrive. They come in the big truck from Moskva.

"Colonel Essmann is here," the maid reported. " 'Ch'aim,' he says up the stairs to you. 'Love.' Oh my goodness, here he is coming up the stairs himself!"

Which was when Alix thought of David for the first time all that day.

52

The Strauss house on Upper North Avenue in Scarsdale reminded David of a great landlocked sailing ship. It existed with no apparent purpose. There were no lights. Over the summer the grass had grown knee high. No one came or left except for a single gimpy sailor: the Strauss housekeeper.

That morning David lather-shaved and showered in the downstairs bath, with its view out over the Four Corners Texaco station. As he stared down on pretty Lincoln Avenue—the hair dryer parting his hair in great clumps, showing patches of pale-white scalp—things that Harry Callaghan had recently told David flashed into his mind.

First of all, Harry had told him that the Jewish terrorist group had been the ones who had killed Elena and Nick. The shooting of Heather had been an *accident.*

The Strausses had been supporting the secret group—which David knew. Then Nick had apparently convinced Elena to stop her heavy financial contributions. In early April, Nick and Elena had actually begun preliminary talks with Intelligence people in Washington; they'd broken the thirty-five-year silence of the secret defense group. They had been fully prepared to expose what they knew of the ultimate plot.

Elena and Nick had been that frightened by the final plan for Dachau Two, David thought now. *What in the name of God was it going to be? And wasn't it insanely ironic that Elena had kept him out of the dangerous group, while Alix had been recruited by the German Jew Ben-Iban.*

He played a little jazz on the living room piano. When that didn't help his head case any, he decided to go for a drive in the Gray Ghost.

As far as David Strauss was concerned, Frankfurt, Germany, Alix's situation, the bizarre shooting spree at the Kleine-Garten, marked the absolute end of it for him.

Anything that remained of the Nazi/Jewish/Strauss family melodrama could go on very well without him now. It would just have to.

At School Road, David sat in the gray Mercedes with the motor running. He lit up a cigarette, smoking it without moving a muscle or even an eyelid.

David was looking down on the field where his friend Hal Friedman had once made the most incredible diving catch in the history of American sandlot football. Christ, what an unbelievable fool he'd been with Alix, he was thinking at the same time. What had Alix been thinking of him all that time in Europe?

He saw a little girl in a tan Friendley's uniform walking down School Road, going to work.

Against his will, he could see Alix moving down the same street twenty years before. Wearing penny loafers, argyle socks, Ambush perfume; maybe his ridiculous school sweater with the big gold S; one of those gold circle pins. The memory was like a good hard punch in the stomach.

Paul Simon was singing on the car radio. "Slip-Sliding Away." The radio station was devoting the whole hour to Simon—and to sending David snide messages about the condition of his life.

He lit another cigarette with the stub of the last. Delicious tobacco flavor.

David remembered Chaim Rabitz. Deserting the young Hasid boy up in the woods at Mountain House. Letting him cry his heart out. Hurting another Jew.

That was about the worst fucking thing David could ever remember doing to anybody.

Other than punching some troglodyte German photographer in the teeth, that was.

And killing Michael Ben-Iban in Frankfurt. Actually killing another man.

David's cigarette had burned all the way down. He released the Mercedes's hand brake and drove back home.

Twenty-five Upper North Avenue. Where he and Nick the Quick had been little goddamn boys together. Where Elena had made them onion and garlic bagels every Sunday morning for about twenty years in a row.

Two dark Oldsmobiles were sitting out in front of the house when David turned the corner.

The lonely old sailing ship had visitors all of a sudden. Something didn't look right.

David switched off the radio and climbed up the front steps to find out what in the name of God was going on now.

"Slip-Sliding Away" was playing at full volume in his head.

53

Harry Callaghan had come to Scarsdale with two newcomers from Washington.

The two men didn't look like agents or interrogators, David was thinking as he accepted their handshakes. They were slicker, big-business types. *Suits.* They looked like they ought to work for E. F. Hutton or Paine Webber.

They made David remember something his grandfather had told him once while they were strolling along Park Avenue near 48th Street in New York. *"The American businessman is a peculiar animal, David. See there, that businessman in front of the Waldorf. Everyday he puts on his nice three-piece suit . . . to go and shovel horse manure."*

"We're just here to have a little chat," the more affable of the two men said to David.

"There have been a few significant developments in the past day or so," the more aggressive government man said.

"I'm not interested." David shook his head. "If I can help by talking to you two, good. But I'm not interested."

"Look, I've got something to say here. Maybe you won't want to hear this, Dr. Strauss." The tougher of the two men from Washington spoke.

"You see, we're fairly certain we know what Dachau Two is all about now. Both our Arab sources and Mossad feel that it's a very large-scale strike. Something to put the Jewish terrorists way, way up on the hit parade. Something important, like Lod, or Munich. Only *bigger* than Lod or Munich."

David put up his hand to stop the man from saying any more. "I don't know if you people can understand this, but I don't believe I have any more to give to this particular cause. What do you *think* you want from me now?"

"I want to try and make you feel the meaning of *massacre*. Do you *feel* massacre, doctor?"

What David Strauss thought he felt was uncontrollable anger, plus some kind of terrible electrical overload in his brain.

He was beginning to understand that he couldn't just leave things now. He couldn't simply bow out of it. They weren't

174

going to let him. And that meant unbelievable, unendurable pain coming up ahead.

He looked to his left at Harry, and the older man bowed his head slightly.

David's mind quickly ran over the events leading up to this point. The initial attack in Scarsdale; Heather and Elena's deaths; Nick and Beri's deaths in California; the trip to Europe with Alix; the shooting of Ben-Iban; Alix's connection with the secret revenge group.

David thought about how Elena had felt he ought to be spared from knowing about the revenge group right from the first. How Nick had shouldered that family responsibility, and died because of it.

After the Frankfurt shooting, the American intelligence people had really given him no choice in the matter. They had shipped him right home, gotten David away from the scene of danger.

Thousands of miles away, he had been able to accept being out of the affair. More than that, it had begun to seem impossible that he ever might get involved again. David had settled into a slightly unreal, numb, but passable daily routine.

Now, David understood that the period of adjustment was over. He felt a terrible squeezing sensation in his brain. He felt nauseated all of a sudden.

"We have space booked for you on Aeroflot this evening, Dr. Strauss. . . . Early this week the Russians found the wreck of a small plane near Odessa that was loaded with arms and equipment. Two Storm Troop members were found dead near the wreck. . . . We'd like you to go to Moscow for us, Dr. Strauss. There's always the chance you might recognize one of them. More important, we want you there in case there are any negotiations, any important communications. You might very well be able to help then."

David looked over at Harry. "Are you still in this thing with me?"

The pipe-smoking man nodded in his quiet, confident way. Of course he was going to Russia. Harry Callaghan was committed *until the job was finished.*

They sailed to Russia together, David and Harry did.

They were going to hunt down Alix and the others, David knew.

Her word *"shee-oot,"* came into his head, and it just wouldn't go away.

54

Time and *Newsweek* would eventually construct neat, red-lined boxes on the Dachau Two strike team.

One cleverly entitled its piece "Black Sabbath: The Last Olympic Team," and therein described the commando group in thriller prose worthy of John Le Carré, or at least Frederick Forsyth.

> *The Dachau Two group, a.k.a "Storm Troop," was a highly motivated and very well financed Jewish terrorist team.*
>
> *It was the first Jewish version of PLO's Black September, and as such, had learned its history lessons extremely well. The group was lean and very sharp, with nearly all of its members handpicked from top Intelligence agencies or armies. Mossad, Shin Beth, the CIA, M.I.6, and Grenzschutzgruppe 9 (West Germany's anti-terrorist specialists) all contributed personnel to make the* Dachau Zwei *team the most awesomely professional and fearsome group that has been assembled to date.*
>
> *All in all, twenty-nine potentially kamikaze Storm Troop members went to the Moscow Olympics to avenge wrongs committed against the Jewish people. They included:*
> Code name: Storm Troop Main.
> Ben Essmann. The Soldier. Colonel Essmann was a decorated and widely known war hero in Israel. Joined the army when he was seventeen and just out of Jerusalem's Rechavia High School. Mossad agent for four years. Then left the company because of concerns over political intervention. Father and sister killed in a PLO bombing. Two cousins murdered at Munich Olympics.

There are Arab allegations that Essmann was still following orders from the Menachem Begin government when he went into Russia. (Other reports have Ben Essmann listed No. 3 on Mossad's secret death lists.)

Joseph Servenko. The Architect. A Russian Jew and leader of past movements to recognize Jewish human rights in Soviet Russia. Three of Servenko's brothers are in Soviet prisons. Servenko's wife was reportedly killed during a raid by the Russian secret police.

Gary Weinstein. The Engineer, or "Einstein." Came from the CIA by way of Harrisburg, Pennsylvania, the Virginia Institute of Technology, and Honeywell Corporation. The most brilliant of the terrorists. Also the most unstable. Weinstein worked in a Washington, D.C., garage for 2½ years perfecting the electronics for Dachau Two.

Anna Lascher. The Weapons Expert. Came from Britain's M.I.6, where she was also a linguist. Expert in the use of small arms and explosives. Anna Lascher was part of the British team's security force at the Munich Olympics.

Alix Rothschild. The Actress. Former fashion model and Hollywood actress. Recruited by Michael Ben-Iban, at first solely as a money-raiser among wealthy American, Israeli, and French Jews. Was a spectator at the Munich Olympics. Mother and father killed at Dachau and Buchenwald, respectively. Came to Moscow to be the group's spokesperson. (Also, see story on Dr. David Strauss.)

Arthur Silver. The Newspaperman. Former subagent for OSS, then for the CIA in both France and Germany. Met Nazi-hunter Michael Ben-Iban on several occasions and was very impressed by the man. Attended Munich Olympics as journalist for the *New York Times*.

Malachi Ben-Eden. The Weapons Expert. Former Shin Beth agent. Once named "Father of the Year" by a Jerusalem newspaper. Also, a ruthless guerrilla fighter.

Shlomo "Sam" Herschel. The Dentist. Entire family of nineteen members killed at Dachau. Arrested in Argentina after "avenger style" strangulation of former SS Colonel in back of furniture delivery truck. Arrested in Paris for similar "avenger style" murders. Never brought to trial on any of these charges.

Marc Jacobson. The Medic. Youngest member of the Dachau group at twenty. Lived in Israel (Hayelet Ha-

Schachar Kibbutz) on and off since he was ten years old. Attended UCLA, where he was a premed student. Minored in advanced weaponry.

Plus . . . Code name: Storm Troop Minor—the cover team. Code name: Blitzkrieg—the attack team. Code name: Eagle—the setup team . . . Twenty-nine members in all.

During their final dinner together at Lev Ginzburg's dacha, Alix found herself being called upon to stand at the table, to make a toast that brought on sadness, joy, cheering, and confusion.

"For century upon century," the beautiful actress said with a glass of red wine up to her eye, "the Jewish nation has learned from catastrophe. Now I fear the others must learn something from this terrible lesson.

"May this be the final Dachau, please God. *L'Ch'aim! Chazack v'amotz!*"

Tears were in her eyes when Alix sat down. Mixed in with all of her raging confusion, she was thinking about David. Alix missed David more than she would have believed possible. For the first time in her life, she thought, she had actually become dependent on someone other than herself.

The entire Dachau group was bedded down by nine-thirty that night.

Starting at 3:30 A.M., they began to leave for Moscow. Traveling separately, they boarded the Russian-Latvian Railroad. They got into sputtering Fiats and fuel-spewing Russian trucks. The Medic and the Nurse rode motorcycles like two young students going to the Olympics.

Dachau Two was finally ready to begin.

Twenty-nine highly efficient commandos were now speeding toward Moscow, a city of some eight and a half million people that Olympic summer.

"It was like no commando unit that had ever entered a large civilian community during peacetime," a London news magazine would say.

"It augured house-to-house fighting. Night fighting. The ultimate terrors that have become inevitable during the last third of our century."

PART VI

55

"The consummate terrors unleashed in Moscow were so bizarre and unexpected, they were literally—graphic." (From Leslie Wall's *War at Midnight*)

"The war skills that manifested themselves during Dachau Zwei are chilling. Thoroughgoing combat skills. Silent, practical, killing skills. The best weaponry money could buy. Kidnapping subplots. And perhaps most of all, the mad genius of Gary Weinstein, whose unexpected Dachau machine terrified like nothing the world has witnessed in the last thirty-five years."

Very early on the morning of July 17, a blond, fifteen-year-old girl named Marina Shchelokov, a prizewinning member of the Soviet Komsomol youth group, tramped through the black, rain-slicked Moscow Hills.

Behind the willowy girl runner, a convoy of Russian Army motorcycles rode slowly and noisily. Their steady *putt, putt, putt, varoom, varoom* disturbed the peace for several hundred yards in any direction.

Still, the motorcycle headlamps made purplish circles and shooting stars against the slanting rain and dark sky. It was all very pretty and moving.

Hundreds of sopping-wet Russians from nearby suburbs lined the muddy roadside, clapping and whistling for the local girl. It was very much like an American Legion or VFW parade in a small American town.

The petite teen-ager held the Olympic flame tightly in her

right hand. As a surprisingly deep-voiced Marina Shchelokov had explained to Komsomol selection committees and at subsequent Communist Party gatherings, the tradition behind the Olympic flame was a rich and beautiful one. Since 1936, the flame had been transported by some form of relay from Mount Olympus to the site of the Olympics. The eternal flame was the symbol of friendship at the Olympics. For Moscow, the flame had already been carried thousands of miles from Olympus, where it had been lit by six vestal virgins.

And now it was all five-feet one-inch, ninety-seven-pound Marina's. For her one-kilometer—approximately nine-minute—run Marina Shchelokov *was* the 22nd Olympiad.

Her one-kilometer run wasn't a particularly inspiring time for the idealistic Komsomol girl, however.

First of all, there was a cold stinging rain in her face and on the blue satin runner's uniform which she'd labored for weeks to make for herself. Then there was the steep uphill nature of her particular section of the run. Lastly though, worst of all, there was the laughing and the cynical joking by the young Russian soldiers propped up on their husky black motorcycles.

As she ran into the rain, chin thrust out, bare arms stiff and tired, Marina wondered to herself if a glimpse behind other scenes at the grand and mighty Olympics might not be equally disillusioning. Getting her own little peek behind the pageantry, she wondered what all the rest of it was really like.

Such a sad and defeatist way to think, Marina finally decided. Why couldn't people just look for the best in things, rather than the worst? Why was she beginning to think like a jaded Westerner herself?

The comrades from her hometown were clapping anyway: her school friends and neighbors.

She passed her father, who was beaming with tremendous pride. Her mother and small, bratty brother were grinning like *matriochki* dolls from underneath the family umbrella.

In spite of the rude soldiers, in spite of the rain and the steep, unfriendly hill, it was a spectacularly glorious moment. The young Russian girl felt a sudden rush of adrenalin that threatened to lift her straight up into the sky.

The Munich Olympics provided some of the most exhilarating, then most horrifying, moments in David Strauss's life. Right after the Black September takeover, David was flown out of Germany with Mark Spitz and the other Jewish-American Olympic team members.

Marina Shchelokov looked into the eternal flame and tears rolled down her already wet and makeup-smeared cheeks. She was so proud of what she was doing, so proud of Russia, she almost couldn't believe it.

The pretty little fifteen-year-old had just reached the shadowy apex of her last hill when she tripped and fell.

Marina's right knee simply buckled and she found herself performing an unexpected head-over-heels somersault.

She landed hard next to the roadway and her running suit was ruined in the mud. A heavy black motorcycle skidded right past her and fell on its side.

Through blue eyes stained with tears, Marina saw all sorts of concerned people racing toward her from the roadside. She saw her father running as fast as he could. The young soldiers were jumping off their motorcycles. The flame was still burning brightly, though.

Finally, the fifteen-year-old girl put her head down to rest on the glistening mud. Blood from the bullet wound under her blond hair mixed in with the rainwater. Marina Shchelokov was the first to die at the 22nd Olympics.

Carrying a Dragunov rifle, hurrying down a muddy hill some five hundred yards away, Colonel Essmann felt only the slightest regret for the Russian girl's death.

Instead, Ben Essmann vividly remembered an East Jerusalem coffee shop struck by Soviet-made grenades in 1976. Seventeen dead, including his father and sister.

Ben Essmann remembered the Munich massacre with the clarity of a fine Nikon camera reproduction.

Most of all, Ben Essmann thought of the concentration camps right there in Russia. He thought of the Jews being tortured and no nation ever saying a word to stop it. Just like in the 1940s.

The Soldier whispered a single word out loud to the outraged Moscow Hills.

The single word Ben Essmann said was *"Jugenführer."*
Hitler Youth!

56

Alix was spending her first petrifying day in Moscow.

Over the course of two years, there had been a hundred-odd drafts and different versions of the Dachau Two ultimatum. World conditions—especially the Middle East balance—shifted at least that many times. Strategies were changed. Only one factor seemed to remain constant.

This was the group's obsession to get the points of the demands set down with Talmudic precision and accuracy.

It was an obsession to make certain that the important document would finally communicate, or at least *record*, the truth about the Nazis and the Jewish people.

The Dachau Two indictment was to have begun: *"For two thousand years, the world has attempted every possible overt and covert method to try to destroy one nation of people, the nation of Jews.*

Now Alix and Arthur Silver, the Newspaperman, carefully reworked the opening words. They had to get the opening just right. *Perfect.*

The tiny hotel where they were lodged was appropriately anonymous and out of the way. The hotel was owned by a Russian jeweler who had married a Jewish woman, then had seen her taken away to a labor camp in Minsk.

Seated at a worktable from which they could see a snatch of royal-blue Moskva River, Alix and Arthur Silver reworked the important opening.

They polished the section of the indictment pertaining to Naxis in modern-day Germany.

They worked on the long section which dealt with the slave-labor camps inside Russia.

Finally, Alix and the Newspaperman agreed on the shortened version that Alix was to read before the TV cameras.

Then they were ready.

After a snack of cold soup, smoked fish, and sour bread, Alix stood before Arthur Silver. Suddenly she was struck with the fear that she wasn't going to be good enough to deliver the demands. Alix's body felt cold and unnatural; she wished she hadn't eaten anything; she wished she were anywhere else but this cramped, very foreign room.

"Now you have to help me rehearse," she finally said.

"Do you take criticism well?" the Newspaperman asked.

"You have to be very tough with me. I have a tendency to be a lazy performer. I don't concentrate as well as I should."

Arthur Silver nodded. There was no doubt that he would be the judge of all that.

Alix cleared her throat, then she delivered the opening five minutes of the demands. Finally she stopped. She seemed afraid. As vulnerable as a small child.

"So far? The beginning? Not very good," she said. "You have to be truthful no matter what."

Arthur Silver knew that he wasn't easily impressed. He had a well-earned reputation for crankiness, for inflicting his absurdly high standards on anyone who worked with, or even around him.

There was something quite startling happening here, he considered. It was more a gut feeling than something he could intellectualize. There was something about the *presence* of this woman.

She was strikingly beautiful, yes. But she was also very human. He recalled the films he'd seen her in: Schlesinger's, Coppola's, Frankenheimer's. She'd improved in each one. With a stab of sadness, Arthur Silver thought about what a truly great actress Alix Rothschild might have become. Perhaps one of the greatest of their age.

"I feel . . . that you are telling me the truth," the Newspaperman finally said. "You believe what you are saying, and I can feel that. *Here.* In my stomach. My anticipation for tomorrow has never been greater than it is right at this moment. You made me shiver just then, Alix."

57

Once they were inside the Russian Olympic Security Head-quarters, David and Harry Callaghan were led down card-board-gray corridors just ringing with Big Brother Muzak, strongly suggesting a prophetic scene from *Brave New World.*

They were brought to a wood-paneled conference room with a wall of dark-brown windows looking out on a central garden full of dogwood trees in full summer blossom.

David's eyes drifted through muzzy cigarette smoke, across heavy beards and dark glasses.

Gathered together in the tense conference room were representatives from the world's intelligence community: Israel's Mossad; the CIA; France's SDECE; M.I.6 from England; West Germany's BND; and the KGB and GRU, of course. Also in the room were grave-looking ambassadors from Egypt, Syria, and Libya, plus several Olympic Committee members in bright-colored blazers with their five-wheel pocket emblem.

With the possible exceptions of Kim Philby, and Melinda and Donald Maclean, every important intelligence person in Moscow was inside the sleek, modern conference room. David Strauss thought it the single most impressive moment he had ever experienced.

On specially prepared prep sheets, David read that *Moscow's Olympic City is one of the world's ten largest. . . . That it is the world's most densely populated city. . . . That the Olympic Village itself is virtually helpless against any sort of organized terrorist attack.* "Or even a half-assed one," Harry Callaghan muttered under his breath.

For the first time really, the terrifying potential of the second Holocaust plot hit David in the stomach. Something about the happy, innocent faces he'd seen walking through Olympic Park brought it home to him with sledgehammer force.

A nattily dressed, blond Russian man finally called the security meeting to order and attention. This man was Valery Kupchuck, a very *kulturny* gentleman, thoroughly Western-

Parade toward Moscow's Red Square. The Russians had never dealt with terrorists so close to home. Nor had they dealt with large crowds of tourists like those present for the Olympic games. The Lenin Mausoleum is in the background at right.

Red Army T-72 tanks. Millions of people around the world had never actually seen the much talked about Russian war machine before that summer.

ized after three years' duty, first at the Court of St. James's, then in Washington, D.C.

A gracious public speaker (Kupchuck reminded David of John Lindsay before the fall), the gray-blond Russian now began to deliver a clear, concise, *paralyzing* report on the actual state of Olympic Village and environs that Friday afternoon.

"Up to this point," Kupchuck's serious, gray-blue eyes made steady contact all around the room, "we have tried to keep information you are about to hear a top-level secret, of course.

"As you might expect, the situation here at the Moscow Olympics is quite singular and extraordinary with respect to security threats and security precautions. *Even for the Soviet Union*, the situation is extraordinary, ladies and gentlemen.

"Thus far, for example, there have been over one hundred and twenty thousand recorded threats made by telegram, letter, phone, and even in person. The threats are running approximately *forty to one* over those reported in 1976 at Montreal."

Valery Kupchuck paused. "That is accurate data. Forty to one over Montreal. The most serious threats investigated and uncovered thus far ... A professional demolition squad. Eleven fellayeen, apolitical street-fighter types—undoubtedly a reaction to the Jewish group. GRU picked them up at the National and Metropole Hotels this Monday past. The fellaheen had antipersonnel grenades and handguns. Very nasty men and women.

"A cadre of black nationalists was stopped at Sheremetyeno yesterday morning. These six were unarmed, but *wanted* in America. Also yesterday, two armed Jewish men from New York City were detained."

"Probably in the Moscow city morgue," Harry said out of the corner of his mouth. "Rumor has it they don't really care for Jewish people here in Russia. Not at all."

"... And so, at railroad stations and on major highways," Kupchuck went on, "at the Games themselves, there are nearly *ninety thousand* security people. That is three and a half times what the West Germans had at Munich. Or to express it another way, it's a little more than four security people

for every participant, coach, and delegation official in attend-
ance here."

"Not to mention there being five thousand or so security
people for every Storm Troop member," Harry said to David.
"Or forty-five thousand each for you and me."

"And that, ladies and gentlemen, is where we are today.
Our security people are very confident about capturing this
Dachau Two team before any harm is done. But that seems
... an extremely dangerous attitude to me. Extremely dangerous."

Valery Kupchuck sat down then, and for some reason, the
people inside the conference room politely applauded.

58

"We, of course, cannot cancel the 22nd Olympiad. Even if
some of us would like to, we can't."

The second installment of the Security meeting began fifteen minutes after Kupchuck's speech. Frock-coated waiters
had meanwhile served tea, biscuits, and cherry preserves.
Little veal cotelette sandwiches and Beluga caviar with onion
and egg were served.

Thus far, the second segment of the meeting was all Colonel
Alexander Belov of the KGB.

This beefy, broad-shouldered policeman was apparently
Russia's answer to Kojak and James Bond, both rolled into
one. Smoking a Romeo y Julieta Churchill cigar, bluff and
seedy, Belov was known to be tough, efficient, creative, even
moderately fair in his famous investigations of high crime in
and around Moscow.

What Belov had to say on the afternoon of July 17, however,
struck every person in the conference room as both mon-
strously unfair and incredibly inefficient. It struck David
Strauss as typical and par for the disaster course.

"I must inform you of a disturbing situation." Belov was continually relighting and puffing his cigar stub as he spoke to the gathering.

"You see, it is our decision that this investigation and search for the so-called Dachau Two terrorists be conducted exclusively by the Moscow Police, the KGB, and the Russian Army.

"It is our final and irreversible decision that there be absolutely no interference inside Soviet Russia by the countries represented in this room."

Belov rubbed out his cigar in a modern wooden ashtray. "No interference.

"Gentlemen, ladies, there is no need for all this hubbub. . . . You see, there have been few successful terrorist actions inside the Soviet Union to this point. In the next few days, I believe that all of you will see why this is so.

"I encourage all of you to go out of this room, and as best you can, enjoy the athletic events. Enjoy the city of Moscow. I will personally see to the less enjoyable side of the next few days.

"There is no way these terrorists can succeed here," Colonel Belov said.

"Please remember," the big Russian man smiled, "we are the people who stopped both Napoleon and Hitler."

"I think," Harry turned to David, "that we'd better go back to the hotel and pray like hell for snow."

59

It didn't snow during the evening of July 17.

The temperature did go down to 66, and there was a sprinkle of summer rain. A fine mist was blowing down from the mock-Gothic skyscrapers that tower over the Russian capital.

Their spirits undampened, over a million tourists coursed along the absurdly wide boulevards of Moscow leading to Olympic Village.

Russian fur hats were everywhere. So was the Russian doll, Misha the Bear, selected to symbolize the Games. So were a surprising number of automobiles—what Nikita Khrushchev had once called "those foul-smelling armchairs on wheels."

The sheer beauty of over a million people gathered together to celebrate the possibility in the world for friendship and love was truly overwhelming.

That evening, gold medals were won by Muller, Nellie Kim, Comaneci, and Keresty. Russia took an early lead in the coveted medal distribution. East Germany had a surprisingly strong hold on second place. The U.S. trailed in third, and sportswriters began to compose vitriolic features revealing how petty rivalries among American amateur organizations had severely crippled the present team.

The feature spots from NBC Sports made much ado about Moscow's Gorky Street, dubbed "Broad-vay" by the hip, young Russians. The broad, glittery avenue was more like Bourbon Street in New Orleans, though. Especially down around Sverdlovsk Square, where brown bread was whiffed and vodka gulped with exaggerated "*pahs*"; where everyone's clothes seemed to smell of smoked fish and diesel fuel.

American jazz and fifteen-year-old rock 'n' roll blared from the cafes. Pixilated men and women in square Russian suits and dresses by Rudi of Poland danced in the avenues where they couldn't get into jam-packed barrooms.

In his editorial that evening, the NBC commentator pronounced Moscow "a grand Slavic wedding reception going full tilt twenty-four hours a day. A modern reenactment of V-E day."

The Moscow State Circus delighted a full house up in the Lenin Hills.

Maximoya and Vassiliev performed *Don Quixote* for a crowd in excess of 70,000.

The Bolshoi was staged within walking distance of Olympic Village.

The silver blimp of an American tire company floated high over the Russian capital, to the general delight of the spectacle-happy Muscovites.

Not half a mile apart, both Alix and David looked out on the dim-blue city streetlights and gay festivities below their rooms. Neither of them had been able to sleep.

They'd gone to their respective hotel windows to look for some small sense of peace and solace out there in the crowded Moscow night.

The tower bells in Red Square finally struck twelve, and it was July 18.

In just a few hours, the plot known as Dachau Two would begin, flourish, and culminate.

The Jews had come to avenge the six million.

PART VII

60

Directly in front of Alix, almost close enough for her to reach out and touch, the five stars on top of the Kremlin were truly beautiful. Like twinkling rubies from Van Cleef or Harry Winston.

Three hundred feet away, the grand Terem Palace was equally beautiful; it glowed in the silver steam of the fuzzy Russian dawn.

Meanwhile, everything else seemed to be crashing in on Alix.

A thousand different ideas and powerful images: a mental avalanche.

Scenes from the Olympic Village.
Scenes from Munich.
David.
Dachau.
Hollywood.
David.

Perhaps because of the imminent danger, the tension, the terrifying death-camp visions started to come one after the other.

Dachau. The barracks. Watchtowers.
Alix's mother. Nineteen-year-old Nina.
The pathetic lines of prisoners walking to their deaths.

Everything was so sadly beautiful and still in the pinkish early morning haze, Alix thought to herself as she walked. Off to her right, St. Basil's looked like faraway Istanbul. Under her feet, Alix could feel the sound of the Moscow Metro.

The Nazi train doors had opened with a noise like rumbling thunder. The prison guards were screaming contrary instructions. Prison dogs were released and allowed to bite whomever they chose.

All Alix had really wanted was a peaceful walk that morning.

Perhaps the consoling feeling that the events she was about to participate in were necessary and right. Some idea that she hadn't been manipulated to come to Moscow; that her being there was a *positive* sign.

A chill, gritty wind picked up across the rough cobblestones of Red Square. The wind swirled dust up into her face. It brought the unwelcome smell of Soviet diesel from nearby Razin and Gertsen streets.

Once the poisoned stench of the camps had gotten into your skin, your eyes, nose, hair, it was impossible to ever get it out. Alix remembered doing shampoo commercials and thinking about getting the stench out as they filmed her washing her hair. She remembered telling another actress, a Jewish girl, and how the young actress had stared at her as if she were mad.

The hourly changing of the guard between the Savior Tower and the Lenin Mausoleum was just taking place.

Bells tolled in the tower of Ivan the Great and the sound reminded Alix of her last days in Frankfurt with David. Black-and-white photos of Germany, then Scarsdale, then the Dachau images rapidly flashed through her mind. For a moment, Alix completely lost control.

Jewish babies, the smallest babies, were stoked into a blazing furnace.

Jewish men, women, and children were hung like pathetic, tattered clothing down the Highway of Death.

Who would ever think to do such things? Why did no one seem to understand or care? Not now. Not ever, really. How could they still tell jokes about the Jews? Didn't they understand what the jokes revealed about themselves? About their own horrifying lives and minds?

Alix looked away from the Savior tower. Her mind cleared of the terrible images.

She saw the Soldier striding into view.

Dear God, have mercy on me. Alix Rothschild whispered. *Have mercy on us all.*

It was time now, even if she wasn't ready.

61

Begun in the early thirties, the dazzling Moscow Metro system currently holds more gold and marble than there was in all of the Romanov palaces together.

The subway fascinated Marc Jacobson and Anna Lascher nearly as much as a block-long Hollywood record shop where they'd once spent the better part of a week while out in California.

The Medic and the Weapons Expert strolled at a leisurely pace through the crowded, underground cathedral. They examined mosaic masterpieces, towering colonnades and sculptures, the overhead chandeliers that overhung the bright tunnels.

They appeared to be tourists, by actually being tourists. On their way to purchase a horde of small arms, rifles, and *plastique* explosives for Dachau Two.

Because it is a model restrictive police state, Moscow presented the Dachau attack force with unique tactical problems, of course.

Coming up out of the Metro, the Medic and the Weapons Expert hoped they were about to solve one of the biggest problems of all.

Holding hands and sometimes kissing, they went inside the GUM department store near Red Square.

Once inside, they sat down next to the famous mahogany-colored fountain situated at the center of the basement floor.

The two terrorists looked like lovers, by actually being lovers. They looked like two obnoxious college brats ensconced in town for the Olympic Games.

High above their heads, in layered, two-hundred-meter-long shopping galleries, Muscovites and Olympic tourists were already standing on long queues, waiting to buy specialty foods, shoes, and clothes.

Before the day was over, nearly five hundred thousand people would have shopped in the large, Moscow-style Macy's.

Marc Jacobson and Anna Lascher looked straight up at the heavy, Lenin Gothic bridges crossing between the galleries; they stared at the impressively high, all-glass roof.

GUM resembled a Middle Eastern souk, the English Weapons Expert observed. Which was perfect: it was proof that the dirty Russians were descended from the dirty Arabs.

The two men from inner-city Moscow finally arrived. The same two Colonel Essmann had met near the Rossiya Hotel.

Today they were carrying long canvas bags like the ones used to transport team sporting equipment across Moscow's sprawling parks. The two men were Russian hoodlums, a human category one seldom reads about in *Pravda* or *Sputnik*. For unconscionably large fees, they had previously helped Soviet Jews to escape from Russia through the seaport towns. Now, for another prohibitively high price, they were going to help the Jews in a way they didn't need or want to understand.

When the two men got up from their brief rest at the fountain, they left the canvas bags behind. They left stolen Army rifles; they left enough *plastique* to raise Lenin Stadium right off the Moskva riverbank. In exchange for the bags, the two Russians walked away with over eighty-thousand rubles for their early morning's labor.

The Dachau Two team was now armed to the teeth.

At 7:45 that morning, Alix and Colonel Ben Essmann, Gary Weinstein—the Engineer—and Rachel Ziegler, crossed the pretty, barbered lawns of Pushkin Mall.

A few blackbirds were out, pecking their gold beaks into

the ground. A few female leaf-sweepers wandered about in their familiar bright yellow babushkas.

Otherwise, the Mall and the park were empty.

Beyond the park, Olympic Village looked nearly empty.

Above the jagged tree line, the famous Moscow Hills seemed deserted as well.

In the cold shadow of a row of fir trees, the four terrorists entered a public toilet marked with thick black Cyrillic letters and spread-legged stick figures representing man and woman.

Inside the rest rooms, four hirsute Russian men and three husky women stood in their stocking feet on the tile floor. These were *fartsovshchiks*—Russian black marketeers.

The seven Russians were quickly stripping down to their grimy underwear.

"Prieveton! Salute!"

A man with a black beard—a dancing bear straight out of the State Circus—grinned and raised his mitt in an earthy greeting.

"Welcome to toilets, comrades!"

Colonel Essmann and Alix smiled back at the Russians. Then they too began to strip off their clothes.

What they were now doing had already become commonplace at the Moscow Olympics. Several news stories had made note of the curious, sometimes humorous phenomenon.

In any wooded place, there was a chance you might suddenly come upon an American boy or girl shucking off his or her favorite dungarees or a man from Paris literally selling the designer shirt off his back.

From the Russian point of view, they were receiving Western clothing worth two or three times its retail value. They would subsequently be able to resell the clothes for two or three times what they had paid. And the Russians who eventually bought the illegal clothing would still be better off than those who bought suits and dresses at GUM or TSUM.

As for the Dachau Two team, they were only interested in the poorly made Russian clothes they would be getting in this deal.

Sixteen security-police and maintenance-worker uniforms from Olympic Village. Both male and female uniforms.

All absolutely essential for access into the closely guarded Olympic Village that day.

The Russians began to step into their Levi and Sasson blue

jeans. They proudly buttoned their new French and California designer sport shirts and put on Bally and Florsheim slip-
ons.

At five minutes to eight, dressed like Russian workers or
Russian police, carrying satchels filled with still more uniforms, the four terrorists walked back across Pushkin Mall as
if nothing had happened.

Comparatively speaking, nothing had.

Olympic Village was still quite asleep on the morning of
July 18.

10:30 A.M.

The Dachau group wisely split off into ones and twos at a
prearranged time. In that way, over twenty individual arrests
had to be made to defuse the ultimate strike plan.

The Newspaperman strolled along with the tightly packed
crowd moving toward the Luzhniki Sports Complex.

The Architect sat and watched the first qualifying heats of
the bicycle races.

The Medic viewed a curiously nostaglic folk-singing group
in Karl Marx Park.

Alix was hidden away in the rear of a Soviet maintenance
van. Beside her, the leader of Dachau Two, the Führer, looked
down at a handsome gold wristwatch.

"Ten-thirty. Time for the very first of our many surprises
for the day."

From three-thirty in the morning on, risking arrest and God
only knew what other KGB punishments, David and Harry
had unofficially patrolled the Olympic Village area of Moscow—first on foot, then in a Zhiguli Fiat that was as nervous
and jumpy as they were.

The two Americans made all the obvious stops, and they played a few wild hunches as well.

They checked both U.S. dormitory sections; the dorms for the East and West Germans; the Lenin wing, there the Russian athletes were stabled, nine to a room.

They also visited the 103,000-seat Lenin Stadium, where the track-and-field events would begin as early as 7 A.M.; plus the Rossiya and Metropole hotels, where several million dollars' worth of American TV and film talent was getting its beauty sleep and ego massages.

Around ten-thirty, the two bone-tired men slumped into a Russian steam bath—a *banya*—located in the vicinity of the beautiful Novodevishy Convent. Harry and David decided they had to rest for a moment now; the Russian steam bath would have to substitute for a night of sleep.

Minutes after David and Harry Callaghan entered the Russian *banya*, Arthur Abrams Silver, occasional columnist for the *New York Times*, author of the best-selling Washington *roman à clef Kingdom Come*, made his seemingly fumbling way alongside a row of aluminum press tables set up on the grassy tribune inside Lenin Stadium.

"Arturo! Arturo!" An old Algonquin Hotel drinking companion from the *Times* tried to get the myopic writer's attention as he hurried past.

"Hey, yo, Arthur!" someone from the *Daily News* yelled— Pete Hamill's younger brother, Silver thought; *some* youngish long-haired man.

In the meantime, Arthur Silver had been almost completely mesmerized by the blazing green athletic field spread out before him.

His mind was already composing one of his famous columns. *Sempiternal Lenin Stadium in the Luzhniki Sports Complex. Giant main arena. Sports palace: seven over-Olympic-size swimming pools where the people of Moscow could swim, even when it was forty below freezing. Ten gargantuan football patches. Four separate field houses. And never closed to the public a single day since it had opened in 1956.*

Over the slanting rooftop, flags from one hundred forty countries snapped in the crisp breeze blowing up from the nearby Moskva River.

Out on the buzzing green field, gifted Olympic athletes were sweating and grunting, sprinting and leaping under the high Moscow skies. It gave Arthur Silver goose bumps just being there.

Here was the real Olympics. Track and field. Frank Shorter, Valerie Borzov, Victor Saneyev, Mike Boit, John Akii. Silver actually knew most of them. Just as he had known Bill Russell, Wilma Rudolph, Cassius Clay. He even loved some of the young amateur athletes, he thought, with a sudden twinge of sadness.

Halfway down through the jumble of reporters and announcers, Arthur Silver suddenly stopped his sentimental turtle walk.

He stood directly behind two Russian TV personalities. A man and a blond woman, both dressed as if it were 1954 again. These two were in charge of announcing all events and their results to the enormous crowd packed inside Lenin Stadium.

The descriptions and results were announced first in Russian, then in English, finally in German. Occasional special announcements were made in Japanese, French, Ethiopian, or the native language of anyone winning a gold medal.

"I am Arthur Silver of the *New York Times*," the columnist said, insinuating his body between those of the two Russian announcers.

At the same time, he was pressing a 41-magnum Luger against the woman announcer's right temple, just below the sloping rim of her wide-banded beige hat.

"I want the two of you to listen very carefully now. Are you both comfortable conversing in English?"

A most cautious nod from the Russian woman. A curt nod from the feather-hatted male announcer.

Word began to filter around the reporter's plaza that someone up there had a gun out.

"Who has a gun out? Where?"

"Oh my God, it's Arthur Silver."

"It's Arthur Silver from the bloody *New York Times*!"

It was also the Newspaperman from the Storm Troop, formerly from Dachau *Konzentrationslager*.

The Newspaperman spoke very slowly, careful that the Russian man and woman understood every important word.

"At this moment, there is a large, professional, Jewish attack force inside Lenin Stadium.

"We are located randomly in this large crowd you see here. Each of us has a plastic bomb. Each bomb has the capability of killing thousands of people. Why are you shaking your head?"

The Russian woman looked into the cloudy bifocals of Arthur Silver. "We happen to know that Lenin Stadium has been electronically checked for explosive devices," she said to him. "What you say cannot be true. It is a bluff."

The Newspaperman smiled; he then snapped open his battered brown briefcase.

Inside the case, the Russians could see, was a maze of twisted white, blue, and red wires; a complicated little generator; a puddle of pinkish *plastiques*. It certainly appeared to be a small, potent bomb, just as the Newspaperman had said.

Arthur Silver now put away his revolver. He placed his hand on the bomb's detonator instead.

"Before we discuss this any further, I would like you seriously to consider what happens if all of these nonexistent bombs are detonated. Please look around you at the thousands of people in these grandstands."

"Bastard," the Russian woman said.

"We will do whatever it is that you wish," said the man.

"All right then." Arthur Silver took a deep breath. He looked around at the brilliant colors shot all through the stadium and he felt slightly dizzy.

"We would like all the track-and-field events stopped first. Please ask the athletes to sit down wherever they are on the field at this moment.

"After that, one of you will telephone General Iranov at the Olympic Security Headquarters. You'll tell General Iranov or Colonel Belov what has happened here. You'll tell them the danger is considerable. And imminent."

The Newspaperman had to stop for a second. His teeth were actually chattering as he tried to make his mouth work. He was shivering as if it were zero-degree weather. He said one final prayer that what they were doing was the right thing.

"All right." Arthur Silver managed to speak again. "I'd like you to make the first announcement. I'd like the lady to speak to the crowd. Would you please stop the Olympic Games now."

65

Settling into the Russian *banya* was a little like taking a sauna in the boiler room of a big-city apartment building, David considered.

It was like bathing in the gray concrete tunnels and cracked-plaster mystery rooms beneath his and Heather's old New York apartment building on Central Park West.

Inside the steam-bath rooms, there were strange Russian men ranging from thirteen to maybe a hundred. They sat like zombies on stone steps which were arranged like miniature grandstands around red-hot coal stoves.

Dripping flesh hung on sloping shoulder bones. Flesh hung on wide hips and ribs like so much wet cloth.

Brownish penises and testicles lay between withered legs like small, dead sea creatures.

Some Russian grandfathers, *dedushkas*, were congregated near the central stone oven. A few of the elderly Russians were flogging themselves with leafy twigs which turned out to be birch, and which were *de rigueur* if you wanted to smell like a birch tree after your *banya*.

Harry Callaghan sat on the lowest stone step and ordered two Zhigulsky beers from an appropriately shriveled Russian bath attendant.

"Tell him just one." David found that he could barely whisper in the heat. "No beer for me, thanks."

"You'll want it when it comes."

"Never mind. I'll want it when it comes," David said to the uncomprehending attendant, who said *da, da, da,* turned, and shuffled away.

As it happened, David wanted the beer much, much sooner than it came.

Not twenty seconds after he sat down on his burning step, the bathhouse air was so bad it began to sear his throat and nostrils.

"So *you're* the one who's trying to kill me," David rasped to Harry Callaghan. "*Here. Now.*"

The agent shrugged. Maybe yes. Maybe no.

The beers finally came and David let a thin, cool stream roll down the blistered insides of his throat.

All of a sudden his head cleared rather violently. His ears popped the way they can after a tricky airplane ride.

David could smell ammonia way back inside his brain. It was a good feeling for about thirty seconds. He felt real smart.

More comfortable now, David settled back on his stone step. It was an odd, odd feeling, this being a sort of pathetic junior-grade detective, he was thinking. Realizing that you were probably going to understand a particularly disturbing crime case, *not* because you'd succeeded in catching the offenders, but rather because the criminals were about to brazenly commit the offense, then rub your nose in it.

David looked up, and Harry was in the middle of saying something.

". . . You see, I should be racing all engines now. Instead . . . I just feel tired of the whole thing. . . . I see Alix's face sometimes. Your brother's face from television that first night . . . I just feel bad, and very tired. It's never been this way for me before. Not in nineteen years of this kind of work. A career of it. When I got up at three I felt very very alone in the hotel room."

"Everybody feels like shit right now," David said. "This is the most frustrating time of all. I want to go punch in the Kremlin walls. The Russians are acting so stupid I can't believe it."

Right then, Harry Callaghan suddenly punched David hard

in the thigh. It was like strange, locker-room camaraderie. Something very weird. David's right leg cramped up as if it were part of the stone stairway. The muscle hurt like hell.

Then David surprised himself a little.

He hit Harry back. A reflex action. *Get hit; hit back.*

David caught the veteran government man right on the point of his dimpled chin. Harder than he'd meant, or thought he'd meant.

Harry Callaghan spit out a mouthful of blood and foam. His eyes were all watery.

Harry laughed. Then both Harry and David started laughing like certifiable maniacs in the cascading steam of the *banya*.

"Shit, I'm sorry," David said, finally managing to speak. "I must be completely nuts already. I'm gone. Say good night, Gracie."

"We've just gone a little cuckoo," Harry explained to the ancient Russian men who were gaping at them. "Just two American madmen. *Moohahaha!*"

It was the only escape they had left. The short burst of manic laughing was the only thing that made any sense at all.

Somehow, David and Harry managed to get their clothes on again. By eleven o'clock they were back out on one of the broad Moscow avenues.

Right there, they met an American father, mother, and two kids in Disneyland shirts, rushing back from the direction of Olympic Village.

"Are you Americans?" the father said to David.

"Yes, we are," David answered.

"Terrorists have just seized the Olympics," the American man said, the most unbelievably pained look coming over his face.

David's heart started to pound and jump up and down. He tried to walk beside the family.

"What happened? Please stop and tell us what's happened. Please."

The man's wife slowed and turned to face David.

"They struck at the hotel where all the NBC-TV people are staying. They're supposed to have bombs. Everything is suddenly unbelievably confusing and horrible."

David Strauss stopped walking. He let the family go on. That was when he noticed that everyone else on the streets of Moscow was running.

66

Twelve noon, the Kremlin.

The eleven men in the windowless, olive-green conference room were all "super-comrades." Some of them were dangerously overweight. They had short haircuts, oatmeal-white faces, square-shouldered suits straight out of American gangster films.

The eleven men were bureaucrats of the very highest rank and order. They ruled Soviet Russia.

"This was clearly a show of force," said General Yuri Iranov, a Politburo member by virtue of being chairman of the KGB. "The Jewish terrorists are trying to demonstrate their power over us, you see."

"An impressive demonstration," one of the other Russian leaders mumbled angrily.

"What exactly has happened?" asked Leonid Brezhnev. "Will someone please start at the beginning for me? At 10:45 this morning something terrible happened that I still don't quite understand."

"From the beginning then," said General Iranov. Relative silence took over in the drab rumpus room.

"At 10:45 this morning, Jewish commandos—"

"*Not Mossad*. Free-lancers. Tel Aviv is sending us screams saying that they have no part in this. They want to know how they can help us. They want to send Mossad operators."

"Yes. Clearly. At 10:45, the Jews attacked Olympic Village as well as some of the more vulnerable athletic sites. A show of force, as I said a minute ago. . . .

"Premier, it was simply impossible to prevent this, with one million tourists roaming through Moscow like some untamed traveling circus, some gypsy carnival. We would have had to arrest every one of the tourists, and taken them down to the cellars in Lubyenko for interrogation."

The other leaders and Politburo members nodded either sympathetically or politely. Yuri Iranov was known to protect his flanks at all times, but he was also a proud, solid policeman.

"Yes, yes, please go on," said Viktor Tvardevsky, the First

Secretary of the Communist Party. "You don't have to make any excuses for your work, General. Not to me anyway."

"The Jews claimed to have plastic bombs scattered through a hundred thousand spectators in Lenin Stadium. They claimed to have a nuclear device in the Rossiya Hotel, plus canisters of nerve gas placed all around the city. Right on Kalinin Prospekt, for one.

"They have already demonstrated technological proficiency, as well as unusual discipline and organization for a guerrilla group. They include experts from Mossad, M.I. 6, Shin Beth. They appear to have one of the CIA's technicians with them."

Vasily Rublev of the GRU winced. "Oof. All of those bastards are madmen, anyway. They recruit actual mad boys from American high schools. Boys who try to blow up their hometowns wind up working in CIA laboratories."

General Iranov crushed out his Papirosi cigarette. "Among the Jewish group, we know Colonel Essmann, formerly of Mossad. Malachi Ben-Eden we know also. Some Russian Jews are involved, of course. The American actress Alix Rothschild is here to get them some support and sympathy."

"What is your estimation of the terrorists?" Brezhnev asked. "How do you sum up what has happened so far?"

Yuri Iranov paused for a moment. The Russian general understood that if he made a mistake now, the others were going to remember it for a long, long time.

"If they are willing to die, we are in for terrible troubles. Even beyond what you are all imagining now."

The KGB leader groped for an appropriate image.

"Consider, if you will, that all of our agents inside New York City suddenly ran amok. How would the New York City police be able to stop them? How do you begin to find them in such a large city? The answer is, *you don't*. You suffer terrible casualties.

"Personally, I suspect that the Dachau Two plot has to do with their trying to reproduce some aspect of Germany's prison camps right here at the Olympics. In Russia, we've never really dealt with anything like this before. Do we arrest all of the tourists?"

Brezhnev was shaking his head from side to side. "Have we actually spoken with the Jews yet? What do these people have to say for themselves? Where are they now? Please go on, General Iranov."

"They strike, and they run. We don't know where they are. We don't know how many they are. They are somewhere among the million tourists inside Moscow. They've sent us a document listing their demands and they say they'll contact us again."

General Iranov glanced at the faces around the conference table. "Would you all like to read the wonderful demands of Dachau Two? I must warn you first, that they will make you sick with worry. These are intelligent people we are dealing with. These are not adolescents with a few machine guns and a death wish."

Iranov gestured and one of his lieutenants handed out mimeographed copies of the demands.

"Oof, oof, oof," Rublev of the GRU was complaining before he had finished half of the first page.

General Iranov was right. It was far worse than any of them had been imagining.

67

The original demands read inside the Kremlin that afternoon were reportedly censored severely before their general release to the public. As they subsequently appeared in major newspapers around the world, the famous demands of the Dachau Two were as follows:

> Yes, the Jewish nation has finally learned the sad and tragic lessons of our fathers—"*Yea, when a man rises up to strike you, rise up and strike him down first.*"
> This was critical dogma we should have learned in ancient Rome, when the legions destroyed and desecrated our land, exiling us, forcing us to live in the desert for the first time.
> It was a sad lesson we should have learned in Spain

during the Inquisition. Or in Poland. Or in the Russian Pale.

But most of all, this was an object lesson that should have consumed each and every Jew with a burning hatred for you after the fires of Dachau, Treblinka, Mauthausen, Auschwitz, Belsen, Ravensbruck, Buchenwald, Maidanek, and Riga consumed the bodies of our mothers, our fathers, our sisters and brothers, our precious little babies.

This *holocaust*, this attempted extermination of an entire race, horrified and fascinated even you. Yet you could not begin to understand or, more important, to *feel* what it all meant. . . .

. . . As of July 18, however, we believe it will be seen that the Jews have finally learned the lesson of history.

It will be seen by all that we have shed our "sheep-to-slaughter mentality and traditions."

The world must now learn to reckon with us on its own brutish level. The docile, acquiescent, "moral" Jew has undergone a metamorphosis. A new, stronger breed of Jew has emerged. The Warrior Jew. Ready to combat racist hatred with force, with power, with our lives.

This has become necessary because Gentile hatred of Jews has not diminished since the fall of Hitler and Nazi Germany.

Rather, all over the world, there has been a subtle Nazi rebirth—a rebirth of vicious anti-Semitism.

Civilized countries have knowingly permitted former Nazi war criminals to live and prosper within their borders. Former SS officers have become influential members of the Austrian Parliament, the German Bundestag, the United States House of Representatives. In Germany alone, over seven million Nazi criminals remain unpunished. Of the men and women who once staffed Dachau *Konzentrationslager*, to take just one example, only one hundred forty of over seven thousand have ever been brought to justice.

Note this well.

The Nazis did not suddenly appear in 1933, then disappear in 1945. Any man or woman who can think at all must know that.

The Nazis are ever with us.

On September 2, 1972, the Federation of West Germany was informed by Rabbi Dr. Michael Ben-Iban that heavily armed bands of PLO terrorists were preparing to attack the Israeli athletes at the Munich Olympics. *Germany, however, did nothing to stop these murderers.* Furthermore, the West German government subsequently participated in the "staged" hijacking of a Lufthansa 727 airliner at Zagreb. During this charade, the surviving fellaheen who had participated in the Munich massacre were released back to the PLO.

For these and innumerable other crimes against all Jews, the German people must now pay a fair penalty, a long overdue penalty.

As *symbolic* payment for Germany's injustices, we demand:

THE GERMAN AND AUSTRIAN GOVERNMENTS MUST IMMEDIATELY EXECUTE THE FOLLOWING NAZI CRIMINALS PRESENTLY LIVING IN THEIR RESPECTIVE COUNTRIES.

1. Friedrich Peter—present chairman of the Austrian Freedom Party, this former commander of the infamous SS "Murder Brigade" took part in massacres of civilians resulting in approximately 20,000 deaths.

2. Hermine Braunsteiner—the notorious murderess of Majcenek, who is now supposedly standing trial in Dusseldorf.

3. Dr. Josef Muller—a former high-ranking Gestapo officer, Muller is presently the director of a high school in Kelkheim, Germany.

4. Hans Gogl—former officer in the Mauthausen concentration camp. Gogl was responsible for the murder of thousands of Jews as well as airmen from the Royal Dutch Air Force.

5. Manfred Roeder—a modern-day advocate of Adolf Hitler's plan to destroy the Jews, Roeder practices this art where it is easiest—in Austria. Although brought to trial in 1963, Roeder has never spent a single day in jail.

More facts!

While Germany and Austria continue to participate in thinly veiled anti-Jewish activity, so does a more subtle offender—the United States of America.

Let it be known by the world, therefore, that, since 1945, the United States has pursued a policy of nonprosecution of Nazi war criminals in the Americas. Of protection of neo-Nazi organizations. Of racial discrimination against Jews.

So be it. We have learned to expect as much from the Gentile countries of the world.

What we will not allow, however, is American participation in the economic strangulation of Israel.

American corporations have religiously followed the Arab boycott. American corporations have kept Jews from top managerial posts at Arab direction. American corporations have refused to deal with Israeli firms such as Clal Israel, Israel Discount Bank, Ampal Development, Israel Paper. . . .

EXXON CORPORATION, PEPSICO, ITT, CHRYSLER MOTOR COMPANY, MOBIL CORPORATION AND OTHERS MUST THEREFORE MAKE PAYMENT OF TEN MILLION DOLLARS EACH TO THE STATE OF ISRAEL. . . . ONCE AGAIN, THIS PAYMENT OF MONEY FOR LIVES IS SYMBOLIC, A TOKEN THAT IS FAR BELOW THE COST OF THE ACTUAL DAMAGE INCURRED.

. . . And finally, we turn our attention to our hosts and comrades—the self-acclaimed "leaders of the people's revolution," the Soviet Union.

If "Mother Russia" was ever a mother to the Jew, then may God make us all orphans.

From our earliest experiences with the Russian people we have been treated to violent hatred, pogroms, discrimination, physical and spiritual murder. Inside Russia, Jews have never been allowed to own land. A Russian Jew wishing to return to his homeland of Israel must request "permission." However, the mere act of requesting an exit visa means loss of job and livelihood, which is in itself a crime under Soviet Law.

Russian Jews are stripped of all their human rights. This includes constant harassment by Soviet police; separation from family; eviction from their homes; arrest and imprisonment in Siberian corrective labor camps for unspecified "anti-Soviet activities."

We will no longer tolerate the imprisonment of Jews for practicing Judaism, however. We will no longer tolerate the denial to Russian Jews of their right to leave Russia and live in Israel.

WE THEREFORE DEMAND THAT THE SOVIET UNION RELEASE IMMEDIATELY THE FOLLOWING JEWISH POLITICAL PRISONERS.

1. Anatold Altman—a simple, honest engraver now serving ten years in a Siberian labor prison.

2. Hillel Butman—lawyer and engineer, serving ten years under strict regime for anti-Soviet activities.

3. Mark Dimshitz—pilot, serving fifteen years for anti-Soviet activities.

4. Arye Khnokh—electrician, serving seven years for anti-Soviet activities.

5. Edward Kuznetsov—translator, serving fifteen years under "specially" strict regime in a labor camp for anti-Soviet activities. Also accused of being a Zionist.

6. Mikhail Korenblit—dentist, serving seven years.

7. Iosif Mendelevich—student, serving twelve years.

8. Boris Penson—artist, serving ten years.

9. Israel Zalmanson—student, serving eight years under strict regime at a labor camp for anti-Soviet activities. Also accused of being a Zionist.

10. Vladamir Slepok—engineer, serving five years for hanging a banner from his Moscow apartment saying, "Let us join our son in Israel."

(*The complete list of Russian Jew POWs, supposedly over one hundred pages, was never released by the Novosti Press Agency.*) The nations implicated in these pages have twelve hours in which to begin to comply with our just demands.

If there is no compliance after twelve hours' time, we will begin to execute our harsh but just plan of vengeance. After twelve hours what happens inside Olympic Village is your responsibility.

THERE WILL BE NO DEADLINE EXTENSIONS BEYOND TWELVE HOURS.

In the first twelve centuries of the Olympic Games, the sacred trust was broken just once, by the Arcadian Army during the 103rd ancient Olympiad.

Now, in our century, the peace has been broken twice within ten years.

Truly, it is a sad time for all men.

May God save us all.

FOR THOSE WHO DARE TO CALL THIS ACTION AN "ATROCITY," LET THEM RECALL THE SIX MILLION "ATROCITIES" WE HAVE FINALLY COME TO AVENGE.

68

Noon until 6 P.M., *Moscow*.

Along Moscow's broad, Leninesque boulevards—Kropot-kin, Gorky, Pirogovskaya—on the pretty, lime-tree-lined plazas around Olympic Village, the horrible shock and confusion was unprecedented, nearly grand enough for Tolstoi. The hostile, confounded street noise suggested a simultaneous playing of *Boris Godunov* and Gershwin's *An American in Paris*.

Well-heeled tourists, athletes with their colorful sweat-gear, and gray, befuddled Moscovites staggered about the avenues with half-open mouths and dazed, dark expressions.

Necks were craned severely as people searched for hidden rooftop snipers and bomb-throwers.

Lovers and families were held and hugged.

Religious people sat, or knelt, and prayed for the first time in half a century on the streets of Moscow.

Occasional knots in the crowd would suddenly bolt from a meeting square like pigeons kicked at in a park. "Please help me. My husband is sick. My husband is dying," a woman moaned on the sidewalks of Kalinin Prospekt.

Pushing his way through the crowds, David watched crack Russian soldiers in their brown uniforms with red trim. Troop trucks were roaring down the streets; so were bounding jeeps full of Russian officers. Some sort of correspondent sat on the lawn at Pushkin Mall, his portable Olivetti in his lap, looking at the passing crowds, typing a sentence, looking at the people again. For some reason, David felt an urge to go over and punch some sense of dignity into the man.

Everyone was studying everyone else in the crowds, he noticed. *How could this be happening to me*, was on at least every other face that passed him.

At 2:55 P.M., with swarms of unstrung, war-weary tourists streaming into Sheremetyvo Airports I and II, Aeroflot Flight # 101 majestically burst into flames and black billowing smoke clouds where it sat on the crowded tarmac.

The nose blew five hundred feet out onto the runway. The wings flew off. Several other nearby jetliners caught fire.

The planes were *empty* at 2:55.

Moments later, over three hundred people would have been boarding the Olympic Special scheduled to fly to Kennedy Airport in New York.

A stern warning from the Dachau group was left in communiqués at both air terminals.

"NO ONE IS TO LEAVE THESE OLYMPICS UNTIL THE DEMANDS OF DACHAU TWO HAVE BEEN SUCCESSFULLY NEGOTIATED. NO ONE!

IF A SINGLE PLANE TAKES OFF, HUNDREDS OF LIVES MAY BE LOST. THIS IS A FINAL WARNING."

Gary Weinstein, meanwhile, was feeling somewhat like a teen-age hell-raiser back in his hometown of Harrisburg, Pennsylvania.

Dangling his long, skinny legs, he sat on a green metal children's swing in Marx Plaza. Weinstein calmly watched the unending procession of saris, dashikis, Levis, drab Russian suits and dresses, and very frightened faces.

When Colonel Alexander Belov and General Iranov finally appeared on the Security Headquarters front steps, the Engineer pressed a wallet-sized detonator inside his trouser pocket. Not fifteen feet from Soviet Russia's top secret policeman, a duffel bag planted beneath the bronze figure of a heroic farmer blew the heavy statue fifty feet into the air. It was the first time Gary Weinstein had actually watched his own handiwork and he was momentarily pleased.

Both Belov and Iranov were kissing the pavement; both had a completely new awareness of the seriousness of their situation.

At 6 P.M., a blue-and-white Russian maintenance truck rode very cautiously down a side street that abutted the northwest corner of the Olympic Village.

The truck swerved onto a parking apron in front of Numbers 110–125.

First Alix, then the Führer stepped out of the van. They were immediately approached by Russian soldiers with Kalashnikov assault rifles raised.

These particular soldiers, however, were the Architect, the Medic, the Dentist, and the Weapons Expert.

"If you are frightened and very unsure of yourself," the leader of Dachau Two whispered to Alix, "then you are exactly the same as me. Believe me though, the large numbers of police and other officials begin to work for us from now on. These people are confident they are trained for every kind of emergency, and that too works in our favor."

Alix watched as the others began to filter onto the small, important street.

She saw the Engineer, Nurse, Housewife, Lawyer. They were all indistinguishable from the Russian security force; some of them were actually checking identifications themselves.

"You must be a truly great actress for the rest of this day," the Führer was whispering to Alix. "You must trust me."

They all began to walk in the direction of Olympic Village.

Having left Harry Callaghan and the rest of the American intelligence people in a hopeless strategy session, and feeling unbelievably frightened and confused now, David reeled through the swelling crowds. His ears were full of the insistent wailing of the police and ambulance sirens. All of David's senses were offended by the truly awful, hospital-emergency-room ambience.

Walking across a flat, grassy plain above Olympic Village, he happened upon a ragged circle of Russian grandmothers in heavy gray-and-black babushkas.

The women were leaning on their canes like tired dancers; they were kibbitzing like Jews, it seemed to David. The assortment of grandmothers made him think of Elena. *Hello, Grandma, David said in his mind. How are you, Elena? You understood what was going to happen—you and Nick did—and you were right. An isolated cell of your Jewish defense network got out of control. A few Jewish defenders finally went mad!*

David finally found a grassy space for himself on the hillside. His own little niche, looking down on the Village proper. Which was beginning to resemble a Hollywood disaster movie set, David couldn't help thinking.

Lighting up a cigarette, he watched two Russian helicopters hover between the starkly modern athletic dormitories. A nearby observation needle pierced the Moscow skyline. *Dachau Two*, David thought for the eleven-millionth time. *Why Dachau Two? A prison here? A death camp? Did that make any sense at all? Did he want the Jews to have some revenge for the Holocaust?*

As David's eyes traveled down the steep, cool slope of the hill, he suddenly found his body jerking straight up again on its grassy seat.

His heart was pounding as if he'd been slapped awake during a vivid nightmare. The fear that was spreading through his body was absolutely paralyzing. David actually *wanted* to disbelieve his eyes.

Sauntering calmly through the hillside crowd was a man David recognized at once.

David recognized the man from glossy photos and a film shown at the Security Center meeting the day before.

Even dressed as he was, in the brown-and-red uniform of the Russian Army, David recognized this man with absolute certainty.

Colonel Ben Essmann, the Soldier, was heading down toward Olympic Village.

70

David tried to watch both his own unsteady step and the back and bobbing black head of the retreating killer.

Fear clouded his vision, badly fogging the edges out of focus.

The blinding-bright red sun didn't help, and at one point the Soldier stepped right into it.

But the Israeli commando quickly appeared again. He stopped to light a black Russian cigarette, looking around casually to check his flanks.

David crouched on one bended knee as Ben Essmann's eyes slowly crept back up the hill. The young doctor's heart was crashing big bass drums and he'd begun to sweat uncontrollably. David's shoulders and the back of his neck were already soaked.

Finally, the Israeli man looked straight at David. Their dark eyes met and held for no more than a split second.

Then the Soldier bolted away.

David began to run as well.

He began to scream at the top of his voice.

"One of the terrorists. Stop him! Stop that man!"

Some people who understood English looked around. A Russian policeman tried to grab Ben Essmann and was shot in the shoulder. A Russian soldier was wounded in the chest by the Israeli.

Then Ben Essmann was scrambling down into the nearby tunnels that ran under most of Olympic Village. He was getting away, David saw, and he just couldn't let that happen.

Down in the tunnel David found a rushing four-lane highway lit with overhead sodium lamps. For maybe two hundred yards both David and the Soldier ran at full speed against the flow of traffic. They sprinted down the right-side lane of the highway.

Fiat and Chaika horns screamed. Brakes screeched. Moscow drivers cursed. David continued to yell out that one of the terrorists was getting away.

"You crazy asshole!" A VW van with "U.S. Olympic Team" on the side paneling just missed hitting David.

David actually felt the speeding van nip his shirttail.

"One of the terrorists!" David continued to shout and point.

Off to the side of the main road were shadowy delivery routes which snaked out beneath specific sections of the Village. Suddenly the Soldier veered off onto one of the side routes.

Not far behind, David followed the Israeli. He ran at three-quarters speed down an eerie cigar-tube tunnel. Listening to his own steps. Listening for the Soldier.

At the tunnel's end, David had to turn right or left along a greasy wall marked with sprawling red Cyrillic letters.

Colonel Essmann suddenly stepped out of the shadows behind David.

The shock made the whole right side of David's body seem to die.

His heart jumped up into his throat and stayed there.

"Not another word, Dr. Strauss. Not a peep or you're very gruesomely and needlessly dead."

Without giving it any real thought, David Strauss turned, lunged, struck the Israeli man in the chest. A Russian service revolver went skidding off across the concrete pavement.

Then Colonel Essmann was standing in a flat-footed crouch, confidently waiting for David to move on him again.

David desperately wanted to strangle the dark-haired commando, but he understood that his real job was to keep from getting killed. The absurd phrase, *Float like a butterfly*, ran through his head and seemed like moderately good advice.

Stay away from him.

Survive.

Somehow.

Surprising both of them, David hit the terrorist with a good right hand to the lower jaw. It was six feet one and a hundred ninety pounds behind a shot David would have described as just about his best punch.

The Israeli shrugged off the solid blow. He maneuvered even lower in his crouch.

David hit him again.

A cracking hard left jab to the nose.

"Come," Ben Essmann whispered with excitement in his voice. He smiled at David, and the American understood that they were playing a game he didn't understand.

"You love Alix still?" Colonel Essmann asked. "I love Alix as well. Come, David."

The Israeli threw a sharp right cross and David's head snapped back hard. *So*—he was a boxer after all.

David could taste thick, warmish blood in his mouth. His legs were feeling wobbly and unreal.

He was trying to remember every boyhood street-fighting trick he'd ever known, but he wasn't getting very far. *Survive. Somehow. Anyhow!*

David hit the Soldier's forehead with a tremendous right hand, and he immediately wished he hadn't. It was like trying to punch out a steel door.

Nevertheless, the other man's knees buckled. For the first time, Essmann's face showed doubt, fear. He'd *hurt* this man, David understood.

David attempted a quick combination, and very suddenly the Soldier exploded into his stomach, head and shoulder first. He chopped David across his collarbone and the American went down hard.

David tried to focus on the wet concrete. Pebbles. Russian cigarette butts. He couldn't hold focus, and he couldn't get up.

Then David Strauss was being pulled roughly to his feet.

"Stronger than you look." The military man from Tel Aviv was short of breath, at least. Ben Essmann stared at David and seemed to make a difficult decision.

"Elena Strauss's grandson! You want to come with me? You wish to see Dachau Two for yourself?" the fiery Soldier challenged.

David nodded weakly.

"So come . . . *David*. Son of Saul, King of all Israel. *Jewish* boy from America. I can't kill you; and I can't leave you. Come and meet the Führer. He'll make the decision."

David Strauss went along with the Israeli. He didn't have a lot of choices. Just questions, questions, questions.

6:15 P.M. *inside Olympic Village.*

"Happy Hanukkah!" Marc Jacobson from Los Angeles—the Medic—called out in his clear California schoolboy's voice.

More than eighty women looked up from steaming platters

of eggs and biscuits, from large beakers of bubbly milk and juices, from an extraordinary amount of juicy prime beef.

What these women saw was not one, but eight, very frightening terrorists who had somehow gotten into their private cafeteria.

The intruders wore brown policeman's uniforms or blue Olympic Village maintenance coveralls. Some of them carried duffel bags or toolboxes. They had handguns or Uzi machine-gun pistols pointed in every possible direction around the dining room.

"They appeared like an idiosyncratic holdup gang," Jane Vreeland Hall said in her Harper & Row book, *The Midnight Survivor.* "They had obviously shot their way inside, with very little hope of getting back out again. They were as scared-looking as we must have been—seeing them for the first time, not believing that they had broken through to get us, wondering what they could possibly want."

Standing in the midst of the seven terrorists, Alix tried to quickly take in the rows of frozen, petrified faces lining the cafeteria tables. All in all, there were eighty-three women and teen-age girls inside Yuri Gagarin Hall when the Dachau team attacked.

All members of the United States Olympic Team; the U.S. Women's Team.

"To put it in terms he Americans and others will understand," the Führer had said just before the attack. "It is a five-hundred-million-dollar kidnap package. We have taken the best of their young people. *Just as they once took the best of ours.*"

As they stood grouped at the center of the dining room, the Führer asked Alix to try to speak to the teary and anxious American women.

Suddenly beginning to shake all over, Alix stepped forward.

"I am Alix Rothschild." As she spoke, Alix was thinking that she was obviously as frightened as the young athletes. She wondered what they must be thinking about her. She tried to imagine their confusion right then.

"Once upon a time, I, uh, I made a movie called *Sara, Sara.*" Somehow, Alix was managing to produce a soft, pleasant speaking voice. She was thinking that she didn't want these women and little girls to be so afraid. She didn't want them to suffer any more than was necessary.

"We," Alix gestured around to the other Dachau team members, "we are part of a Jewish army. We're here partly because of terrible things that happened many years ago. Things that you've heard about, read about. And we're here partly because of terrible things that are happening right now in the world. Things that you *don't* realize are happening. None of this has to concern any of you right now, though. All you have to remember now is that you must obey any orders that are given to you."

"I am *also* Jewish."

A thin girl with red, frizzy hair—a twenty-two-year-old gym monkey from Houston—had broken the petrified silence inside the dining hall.

"And I think you're all shit. All terrorists are shit! You, too, *Miss Rothschild!*"

Alix nodded in the direction of the wiry, red-haired girl. "I don't completely agree with you," she said simply. Already, Alix knew, she was winning over some in the group. Already some of the girls trusted her. The famous Rothschild smile was overtaking reality one final time.

Alix and the others now began to strip off their coveralls and police uniforms.

The Dachau team men wore conservative suits. The women had on loose white blouses and dark pants. The men now pinned on ritual Jewish skullcaps.

"We would like all of you to please get up slowly," Alix spoke again. "Table by table. Please, please, don't attempt to be heroic. If these machine guns are fired, people will die. *Please* be careful.

"We're going upstairs to the bedrooms and suites on the third, fourth, and fifth floors only. This table first. You girls here.

"No one will be hurt, I promise you," Alix said, and regretted it immediately.

Between 6:15 and 6:30, while diversions were going off all over Moscow, separate attacks were made on three other Olympic Village dormitory sections.

The West German Women's Dorm was taken with relative ease.

At the Russian Men's Dormitory, a gun battle claimed the lives of nine Red Army soldiers and two terrorists.

On two floors in the Pushkin Center—where Syrian and Egyptian athletes were being housed—the entire Jewish team was killed by Moscow police and Red Army marksmen.

The mysteries of Dachau Two, of Alix Rothschild, of the Strauss family murders, were all about to unfold, David understood as he was pushed past two terrorist guards and entered the hostage section of Olympic Village.

Astonishingly, the main subject was what it had been right from that first terrible night on Upper North Avenue in Westchester.

Nazis.

In 1980.

72

The first of the demands was met with deceptive speed and a sense of cooperation.

A blue Soviet police van came weaving up to the hostage dormitory like a New York City cab in rush hour. There was a dramatic screech of tires as the van stopped.

Every newscaster in Moscow immediately began to speculate about the police van's contents.

Finally, the Russians announced that a sophisticated video-taping unit had been delivered to the hostage dorm.

They were going to make an important movie inside 110 Yuri Gagarin.

Once the equipment had arrived, the camera and lights were quickly set up. It was time for Alix to perform, to read a concentrated version of the demands for the huge TV audience. Somehow, Alix had to make them all understand now.

"In your hearts," Alix began as she'd rehearsed it so many time with Arthur Silver, "you must know that the Nazis didn't suddenly appear out of nowhere in 1933. The Nazi ideas didn't suddenly disappear in 1945.

"You must know that what is happening today was inevitable unless drastic reforms were made."

Alix Rothschild spoke softly; she spoke humbly, sadly.

During the fourteen-minute speech she was often eloquent.

"Sometimes I've wondered if a number such as *six million killed* is too difficult to grasp, too abstract in a strange way. Think about the murder of just two human beings for a moment. My mother and father were murdered in Nazi death camps. They were good people, they never hurt anyone, and then they were murdered. Worse than murdered. They were tortured, they were disgraced, they were dehumanized.

"The men and women who did this, men who killed a hundred thousand human beings apiece, walk free today!

"Jews are suffering in concetration camps again. Right now. Right here inside Soviet Russia.

"Do you remember the first incredible stories of of the death and torture camps in the 1940s? Do you remember how no one wanted to hear? I'm telling *you* now. All of you! There are concentration camps for Jews inside Russia today. This is not speculation; this is not television drama; this is the truth! Are you going to sit and do nothing about it a second time?

"I am personally afraid; I have nightmares that the next Holocaust will take place in Israel.

"I am desperately afraid that nuclear bombs will be dropped on the state of Israel. Three million more Jews will die in the fires.

"I am convinced this will happen unless drastic reform is undertaken now. I am certain of it. The bombings are inevitable as things stand right now.

"Please understand. Please listen and understand.

"As another human being, I ask this of you."

For a moment at least, for fifteen minutes, people all over the world listened and understood. Inside Russia, all over Europe, in the United States, down through South America.

"Oh Jesus." David shook his head and whispered hoarsely.
"You bastard. You *incredible, pathetic* bastard."

Some delicate balance mechanism inside his head was
doing flip-flops; awful, three-hundred-sixty-degree spins and
loops. Blood raced to David's face. Adrenalin swept through
his body like a flash flood.

"You bastard."

One of the final pieces of the horrifying puzzle had just
dropped into place, severely jarring David's psyche, warping
what remained of his sense of reality.

"Sit?" David asked. "May I? Am I allowed?"

The Führer nodded. "Smoke? Coffee? I would like to say
one thing only, David. We *pleaded* both with Elena and your
brother. They chose to break our vows. They threatened
everything we solemnly believe in."

David accepted a nonfilter cigarette. As he lit it, an elaborately detailed scene from the past was flooding over him like
a loss of consciousness. In the scene, *Harry Callaghan was
stepping into a dark sedan. The ceiling light inside the car
apparently didn't work. The agent Thomas Hallahan turned
the car's ignition over once. David was looking into a tilting,
smiling face that was back-lit by a reddish gin-mill sign.*

Now the same face was looking into his eyes again.

*Benjamin Rabinowitz, the American Nazi-hunter, the
Führer, was sitting across from him in the American Women's
Team Tormitory. The man most responsible for the deaths of
his wife, his brother, his grandmother.*

"I truly appreciated your concern for my life back in Wallkill," Rabinowitz said. "You screamed out several times after
the gunshot. Right then, I knew that you were truly a good
man. Concerned about life and death. A true grandson of
Elena. At the time, I needed to know how much you knew
about our group. After that, I had to disappear from sight. I'm
sorry for the scare, David. I'm sorry for a great many things."

David had a jumble of questions about the Wallkill incident, but he slowly let them slip out of his mind. He simply stared into the old Nazi-hunter's eyes.

"Tell me about Dachau Two," David finally whispered. "What are you people going to do here? What is all this leading up to?"

Rabinowitz shook his head back and forth. "Not right now, Dr. Strauss. You'll understand the whole thing soon enough. If you stay here with us."

David caught a quick movement going on to his side. He looked toward the doorway of the Olympic Village suite and saw Alix.

She looked much the same as she had during the TV appearance. Alix looked very pretty; very serious.

"I'm sorry, David," she said tentatively. "I'm just sorry."

Benjamin Rabinowitz rose up from his chair.

"If David wants to leave here, Alix, we may let him go. Whatever he wants. Let him read through our demands. Answer any of his questions. I think Dr. David Strauss wants to leave, though." Rabinowitz shook his head. "We're a little too Jewish for him."

David stared back at the old man. "Actually, you're a little too Nazi for me."

As soon as Rabinowitz had left the room, Alix began speaking very rapidly to David. At the same time, she tried to avoid looking into his eyes.

"I tried to tell you so many times when we were together, David; Ben-Iban had told me to *tell no one*... I'm sorry....

"*I* want you to leave here, David," Alix said. "Come with me. Right now. Ben Essmann only got you in here to let you die. He believes all good Jews ought to be ready to die today. He thinks this is Armageddon day."

David pulled away from Alix.

He sat down and thrust his feet up on a chair. He stubbornly puffed his cigarette.

"You said in your little telegram to Frankfurt that I'd understand everything soon. So explain it all to me. I'd like you to make me understand all of this."

Alix's head dropped and she sighed out loud. Something had begun to go wrong. In the last few hours especially she'd begun to feel it. Something in the eyes of Rabinowitz.

"David, I *can't* make you understand. *I'm afraid* of what

they want to do here now. I'm afraid of Rabinowitz, Ben Essmann, the one called the Engineer. When I first became involved—one of the reasons I let myself get involved—no one was supposed to be hurt except for a few very deserving Nazis. That's the truth. That's what Dachau Two meant when Ben-Iban explained it to me. But David, I've been with Benjamin Rabinowitz all day today. He wants revenge! That's all he seems interested in."

Alix shook her head and David thought that she looked bruised. The way she'd looked after they'd visited Dachau together. Alix looked terribly afraid now. Which was exactly the way David felt himself.

"I wanted to make people understand about the Nazis," Alix said. "I wanted to avenge the murders of my mother and my father. I wanted to stop the nightmares of thirty years. I *don't* want to hurt innocent people."

Allegiances and conditions began to shift and change dramatically soon after that. Somewhere along the way, David Strauss thought that he finally became a Jew himself.

1 P.M. Washington, D.C.

"Yes, I've read the demands. . . . Yes . . . Absolutely . . . I've read them over and over, in fact. Personally, Premier, I don't see how we can do anything meaningful in the time allotted. Or even if we were given more time, to be frank. What are the others saying?"

"Oh, the same as yourself," the Premier of the Soviet Union said to the American President. Previous to this moment, their private telephone connection had been used by John Kennedy calling about Cuba; by Lyndon Johnson attempting to unravel the puzzle of Vietnam; by Nixon, announcing that Mr. Kissinger thought he ought to make a visit to Peking.

"Do you have any idea what you plan to do, Premier? The current American President, though often simplistic and parochial, was known as a sincere and honest man at least; his concern for the Olympic athletes was real, personal, somewhat touching.

"Yes, we have lots of ideas, Mr. President. All of them bad, I'm afraid. We are in a terrible bind, as you might well understand!"

"If there is anything any of our people can do ... I'll pray for you, and for all of our athletes," said the President of the United States of America.

He hung up the telephone then; he swung around to look out over the Harry Truman porch, over the lonely White House lawns.

What would I do if the terrible decision were mine instead of the Russian Premier's, the President considered briefly.

The answer was painfully obvious and the gray-haired American man shook his head sadly.

He knew that an attack would have to be ordered on the athletes' dormitories.

75

For an instant, Alix saw the David Strauss and a whole world she'd known in some other place, some other time. Familiarity and tenderness, regret, fear, all lumped together in her throat—at least, something substantial and powerful was raging there. She'd finally realized that she did love David— probably, that she'd always loved him.

Only now it was obviously too late. Now it didn't even matter.

Still, Alix felt that David deserved to know a little of what had happened. . . .

What she didn't know was that she had far more to learn than David did.

"Your grandparents, I suppose your father and mother, too," Alix said, speaking in an embarrassed whisper, groping for the exactly right words. "They had contributed hundreds of thousands of dollars to the watchdog defense group. Much more money than you were ever told about. This went way back into the forties and fifties. The group was called DIN in the beginning, *Dahm Y'Israel Noheam!* 'The blood of Israel will take vengeance!'

"DIN was eventually called the 'Council of Leaders,' or simply 'The Council,' " Alix went on. "In the 1940s, some of the more radical members had plotted to poison over a million Germans as retribution for the Holocaust. There was a brief financial sponsorship of 'The Wrath of God,' which Ben Essmann supervised. Chaim Weizmann and Moishe Dayan were supposedly members at one time. Several rich, well-intentioned Jewish-American families contributed heavily."

"Like the Strausses," David said.

"And the Rothmans," Alix countered. "My aunt and uncle understood the problem of genocide in their hearts. They also read Saul Baron, Elie Wiesel, Lucy Dawidowicz. In our house, not a day went by that someone didn't bring up the Holocaust.

"The extermination was more subtle in the late fifties and sixties, but it was still going on, David. Not only in the Middle East, where attention was focused. In South America, Brazil and Argentina especially. In the United States. Here in Russia, of course. That's what held the watchdog group together for thirty-five years. Concerned Jews, mostly survivors, they understood how it could start all over again.

"Eventually there were thousands of loosely connected members all over the world. In nineteen different countries. There was a main steering group; plus subgroups based on differing religious and political beliefs. That's how things ultimately got out of control—*one of the subgroups.* The important thing was that Jews were protectiong Jews."

David suddenly cut in on Alix.

"*I am a concerned Jew, Alix.* No one ever tried to exterminate me until your people came along and decided to play God. Until Benjamin Rabinowitz ordered my grandmother and my brother killed. Why don't you try explaining *that* to me."

Alix's mouth went completely slack. Her head began to shake from side to side. Alix's eyes rolled involuntarily, then closed shut.

Her look was part incredulous shock, part pure amazement. "David, what are you saying? Please. That isn't possible! No!"

Confronted with Alix's shocked reaction, David suddenly *knew.* He understood everything he needed to understand. All the suspicions about Alix that had never rung true for him. *They had never told her about the killings.* Perhaps they'd thought Alix wouldn't have gone through with the rest if she'd known. David suspected they'd kept the entire neo-Nazi plot from Alix.

Alix was crying now, sobbing. All the tension and strain was bursting out at once.

"Harry Callaghan told me, Alix. The FBI and the CIA finally solved most of the Storm Troop puzzle last week. I was able to fill in a few of the details. . . ."

Alix was holding her face in both hands. "Oh David, believe me, *I didn't know. I didn't know. I didn't know.*"

Alix had no idea how to communicate to David what she was feeling now. Her usual guilt was doubled, tripled. She felt as if all her insides had suddenly been ripped out with a sharp knife. *The murders of Elena, Nick, David's wife, Heather.* It was *impossible* to comprehend.

Now it was David's turn to try to explain.

"My grandmother, Rabinowitz, Ben-Iban—they had all worked together for years. Ever since they'd met in the confusion of the DP camps. Much, much later, my brother Nick became involved. Nick was the obvious choice because Elena always thought I was too Americanized to really understand. Especially the brutal Nazi-hunting. The revenge murders . . . besides, I was Elena's doctor. That was a holdover from her experience with 'Materials for Israel' in the forties. My grandmother had always wanted me to go to practice medicine in Israel. For as long as I can remember. So I was kept out of the secret group. To protect me, I suppose."

"Was Nick that heavily involved?" Alix asked. "Did they have to? Oh my God, David!"

"My brother Nick believed that his films could win important support for the Jewish people. Change some misconceptions, maybe a few of the terrible biases. Nick didn't really believe in Nazis. Not the Fourth Reich kind anyway.

"In the beginning, Nick got my grandmother to give him money for his film projects. My grandmother diverted money away from the group and its work. Then, Nick wanted our family to go to the FBI. Ben-Iban and especially Benjamin Rabinowitz were apparently beginning to frighten him. What he heard about the Dachau plan frightened him. There was the pledge of death to anyone who revealed the group's secrets, of course. Jewish *omertà,* which I suppose was necessary for the group's survival. Nick and Elena knew that when they tried to contact the government last spring."

"Everything was so professional. So very clever in an espionage sense," Alix said. "Except—who watches the watchdog group? That old problem."

"Oh David, everything we wrote in the demands is true. That's the horrible part. *The economic sanctions against Israel; the nuclear threat always hanging overhead. The Russian POWs—the Russian slave camps that exist right now. Nazis in high government positions all over the world. Nazi mass-murderers still walking free.*"

Suddenly Alix's mind flashed a terrible step ahead. To another part of the Dachau Two plan. To the deadly device that had put necessary strength and muscle behind the Dachau group's threats.

"There is another factor operating here in Moscow," she said to David. "A complicated mechanism was designed to ensure that the demands were treated seriously. Now, Rabinowitz and Ben Essmann are planning to turn it into an instrument for revenge. I'm certain of it now. What's happening is exactly what your brother and grandmother were afraid of! Do you remember that *Der Spiegel* researcher saying that the Nazis were old and this was their last chance to establish the Reich? Well, the Jewish survivors are old, too. This is their last chance for revenge. They want to avenge the six million, David. I'm just beginning to understand the whole thing myself. Suddenly all the different pieces are making sense to me."

"There has to be something that can be done," David said. "I keep thinking of Operation Thunderbolt. All those spectacular rescues. That train in the Netherlands. . . ."

Alix put her hand on David's arm. "*You* have to leave the dormitory. You have to tell the Russians what you know about the situation here. Maybe if they know . . ."

"And what are you going to do if I refuse to leave?" David finally asked. "Because first of all, the Russians have already been warned about a disaster here. Secondly, they're not going to listen to me. The Russians don't listen to anybody."

David Strauss and Alix Rothschild stared at one another for a long, uncomfortable moment. Then they reached for each other. They held on as tightly as they could.

They began to make a plan. They quickly plotted what they might be able to accomplish working on the inside of Dachau Two.

76

11:00 P.M., *the Kremlin.*

A staggered procession of hand-tooled Zil limousines— side-blinds drawn, trailing small gray rags of diesel exhaust— deposited their important passengers at an oval side entrance to the red-brick-walled Kremlin.

From one of the slick black limos stepped the American agent Harry Callaghan.

Inside a czarist-looking dining area, Harry sashayed among diplomats and other VIPs, all outfitted in dark, expensive clothes, greeting one another in somber, whispery tones. Even *they* had never experienced anything quite like this: champagne and French cognac; Beluga caviar; high intrigue in the night air.

The occasion brought to mind the formal receptions held before and after ceremonial funerals for important or revered heads of state. The one in Paris for General Charles de Gaulle. Franco's funeral in Madrid. The Kennedy funerals in Washington and New York.

By ten minutes after eleven, exquisite rumors about the purpose of the secret meeting had proliferated far beyond the scope of anyone not privy to the whisperings of the hyper-imaginative diplomatic community.

Just a minute or so later, a Russian man, gray-bearded and in a neat, gray business suit, crossed the checked marble floor of the large, formal room.

The man assumed a central position behind a blood-red hammer and sickle on a makeshift speaker's dais.

"As a courtesy," General Yuri Iranov began over the trail-off of diplomatic voices, "as a courtesy to all of the countries visiting Moscow during these Olympics, these particularly distressing times, I would like to make a few important re-marks.

"As far as this situation in Olympic Village is concerned, we are going to ask you to please content yourselves to sit back and be spectators on this truly unfortunate evening.

"At a quarter to twelve tonight," the Russian KGB chairman continued over a rising din, "approximately fifteen minutes before the first Jewish terrorist ultimatum runs out, there will be separate diversions in the streets outside each of the three hostage sections of the Olympics."

A few Russian stooges standing around the chandeliered room now began to nod enthusiastically, to clap.

"These diversions have been carefully designed to get as many terrorists as possible to *go to the windows of their buildings*.... Something, as you shall see, the terrorists have been doing as a matter of habit."

"You're going to *attack* the dormitories?" An American voice sounded in the gallery.

"Secondly," General Iranov continued, "a group of the fin-est Russian Army marksmen—three marksmen for each of the terrorists—are already in position surrounding the four dor-mitories. Sixty seconds after the diversions begin, these marksmen will shoot dead any terrorist careless enough to be at a front window."

The KGB general now held up a recent, blown-up photo-graph of a section of Olympic Village.

The diplomats could see a man—a negotiator—a *diver-sion*—approaching the front of the dormitory.

All over the photograph there were white grease-pencil cir-cles where terrorists had been spotted looking out of upstairs windows. The photograph offered evidence that six of the eight terrorists holding that section of building would have been shot dead at that moment.

"Third and last," General Iranov continued, "as soon as the sniper fire begins, teams of soldiers and policemen will strike at the rear and tunnel entrances.

"In most cases, plastic explosives have already been planted to blow off doors and other possible obstructions.

"Since most of the athletes are being kept in separate rooms, the resulting bloodshed and any deaths should be minimal."

"What about their threat to kill all six hundred eighty-two athletes?" Harry Callaghan was suddenly shouting at the Russian. The professional agent was suddenly making a scene; the quiet American was finally aroused. "What about their threat to create another Dachau here?"

General Iranov, meanwhile, was already leaving the speaker's dais. He appeared very dignified and calm, as if no diplomats or ambassadors were screaming at him from less than thirty feet away.

At 11:40 there was a wild dash for all the nearby telephones inside the Kremlin.

Telephone calls flashed out to Washington, D.C., to Tel Aviv, to Munich, to London, Cairo, Damascus.

Harry Callaghan, meanwhile, was in his limousine, already rushing back to Olympic Village.

Harry wanted to try to derail the speeding, oncoming disaster.

Obscured by a half-open door sporting a life-sized Jimmy Connors poster, a single guard stood in the worst imaginable location. The guard was down at the far end of the claustrophobic fifth-floor hallway. Right about where Jimmy Connors would have smashed his imaginary power serve.

A larger part of the upcoming problem, David concluded as he eyed the guard, was that Marc Jacobson, the Medic, was holding a Stechkin machine-gun pistol in one hand.

The gun was capable of discharging one hundred and five rounds of 9 mm ammunition in ten seconds firing time. It was a menace anywhere, but especially in a narrow hallway crowded with terrified young girls.

"I'm going to try to hold this pistol on you," Alix said as she and David turned down the narrow, dramatic corridor. "When we get down to his end, I'll say something and you hit him. Hit him hard! As hard as you can, David."

David's head twisted around. "What are you going to say to him?"

"I'll thing of something by the time we get there. Go ahead."

"Just say hello," David turned his head and whispered. "Something simple is enough."

"Just *walk*, David. Try not to look like we're doing what we're doing, O.K.?"

His eyes riveted on the young terrorist with the gruesome firearm in the crook of his arm, David marched straight ahead. Some of the United States team girls were peeking out into the hallway. Very frightened young women. David recognized the fifteen-year-old gymnast, Candy Slattery; a black sprinter named Mercy Tallant, who had already won a gold medal; "little Teri Byrd from Muncie, Indiana," who, according to Curt Gowdy, had the best jump shot—man or woman—at the 1980 Olympics.

"If I blow this, you just have to shoot him," David twisted his head and whispered again. His mouth felt wadded with cotton. "Don't hesitate, Alix. Not for a second."

David tried to take a deep breath, but no oxygen seemed to come up out of his lungs. He had no idea whether he could knock this man out, or at least down. More likely, he'd break his hand and get shot.

"David is going out now!" Alix suddenly blurted.

Confused, David started to turn around again.

"Hit him!" Alix shouted.

Too late, though. David having blown the signal, the machine gun was thrust like a bayonet into the pit of his stomach.

Marc Jacobson had started to yell something to Alix, when David's hardest punch cracked into the Medic's nose and cheekbone, breaking the former, turning whatever the young terrorist was going to yell into a sick bird sound like *aarrkkk.*

David quickly spun around and yanked a fire extinguisher off the wall. His ears ringing, he pressed the forty-pound canister straight over his head. He roared out like an Olympic weight lifter.

To his amazement, the scraggly bearded terrorist was unconscious on the floor. David bent and set down the fire extinguisher. He picked up the Medic's Stechkin.

"All right, let's go down to the fourth floor now. Try to think of a little better signal phrase this time."

"Always tearing down, never building up," Alix said.

It wasn't funny; it was just nervous talk. It was as frightening as anything either of them could ever have imagined. It was worse than that.

It was also 11:40.

78

At 11:45, on the order of Dachau survivor Benjamin Rabinowitz, Colonel Ben Essmann raced down the back stairs of their section of hostage dormitory; the Soldier was now to begin Dachau Two.

The tall, dark-haired commando was sweating fiercely. Acidy water was seeping from under his curly black hairline. Sweat trickled down and stung his dark eyes. This one time, even the Soldier was a little frightened and unsure.

The Führer wanted him to help kill a great number of the world's finest athletes. As revenge for the death camps: for Munich; Lod; Ma'alot.

Once he reached the dormitory kitchen, the professional terrorist stalked among the buzzing refrigerators and ovens.

He bent down low among the machines and kitchen worktables.

Holding a penlight in his mouth, the Soldier began to tinker with a wrench, then with a small Phillips screwdriver. For a scary moment the Soldier was beginning to experience his first feelings of genuine doubt and concern.

In the other hostage sections of the dormitory, the Engineer and the Russian Architect were presumably twisting away the same important nuts and bolts.

Each man worked on a sophisticated, less than thirty-pound generator; a black metal electric box that had been sitting harmlessly, without apparent purpose, under the stainless-steel kitchen sinks. An official-looking unit marked # A919-GRT.

These generators had been painstakingly, brilliantly designed by the Engineer, Gary Weinstein. They served only one purpose in the kitchens. The generators would compound, then switch the microwaves flowing through magnetron tubes in each of the kitchen ovens. The microwaves would be transferred into special casing that ran through the air-conditioning system of the dormitories. Josef Servenko, the Architect, and four other Russian Jews, had meticulously built the tubing into nearly a third of all the dormitory space in Olympic Village. *The buildings of Moscow's Olympic Village,* they had all decided, *were definitely not terrorist-proof.* The dormitories were essentially large, high-pressure microwave ovens now.

In less than sixty seconds, the compounded, "fat" microwaves would be shooting out of the air vents and ducts in every suite of rooms in the hostage dorms. The microwaves would bounce pell-mell, helter-skelter off the impenetrable metal around the vents. Then, the microwaves would begin to penetrate and discharge their energy into glass, fiber, stone, plastic, wood, and human flesh.

According to the Engineer, in less than twelve minutes, everyone inside the dormitories would be dead or dying. The six hundred and eighty-two hostage athletes. The terrorists themselves.

As they raced down the stairway to the fourth floor, both of their hearts beating fiercely, David and Alix nearly collided with Malachi Ben-Eden, the Weapons Expert.

"They're preparing to attack us!" the former Shin Beth agent screamed. "They're coming at the building from all directions!"

David's right foot flew out like a star football punter's. It caught the Weapons Expert right on the tip of the chin. David thought he'd broken his foot. The surprised terrorist went tumbling down the steep flight of stairs, then lay in a crumpled heap.

"Not too bad for a broken-down gynecologist," David said as they collected another Stechkin and more grenades. He was at least as surprised as the Weapons Expert had been.

"I wouldn't get too cocky," Alix whispered, proud of David anyway.

Just then a long-haired woman, Anna Lascher, suddenly stepped out of the fourth-floor hallway.

"You traitor!" she said, raising her rifle toward Alix.

A single shot cracked in the tiny stairwell. Alix had fired her own small Beretta. The smell of cordite wafted into her nose like ammonia.

The woman terrorist crashed back hard against the wall. She slipped down to the floor grimacing in pain, clutching her wounded shoulder.

"We're not traitors!" Alix bent and spoke to the stunned Jewish girl. "Think about what's really beginning to happen here. Think, Anna. Don't you see what's happening? Don't you see, brave girl? Don't you see, Anna?"

79

The final twists and turns were the best and the worst.

These were the aberrations which, once revealed, made people shake their heads in wonderment; which made them purchase morning *and* evening editions of their local newspapers.

Skirmish lines of young Red Army soldiers were choking off the tiny cul-de-sacs and side lanes around the hostage dormitory. A regiment of martial-brown uniforms marched down a wider street, like a Red Square parade on May Day. Everything but the towering missiles were on hand.

Red Army helicopters were settling down onto nearby rooftops.

Combat troops were streaming out of stout transport trucks and municipal buses.

Five, seven, nine, twelve armored cars appeared. Their turret lights were blazing balls of fire in the night. The tanks came forward slowly at ten to fifteen miles per hour, but they seemed to be moving faster because of the terrible roaring, rattling noise.

A smattering of cheers rose from the crowd as roving tank searchlights swung across the blank, staring faces. Some Russian women patted the armored-steel shells as if they were faithful family watchdogs.

For a whole generation of Americans, it was the first actual sighting of the much-talked-about Russian war machine.

West Germany's ZDF, the BBC, NBC, the French and Japanese TV networks filmed the live battle scene from every conceivable angle and perspective.

The TV cameramen shot long lens; zoom lens; fog lens for a dramatic smoking-inferno effect.

They shot close, extremely close, and closer still.

Nearly a hundred tense Russian Army and Moscow Police sharpshooters stood at the ready.

Outfitted in dark-gray sweatsuits and peaked hats, the Russian marksmen lay flat on nearby rooftops.

They lay in the dark that stretched behind open dormitory windows facing down on the hostage dorms.

They lay in vacant alleyways; under jeeps and harmless-looking road cars.

The sharpshooters viewed the dormitories through a hundred deadly infrared night-scopes. They very patiently searched out the Jews.

Meanwhile, two important-looking cars—shiny, seventy-thousand-dollar Zil limos—drove at 55 mph in the eerily deserted tunnels directly underneath Olympic Village.

Nearing Yuri Gagarin Square, the Russian-made luxury cars emerged from a wide service ramp. They were like two giant but cautious lizards peeking up from underground.

As the sparkling limos were escorted through peripheral crowds, the Russian people and some tourists suddenly began to shout the names Brezhnev and Podgorny.

The rumor was instantly spread world-wide by the "live" TV announcers and commentators.

"In a surprise move, Russian leaders are going to meet with the Jewish terrorists holding six hundred and eighty-two athletes in Olympic Village," TV stations announced, interrupting al varieties of other programming. "Suddenly there is great hope in Moscow."

Benjamin Rabinowitz sat with his glazed gray eyes looking down on Yuri Gagarin Square. The rest of Rabinowitz was off in another world entirely; he was satisfied that a fitting revenge for the Holocaust of the forties was now guaranteed. He was convinced that this day would prevent another terrible extermination. It would help make the Jewish nation strong again.

Go and smite the Amalekites, Rabinowitz thought to himself. *Destroy all that they have and spare nothing,* the Lord God had said. *Slay both man and woman, infant and suckling, camel and ass.* Begin Dachau Two.

The door to his suite opened suddenly and the Führer just had time to raise his pistol.

Dr. David Strauss hesitated dangerously, then he fired the Stechkin machine-gun pistol. It fired at the rate of one hundred and five rounds for every ten seconds. The bullets tore into Rabinowitz at over eight hundred miles an hour. This time, Rabinowitz wasn't likely to rise from the dead.

"That one is for Elena," David whispered to no one in particular.

80

Douglas Attenborough was to write in the *London Times:*
"The Dachau of Nazi Germany had been quiet, almost bu-
colic, quite peaceful to the eye. Seventeen kilometers from
Munich along the still and beautiful Amper River, the German
Konzentrationslager was a strange, secret village of low-lying,
gray-concrete and wood-slat barracks built on what could have
passed for a quaint, Scottish dairy farm.

"Thirty-five years later—last night—something horrifying
called Dachau Two was a very public, a visual and aural spectacle. It was the worst scene I've witnessed since I was a small
boy, living through the Luftwaffe bombings of London."

Tense and frightened Russian Army snipers listened to
carefully enunciated babble through their headsets.

The brilliant KGB attack plan was suddenly looking rather
ragtag and almost unprofessional to them. The Soviets' lack
of experience in dealing with terrorists was showing through
badly. Thus far, only two of the Jewish men and women had
appeared in the dormitory windows.

In the meantime, some of the American women athletes
were escaping out the front door. What in hell was going on
in there?

The Russian ground-attack forces were jammed triple-file
into the darkened alleyways separating sections of the village.

Down in the underground tunnels, more soldiers waited
like thousands of stone pillars. They smoked their Papirosis
down to the cardboard filters, lighting cigarette with cigarette.

11:46.

11:47.

11:48.

*The scene inside Olympic Village went completely irrev-
ocably mad at 11:49.*

The Russian Army snipers fired on order at the front windows, glass balcony doors, and rooftop escape hatches.

The Housewife was struck twelve times in the face and

chest. As the crowd gasped in horror, the woman dropped straight down from a fifth-floor window.

The twenty-two-year-old Medic was cut up like a paper target on a practice shooting range.

An American assistant swimming coach was killed by mistake.

The crackling SKS automatic rifles sounded like a huge bonfire made from dry pine limbs.

Inside the kitchen, meanwhile, Colonel Ben Essmann was lying in a secure sniper position himself. His own rifle was trained on the swinging doors leading out to the dormitory corridor.

The Soldier's eyes were wide and his mouth was hanging open.

The former Israeli paratrooper, former intelligence agent, former commando was counting down.

"One hundred nineteen. One hundred twenty. Blast off!"

The silent kitchen screamed for Colonel Ben Essmann.

He thought that he could actually feel his blood beginning to boil.

He knew that he was about to become a holy martyr in the name of the six million.

In a way too, Ben Essmann thought, he was sounding a blow against Jewish enemies of all times: Pharaoh, Haman of Persia, the Greek Antiochus, the Muslims, the Nazis, the Arabs. The strange, fiery Soldier silently cursed each and every one of them.

During the first terrifying moments, there was something like the buzzing, hissing noise made by live electric transformer wires.

"It's originating somewhere on the second floor," a Russian

scientist reported. The white-bearded man was speaking over the West German TV network ZDF.

"But this strange light we all are seeing. A fire would not be possible in this building. No, that would be impossible."

Nevertheless, an ethereal white light was coming from the second floor. The crowd of nearly two hundred thousand spectators sent up a loud, sustained *aaahhh*. It was the remarkable collective sound of awe, wild disbelief, bone-chilling fear.

"Perhaps it *is* a fire." The Russian scientist was beginning to blanch underneath his pancake TV makeup. "Could they have set themselves on fire?"

Less than sixty seconds later, the third floor of the building began to give off the same queer, white glow.

Grayish smoke rose from the roof like steam coming off a boiling pot of water. No flames could be seen anywhere, though.

A few young women jumped out of dormitory windows, graceful as prima ballerinas in their falls. A mist-like silver rain began to rise from the building's sloping gray roofs.

A famous American sports announcer was crying as he spoke. "Our Olympic women are dying. Oh my God."

"It is 11:52 P.M. here. It is July the 18th, 1980," stated the announcer for the BBC. "Ladies and gentlemen, young people of England, we in this control booth cannot believe what we are witnessing here in Moscow."

"Somewhere around our booth, we can hear Pëtr Tchaikovsky playing," reported the announcer broadcasting back to West Germany. "This terrible scene is overwhelming me. I can no longer speak."

Great red fire-pumpers had begun to spray streams of whipped foam high up onto the buildings. The snipers continued their rifle fire.

"It is like a sound and light show representing the first Dachau." An American woman commentator was one of the first to approach some kind of primitive understanding of the event. "I never fully understood the death camps or the Nazi furnaces until today. Not really, I didn't. My God, I wasn't even born at the time of the first Dachau."

No wind was blowing in Yuri Gagarin Square. A three-quarter moon sat over Olympic Village like a chipped white coin.

The huge crowd grew strangely quiet, allowing the ambulance and police sirens to come through like banshee screams in the night.

Americans who were listening to ABC News heard the most poignant, at least the most famous single statement of all.

"My God, please have mercy on us. Somehow, they've set everything on fire. *My God, my God, my God, my God, my God.*"

82

Alix and David thought that they were probably going to die in the next few minutes.

David took a combination deep breath and dry, gasping gulp. He was imagining another confrontation with Colonel Ben Essmann. David was regretting it tremendously.

"Those first two men were relatively easy," he turned and whispered to Alix. "The two guards we surprised upstairs. I wasn't thinking clearly then. Now I'm thinking. My imagination is working. Also, I've already had the hell kicked out of me by that Israeli bastard."

"I really want you to try and get out of the building." Alix began to cry. She made an effort not to, but then the tears just came. "No more arguing, David. Please go."

Just the ironic beginnings of a smile formed on David's lips. "I think we went through all that already. Isn't this where I came in on this particular movie? I told you, I'm not leaving you in here."

Giving himself no more time to think, not sure whether they had any more time to delay, David pushed open the kitchen door.

"Ben Essmann!" Alix called inside through the swinging

door. "This is Alix. I have David Strauss here as a hostage. What do we do now, Colonel?"

The large kitchen lay in baffling, scary darkness.

It was full of clicking, whirring machine sounds, though. Electric clocks. Refrigerator motors. The motor of a small walk-in freezer. Ovens.

Alix flipped the light switch, but nothing much happened. The overhead lights wouldn't yield more than a dull-yellow glow.

All the dormitory lights were flickering and dimming, as if they were going through a brownout. The hallways and rooms didn't *feel* warm, but the insulated ceilings were beginning to seep thin wisps of smoke.

"Ben Essmann. It's Alix. Where are you? Are you in here? Colonel Essmann, *can you hear me?*"

Both Alix and David took a cautious step into the eerie kitchen darkness.

The door to the hallway suddenly swung shut behind them.

"Benjamin Rabinowitz is negotiating with the Russians," Alix cried, deciding to try another tack. "The ends cannot justify the means here, Colonel. *I know you can hear me!*"

Still no response came from the kitchen darkness.

Alix tried to catch her breath and she couldn't.

"Oh damn it, David. He's in here," she whispered. "He knows exactly what we're trying to do."

Enveloped in the creeping darkness, the prickly, electric nothingness of the room, David had become aware that his skin was beginning to tingle. He was starting to have flashbacks of the night in Elena's bedroom. He recalled the shooting scene at the restaurant in Germany. Then the killing of Michael Ben-Iban.

David decided that they had to take another approach with Colonel Essmann.

He yelled out at the dancing light spots in front of his eyes.

"These are teen-age girls that you're murdering here!"

Once again, no response came from the Israeli man. There was loud noise coming from outside, though. Screams. Gunfire—like popping strings of Chinese firecrackers.

David lowered his voice to a more conversational level.

"So! How does it feel to be a murderer of young girls, Colonel? What is it like to be a Nazi, Colonel? You are a murdering,

Nazi bastard, you know! You're betraying everything you claim to be fighting for."

"David?" Alix whispered.

Then a hoarse voice came from the other side of the room. Essmann was in the kitchen. He called out to David. He called out in Hebrew.

"Yes, surely I am that—a Nazi! Now why don't you tell me the nice story about the young Israeli boys who died at Munich, doctor? Then tell me about Auschwitz and Buchenwald! All about Maidanek, where forty in my family died in slaughtering pens."

"That happened forty years ago!" Alix found herself screaming.

"He's in the far right corner," David whispered.

At the same time, he remembered that judging the true direction of sound could be terribly deceiving in the dark. That thought gave David the most awful moment of doubt and panic.

But there really wasn't any time for doubt now. He'd already made up his mind.

David quickly swept his arm out along a row of hanging pots and pans in front of them.

The resultant loud clatter, the sudden crashing of pots to the floor, was unexpected and disorienting. It was like missing a step in a dream.

At the same time, David's right hand shot down under the heavy wood cutting table directly in front of him and Alix.

"Here's something from Heather and Nick!" David called out. He grabbed Alix roughly around the waist. He threw her to the floor.

A bright gold flash illuminated the entire kitchen for a millisecond.

One of the Medic's white phosphorus grenades ripped a gaping hole of light in the overwhelming darkness.

A flat, thunderous *bang* pierced the skin of David and Alix's eardrums.

Then they were scrambling to their feet. David and Alix were running to the other side of the kitchen.

Alix pulled open refrigerator doors and they could see Colonel Essmann in a terrible slice of cold light. The Israeli man was dead: a bloody, insignificant heap on the floor.

David ran to the black generator and he reversed each toggle switch. He tried to reverse everything that had been done. As a second step, he turned off the kitchen ovens. Alix turned off the air-conditioning unit in the kitchen. She turned off anything that was electrical.

Then the terrifying room was quiet and still.

Neither of them was sure, but they thought Dachau Two might be over.

"Will you please hold me?" Alix whispered and began to softly cry. "Just hold on for a minute. Just hold me, O.K.?"

EPILOGUE

The morning after, Moscow awoke to severe post-battle conditions: a light, sticky drizzle; fog and cardboard-gray clouds hanging over the city like a wet, dripping blanket; thousands of tourists wandering the streets like war orphans. . . .

In the final accounting of the Dachau Two incident, Tass, *Izvestia,* and *Pravda* reported that thirty-four athletes and forty-nine Olympic security people and tourists died during the thirteen hours of the takeover. All but a few of the casualties were Russians, Germans, Syrians, or Egyptians. All but three of the Jewish terrorists—the Russian Architect, the Dentist, and the Nurse—were also killed, "murdered" according to some eyewitnesses.

Overall though, the deaths and injuries were far less than had been originally feared and expected. No small thanks to Dr. David Strauss and to Alix Rothschild, it was said. Also to the fact that in one of the three captive dormitory sections, the Architect had refused to kill innocent young athletes; the microwave apparatus had never been turned on.

The worst of it was twenty-two young athletes from the West German team. They were found dead in two adjacent rooms on the third floor of their dormitory. "May these young men and women be the last Holocaust casualties," the Chancellor of West Germany said at the state funeral in Bonn.

As for the effect of Dachau Two on Middle Eastern tension, it has been called both a "contributing factor" by Cairo newspapers, and a "symptom" by Jerusalem's *Yediot Aarenot.*

Whether or not the radical Jewish group knew about the

recently revealed P.F.L.P. arms build-up has never been satisfactorily determined. Former war criminals, however, *are* still funding Arab terrorist cells.

In November, agent Harry Callaghan was assigned to a Washington job safeguarding the President's wife and, occasionally, the President himself.

Harry is now said to be writing a rather scandalous memoir about the intelligence community, under contract with a New York publisher. In the memoir, he will undoubtedly tell his version of the Dachau Two affair.

As for Alix Rothschild and David Strauss, most of the evidence is scattered, vague, largely inconclusive.

For one thing, their escape from Olympic Village was never completely explained by the Russians—who are not great information purveyors anyway. One unofficial version had them getting out through the maze of tunnels and roadways underneath of the dormitories themselves (possibly with the help of American agent Harry Callaghan).

Another story (*Jerusalem Post*) was that during the impossible confusion in front of the liberated dormitory—with American women athletes streaming out onto the streets, with other athletes running up to congratulate them, with joyous spectators and news people breaking through the police barricades (and the Russian police doing a bit of rejoicing in the streets themselves)—David and Alix had somehow slipped into the amorphous, unmanageable crowd, and been whisked along to safety.

Subsequent rumors (the *London Observer;* the *Times*) about their living on a farm outside of Eilat in Israel were proven false. So was the story (*New York Post*) that they were both prisoners in the Potma Labor Camp inside Soviet Russia.

Still another rumor had them going their separate ways after Moscow. In this version, David Strauss is now working as a doctor somewhere inside Israel.

A French photographer recently claimed to have a photograph of the two of them taken in the Algarve. The shot appeared in an American men's magazine, but it was difficult to tell if the two swimmers pictured were actually David and Alix.

A California actress claimed she saw Alix in Los Angeles.

Alix was said to be pregnant and very "matronly looking." She no longer seemed to be *Rothschild.*

In late November, Nick and Beri Strauss's movie *The Fourth Commandment* played to an enormously large TV audience across America.

The film is soon due to be seen in Great Britain, Israel, France, Spain, the Netherlands, and Japan.

The movie will also be shown all through South America and West Germany.

As the winter of 1980 settled in, there was one final development. . . .

Early in December, SS General Richard Glucks, Dr. Ludwig Hahn, and the former Nazi SS commander of Auschwitz, Walter Rauff, were enjoying a choice morning sun and ocean breeze on the white stucco dining porch of the Hotel Mercedes Bleu.

The wealthy war criminals were luxuriating over the most delicate French croissants, over very hot and delicious Blue Mountain blend coffee. Dr. Ludwig Hahn was just lighting up his first Havana Corona of the day.

Very suddenly, four men in khaki trousers and white shirts broke the perfect mood of the peaceful terrace setting.

The intruders fired gas-operated rifles on a ring of casual bodyguards sunning their faces at a table not six feet away from the three Nazis.

One bodyguard flipped back over the terrace railing like a circus acrobat. A second man crashed into a pastry cart sending rolls and biscuits flying in twenty different directions.

The immaculate, white-tile floor was stained with blood the bright-red color of bougainvillaea.

Richard Glucks stood up, screaming at the invaders in very bad Portuguese/Spanish.

"We have agreements with your government. Does the Minister know that you're here?"

A dark-skinned man who could have easily passed for Brazilian, showed his brilliant white teeth to the old Nazis. The man then spoke to the Germans—first in Hebrew, then in stilted German. The man, Benny Netanyahn, was a former major in Mossad; also an "Avenger," reawakened by the demands of Dachau Two.

"You scaly old bastards are accused of crimes against the human race, of which I am a part," he announced. "You can have no agreement with any legitimate government! Your names are *Nazi* Richard Glucks, *Nazi* Ludwig Hahn, *Nazi* Walter Rauff. Among the three of you, you are responsible for over two hundred thousand murders.

"You will be hanged at eleven today. No further discussion is necessary. Tie their arms! Keep them out of my sight until eleven!"

Actually, the hangings didn't take place until closer to noon.

Wealthy hotel patrons, native gardeners and maids, dark, breasty Nazi mistresses from Rio—they were all forced to stand out in the lush gardens.

They were forced to look up at the glistening, bone-white terrazzo.

Buzzards flew high over the terrace like minute, black glider planes.

The South American sun was a bleached-white circle of fire; a dollop of melting lard.

Very suddenly, the three heavy hemp ropes jumped out; then they snapped to rigid, straining attention.

The three Nazis were left hanging in the sun like slack-bellied sides of aging meat; like the Jews in the *Konzentrationslagers* of another era.

Similar scenes were enacted in a high school filled with pretty blond boys in Kelkheim, Germany.

In a sybaritic fourteen-room suite inside a Vienna, Austria, luxury hotel.

On the bare concrete roof of an apartment building in Lefrak City, Queens.

On the barber-cut front lawn of a millionaire's house in the Bel Air section of Beverly Hills.

In Rio, an entire street, an expensive sector of the South American city where German emigrants had settled, was razed to the ground one crimson dawn.

James Patterson, New York City
For all those who didn't survive
For Charles Aaron Morris, my grandfather

256